D0828218

MURDER-IN-LAW

Also by Veronica Heley from Severn House

The Ellie Quicke mysteries

MURDER AT THE ALTAR
MURDER BY SUICIDE
MURDER OF INNOCENCE
MURDER BY ACCIDENT
MURDER IN THE GARDEN
MURDER BY COMMITTEE
MURDER BY BICYCLE
MURDER OF IDENTITY
MURDER IN THE PARK
MURDER IN HOUSE
MURDER BY MISTAKE
MURDER MY NEIGHBOUR
MURDER IN MIND
MURDER WITH MERCY
MURDER IN TIME
MURDER BY SUSPICION
MURDER IN STYLE
MURDER FOR NOTHING
MURDER BY SUGGESTION
MURDER FOR GOOD

The Bea Abbot Agency mysteries

FALSE CHARITY
FALSE PICTURE
FALSE STEP
FALSE PRETENCES
FALSE MONEY
FALSE REPORT
FALSE ALARM
FALSE DIAMOND
FALSE IMPRESSION
FALSE WALL
FALSE FIRE
FALSE PRIDE
FALSE ACCOUNT
FALSE CONCLUSION

MURDER-IN-LAW

Veronica Heley

SEVERN
HOUSE

First world edition published in Great Britain and the USA in 2021
by Severn House, an imprint of Canongate Books Ltd,
14 High Street, Edinburgh EH1 1TE.

Trade paperback edition first published in Great Britain and the USA in 2022
by Severn House, an imprint of Canongate Books Ltd.

severnhouse.com

British Library Cataloguing-in-Publication Data
A CIP catalogue record for this title is available from the British Library.

ISBN-13: 978-0-7278-9097-9 (cased)
ISBN-13: 978-1-78029-777-4 (trade paper)
ISBN-13: 978-1-4483-0515-5 (e-book)

All Severn House titles are printed on acid-free paper.

Typeset by Palimpsest Book Production Ltd.,
Falkirk, Stirlingshire, Scotland.
Printed and bound in Great Britain by
TJ Books Limited, Padstow, Cornwall.

ONE

Friday morning

B*ring!* went the doorbell.

Susan ignored it.

After many months of living in a one-bedroom flat, Susan, her husband and baby Fifi had moved into their spacious new home the evening before, and nothing was in the right place.

Carpets were down, the curtains were nearly all up and most of the furniture had arrived in the right rooms, if not in the right places. The previous evening Susan had transferred provisions from cool boxes to the brand-new fridge and freezer and had made up beds so that they could eat and sleep in their new house.

This morning Rafael had escaped to go to work, baby Fifi had been placed in her buggy for her morning nap, and Susan had started to tackle the chaos in the kitchen.

Bring-bring!

Bother! Whoever could it be?

Susan was expecting a food delivery from the supermarket but not till the afternoon, and she had promised herself that her kitchen would be in working order before then. Susan was a great cook and believed that the application of good food helped to solve most problems in life.

Brring-brring-brring!

The kitchen window overlooked the drive. Was that a strange black car outside? And a woman standing at the front door?

Susan had bright red hair and patience was not her strong point. Chuntering away to herself, she picked her way through the boxes in the newly extended hall to find . . .

. . . the Wicked Witch of the North on the doorstep.

Susan recoiled.

Diana – aka the Wicked Witch of the North – was the only daughter of Susan and Rafael's next-door neighbour, Ellie Quicke. Ellie was one of the most delightful, motherly people you could ever wish to meet. Diana, however, did not take after her mother.

Susan had long ago decided that Diana was a grade one bully, to be avoided at all costs.

The newcomer pushed a heavy, pink bundle into Susan's arms and then took a half step back. 'Oh! You're not . . .? Where's my mother? There's no answer next door, so she must be with you. I need her. Now!'

Susan blinked. Diana's sledge-hammer tactics might keep Ellie wary of her daughter, but Susan was no relation and didn't see why she should act the same way. She transferred the damp bundle back to its owner, saying, 'Your mother's not back from Canada yet.'

Behind her, the landline phone rang.

'What!' Diana's blood pressure rose. Her usually pale face turned pink and so, to Susan's amusement, did the tip of her nose. 'It seems' – the words issued from between clenched teeth – 'that you don't recall who I am.'

Susan managed a sweet smile. 'Oh yes. You are Ellie's daughter, Diana, who is married to Evan, the local estate agent. You have two children and a nanny and you live in a big house on the other side of the park.'

Diana breathed through her nose, rather like a dragon snorting fury. 'Then you know I am not to be trifled with. This is an emergency. I need someone to look after little Jenny today, and I need the keys to my mother's house next door.'

Diana tried to pass the damp bundle back to Susan, but Susan wasn't having it. She retreated half a step and reached behind her for the front door, saying, 'Sorry. I have my own daughter to look after, and your mother is not expected back till next week.'

'What?' Diana sagged. 'But . . . she must be. It's on my calendar. The end of the month.'

'If you'd kept in touch you'd know that the Reverend Thomas, your stepfather, was invited at short notice to speak at a conference in Ottawa. It's true that your mother had originally planned to return this week but there's been a hold-up with the plumbing next door and the house still isn't ready. It made sense for your mother to stay on and return with him in ten days' time.'

Diana turned a sickly shade of green. However, she hadn't been nicknamed Deadly Di for nothing. Her eyes switched left and right as she worked out what to do.

Susan, savouring her victory, tried to close the door on the invader but Diana was too quick for her. The bundle, which had been wailing gently to itself, was thrust back into Susan's arms and Diana started back to her car saying, 'Well, you'll have to help me out instead. Jenny needs changing and feeding, and you'll have to fetch Little Evan from the nursery at noon. I've got a few of their things here which I'll leave with you. I have to get to the hospital, now!'

Her voice was high-pitched. At any moment now she was going to burst into flames.

'What? No way!' said Susan, as the bundle wept gently to itself in her arms. And yes, it was damp underneath. 'I can't—!'

Still talking, Diana opened the back door of her car and swung various packages on to the driveway. 'I'll have to move into my mother's part of the house till—'

'What? No, you can't!'

Diana sent her voice up a notch. 'The. Police. Turned. Us. Out. There's blood, everywhere. They only let me fetch a few of the children's things, and the ambulance has taken Evan to Ealing hospital.' She got into the car. 'I'll ring you when I can.'

The car door slammed. Wheels spat gravel as Diana turned into the road without checking for oncoming traffic. A passing taxi swerved on to the wrong side of the road to avoid her.

And then there was silence.

Susan was left holding the baby. She shook her head to clear it. She was still in bed. She was dreaming. This was not happening!

How dare Diana dump her child on Susan! Who did she think she was!

They had never been friends. Susan had enabled Ellie and Thomas to stay on in a house which was far too big and expensive for them simply by paying her rent for Ellie's upstairs flat on time. Diana hadn't approved of Ellie having a lodger and had been a thorn in Susan's side from the start.

Susan was a loving and giving person. She had grown very

fond of Ellie and Thomas, and they of her. Susan loved to cook and to try out her recipes on Ellie and Thomas. In short, Susan had endeared herself to the older couple – and vice versa.

In due course Susan had left to marry her half-Italian businessman, Rafael, who had also come to care for Ellie and Thomas. It was Rafael who had come up with a possible solution to the problem of the older couple living in such a big house.

Some years before, Ellie had inherited money with which she had founded a charitable trust to provide affordable housing for those in need. Rafael suggested that Ellie should turn the big house over to the trust, so that it could be remodelled into two, smaller, more manageable houses: one for Ellie and Thomas to live in rent free for life, and the other which Rafael and Susan would rent from the trust.

It was arranged that Susan and Rafael would project manage the rebuild and live in Rafael's bachelor flat while Ellie and Thomas went on an extended visit to his daughter and her family in Canada.

Everyone except Diana thought this an excellent idea. Diana was always short of money. She'd wanted her mother to downsize to a small flat and hand the difference over. Diana said Rafael and Susan had brought undue influence to bear on their mother to let the scheme go through but gone through it had, despite a host of minor irritations such as the plumbing in Ellie's part of the house throwing up more problems than Vesuvius.

Diana had not helped the project along. No way!

And now, after months of ignoring Susan, Diana had dumped her child on her!

Inside the house, the landline phone rang again, accompanied by a wail from a newly wakened child. Fifi's morning nap was over and she required attention.

The phone stopped ringing. A message was being left.

Susan dithered. What should she deal with first?

Jenny was quite an armful, a chunky child who must be nearly two years old by now. And not potty-trained. And miserable.

Susan looked around for someone, anyone, to help. The work to divide the large Victorian house into two semi-detached houses had been going on for nearly a year. The scaffolding had been taken down but work continued inside. Usually there'd be a workman or two hanging around whom Susan could ask to help her, but today . . . silence.

There wasn't even any sign of the plumber, who was supposed to be working next door to fix the latest leak.

Jenny wriggled in Susan's arms.

Automatically Susan went into Mummy mode. She pulled the child on to her hip and stroked her wispy fair hair. Jenny took after her big-boned, fair-haired father, who had a beak of a nose and a sense of entitlement which didn't endear him to those he considered of little importance – which was almost everyone who didn't belong to the golf club and employed indoor staff.

Neither Jenny nor her older brother, Little Evan, took after Diana, who normally dressed in black, and whose cap of smooth black hair and sharp manner had earned her the nickname of Deadly Di.

Susan tried to put Jenny down.

'No!' Jenny resisted, clinging to Susan's ample frontage. Susan melted; the poor little mite must be bewildered at being plucked from her home and her nanny and handed over to a stranger.

First things first. Babies needed attention, and Susan was programmed by nature to give it. It was beginning to drizzle, but Susan left the pile of bags on the driveway in order to deal with the children. Kicking the front door to, she shifted herself and Jenny back into the hall.

She'd left Fifi in her baby buggy while she slept, but yes, the child was now wide awake. With her spare hand, Susan undid the straps that held Fifi safe, and lifted her on to her free hip. 'There, there. Now what am I going to do?'

Fifi blinked at the strange child occupying some of *her* space. 'Fifi' wasn't her official name. She had a string of first names on her birth certificate. But when her father had first taken her from the midwife's arms, he'd said, 'Hello, Fifi,' and 'Fifi' she'd remained.

Fifi took after Rafael in looks. She was Jenny's opposite in every way, being black of hair and eye, with every movement quick and neat, whereas Jenny was chunky, fair and slow.

The two children stared wide-eyed at one another.

Jenny looked up at Susan. 'Nanny? Where my Nanny?'

'I don't know where she is, love.'

The front doorbell rang again, sharply. Two sharp rings.

'Thank heaven for that,' said Susan, trying once again to put Jenny down on the brand-new wooden floor – and failing.

This time it was her husband, Rafael, who swept in, towing three of the bags which Diana had left on the driveway. He took in the situation at a glance. 'I rang you a couple of times. The plumber's been on to say he's off sick and won't be working today. When you didn't answer, I thought I'd better drop round to see if you were all right. Er, whose child is that? We haven't grown another overnight, have we?'

'Diana's. She didn't know Ellie had extended her stay in Canada and expected her mother to take her and her children in. When I told her Ellie wouldn't be back for a while, she dumped Jenny into my arms with instructions to look after her. It seems there's some trouble at their place and Evan's been taken to hospital.'

'Nanny?' said Jenny, on the verge of tears.

Rafael assessed the problem. 'You cope with the kids. It's starting to rain. I'll bring the rest of the bags in.' He set off to do this task with his usual efficiency.

Susan took the children through into her brand-new kitchen. It was going to be a lovely place to work in, once she'd found places to put everything. Again, she tried to detach Jenny from herself, with no success at all. Fifi, on the other hand, began to make huffing noises to remind her mother that it was time to be fed.

Susan somehow managed to pull up her T-shirt and, kicking a stool free of the central unit, lifted Fifi on to her breast. Fifi wasted no time in getting down to it.

Jenny watched, wide-eyed. Tears spurted. She yowled. She was hungry too, wasn't she?

Susan managed to transfer Jenny, awkwardly, on to a nearby chair, praying she'd not fall off. She reached for the biscuit tin. Opening it one-handed, she handed Jenny a piece of shortbread which she hoped would keep the child going till she could be attended to properly. Yes, that did the trick.

Fifi suckled and Susan relaxed.

Susan wondered if Diana had ever breast-fed her children and answered her own question: No, of course not! Deadly Di would have handed her two over to a nanny from birth.

Susan recalled Ellie saying that Diana was at least a good mother to her babes. Susan had taken leave to doubt that at the time and had seen nothing to change her mind about it since. Fancy dumping her daughter on a comparative stranger!

Rafael dropped bags into the hall and said he'd push the Beast into the garage and come back to help. 'The Beast' was his pride and joy, a humungous great motorbike which he used for work purposes, being faster in London traffic than the stately limo which he'd purchased when Susan became pregnant. But it was the Beast who had the privilege of shelter, while the limo was parked outside in all weathers.

On his return, Rafael shed his leather jacket, saying, 'Diana has a nanny, hasn't she? What's happened to her? Meantime, what does the cuckoo child eat?'

Susan couldn't think straight. She told herself to calm down, or her milk supply would fail. 'An egg? Bread? I brought some with us when we moved in yesterday, didn't I? There's a supermarket delivery arriving this afternoon . . . or there may be some food in the bags Diana brought. She went off to the hospital. She said Little Evan has to be collected from his nursery at noon but I haven't a clue where that is. Nor do I have Diana's mobile number, or her home number. What are we going to do?'

She burped Fifi and changed sides.

Rafael had been well trained by Fifi and knew exactly what to do. 'We feed their faces, and ours. Breakfast seems a long time ago. Scrambled eggs on toast for all of us. I'll make it. Then we check with the hospital.'

'Diana mentioned the police,' said Susan, trying to think clearly. 'And blood. It sounds as if something nasty has happened to Evan.'

Rafael grinned. 'I expect he had too much to drink and fell down the stairs. It couldn't have happened to a nicer person. Um. No. Sorry. Shouldn't have said that.'

But, while assembling food from the fridge, he continued to be amused by the thought of Evan coming to grief. Rafael might be young, but he was a shrewd businessman with a finger in many pies and knew more than most about what went on locally, especially if dodgy dealings were involved.

Susan smiled and shook her head at him, knowing that his sharp words hid a soft heart.

He whipped up eggs, made toast, poured out fruit juice for Jenny and made tea. 'What's the cuckoo child's name? Ugh, she needs changing, doesn't she? I'm not touching her in that state.'

Recognizing her name, Jenny whined, 'Where my Nanny?' But she allowed Susan to change her in the downstairs toilet so that she could sit on Rafael's knee to be fed.

So they ate, surrounded by boxes.

Susan concentrated on Fifi, who usually closed her long-lashed eyes while she fed but today fixed them, wide-open, first on her mother and then on Jenny. Fifi was not fooled. Something was Going On!

Susan burped Fifi again, changed her nappy, replaced her dungarees and put her in her playpen in the big living room opposite so that she could have a good kick and a crawl around. She'd be fine so long as she had sight of one or other of her parents. There were toys and cloth books for her to play with, and she might even try pulling herself up to a standing position, though she hadn't mastered the art of walking as yet.

'What do we do with the cuckoo child?' Rafael tried to stand Jenny on her own two feet . . . at which the child collapsed on to the floor, grizzling.

Susan looked at her watch. Was that really the time? 'Jenny must be tired. She can go in Fifi's buggy for a nap. We ought to be fetching Evan from nursery at this very minute.'

'We ought to be doing nothing of the kind. He's not our concern. He has a nanny, doesn't he?'

To which Susan shrugged. He was right, of course. But.

She tried to put Jenny into the buggy – and failed. Jenny stiffened and wept. However, Rafael's authoritative manner cowed her into submission and he managed to strap her into the buggy and lower the hood to help the child to nod off.

Meanwhile, Susan had been thinking what to do. She reached for the landline. 'I wonder if Lesley knows what's happened to Evan.'

Susan's aunt Lesley Millburn was a detective inspector in the local police force. Susan's father had disappeared at her birth and, perhaps in consequence of this betrayal, the child's relationship with her mother had always been a somewhat distant one. So it was her young aunt, Lesley, who had kept an eye on Susan as she grew up and encouraged her to take a cookery course when she left school.

Lesley had been friends with Ellie and her retired minister husband, Thomas, for many a long year and had observed their struggles to keep the large house going by renting the attic flat out to a series of lodgers. It was Lesley who had introduced Susan to Ellie as a prospective lodger when the girl enrolled at college.

Susan was still slightly in awe of an aunt who was doing so well in the police force, while guiltily aware that she herself had drawn a better card in the marriage stakes than Lesley. Rafael was a loving, practical and attentive husband, whereas Lesley's seemed to think more of his batting average at cricket than of his wife.

Susan dialled her aunt's private mobile number while Rafael fed the dishwasher. Lesley's phone went to voicemail. Susan left a message and wondered what to do next. 'That poor little boy must be waiting to be collected from his nursery. He won't understand what's happening.'

Rafael said, 'I've got a couple of meetings later this afternoon, but in an emergency I can put them both off. Let me see if I can locate Deadly Di. The estate agency will have her mobile number and even if they won't give us her number direct, they can get her to call us about fetching Little Evan.'

'She may not be able to take the call if she's at the hospital,' said Susan. She glanced through the open door into the big room opposite, where Fifi was trying to put her foot into her mouth and not quite succeeding. Fifi was crooning to herself. She liked being in that big airy room. Fifi liked light and space.

Susan left a second voicemail message on Lesley's phone. 'Lesley doesn't like people calling her on her mobile at work, so she'll know that if I call twice, it's an emergency.'

In fact, Lesley did pick up this time. Susan said, 'Sorry to trouble you, but—'

'It's about Evan, right? Look, I'll call you back.' Lesley killed the call.

'Oh.' Susan pulled a face. 'Lesley knew I was ringing about Evan. So it seems he really is in trouble.'

Rafael nodded. He was on his own phone, trying to contact Diana's office. Susan went to check that Jenny was asleep, which she was. Then she attacked the nearest carton which contained cooking pans and began to put them away in a low cupboard.

Rafael was getting frustrated. 'Her office number's engaged. Don't they have more than one line at the agency?' He tried again, saying, 'I wonder if it was Deadly Di herself who clocked Evan on the head? Not that I'd blame her, the way he carries on. Oh . . .' He interrupted himself to speak into the phone. 'My name is Rafael . . . yes, I'm a friend of Diana's mother. I wonder if you can help me. Diana has asked my wife to look after her children this morning. There's some emergency, I understand?'

The phone quacked and clicked off.

Rafael threw his smartphone down. 'Diana's told the office to hold her calls. She said she had to go to the hospital and would contact them later.' He bent over the nearest half-unpacked box. 'I like this new chopping board. Where do you want it?'

Susan turned aside to reach for the box of tissues. Rafael put his arm around her.

She blew her nose. 'I'm thinking of poor little Evan, waiting to be picked up from his nursery, not knowing what has happened. At that age, it must be frightening. Jenny is old enough to know something is terribly wrong, too.'

'So is Fifi.' He held her close. 'You are the most wonderful woman in the whole world. I think you care more for Diana's children than she does. We'll have another of our own someday, I promise.'

'We-e-ll,' said Susan . . . and the landline rang.

It was Lesley. 'Evan was assaulted at home in the early hours. He died an hour ago. We've invited Diana to come down to the station to make a statement. She's beside herself, screeching she can't leave the children, whom she says she's dumped on you. Social Services have been contacted and will take them off your hands.'

TWO

Friday noon

Lesley's phone clicked off.

Susan told Rafael, 'Evan's dead, Diana's being questioned and Social Services are coming here to take the children. They must think Diana killed Evan!'

Rafael said, 'What! I know I made a joke about her doing that, but . . . No, she wouldn't. She's a cold-blooded so-and-so, but . . . No, even supposing that she did take a swipe at him . . . Let's face it, he's not exactly an ideal husband, but—'

'To be fair, he has – did have – Alzheimer's.'

'Sure. I'd have thought that if she had killed him, she'd have set things up so that someone else would take the blame. Intruders? That would be the easiest excuse, or some of the people he's been dealing with might have turned on him. He's been involved in some dodgy deals in the past but not, I think, recently. Or not that I've heard of.' He ran his hands back through his longer-than-usual dark hair and held on to his head.

Susan was thinking of the children. 'Oh, those poor little things. The police must think she's guilty or they wouldn't bother to get Social Services to collect them.'

'I think, if you can manage here . . .' Rafael started down the corridor to his study, saying, 'I'll see what I can find out.'

Susan called after him, 'What about Little Evan?'

'Oh. Yes. All right. I'll get on the internet and see if I can track down which nursery he's at. It's bound to be the most expensive in the neighbourhood.'

He vanished into his den. He had an office at the block of flats he owned and managed, but he intended in future to work more from home. This new study of his – which had once been Ellie's – now contained a lot more technology than hers had ever done. Rafael had spent an hour the previous evening installing and connecting up this and that while Susan had concentrated on food and bedding.

Susan wondered what Rafael had meant about Evan being involved in dodgy dealings in the past. Dodgy enough to get him killed?

Susan knew that Rafael had occasionally sailed too closely to the wind in the old days before they'd met. Before they were married, he'd promised her that he'd never get involved in questionable dealings again, and he hadn't.

At least, not to her knowledge, he hadn't.

He might perhaps have heard something on the grapevine . . .?

No, it was far more likely that Diana had lashed out at Evan, not meaning to kill. No, of course not. But perhaps, in a rage . . . But there was no point worrying about that. Lesley would sort it out.

Susan finished putting the pots and pans away and started on the crockery. She'd been planning where to put this and that in her new kitchen all the months that they'd been living in Rafael's bachelor flat, but her mind wasn't on the job now for worrying about the children. Rafael had laughed at her for being so soft about Evan and Jenny but there, that's the way she'd been made.

The phone rang. Startled, she lifted the landline on the counter. No, it wasn't that one. She'd put her own mobile down somewhere . . . but no. This was a phone ringing in the kitchen. Ah, Rafael had thrown his mobile down on to the table and . . . she sought for it among the crockery and found it. Somewhat flurried, she couldn't remember what his mobile number was, so said, 'Hello?'

A moment of tension, and the phone went dead.

A wrong number. Or one of those dratted cold calls.

She went back to fitting mugs into a cupboard over the space on the worktop where the kettle stood.

She couldn't get Evan's death out of her mind. They'd never met, but Ellie had talked about him now and then, and there'd been pictures of him in the local paper, presenting a cup to some schoolchildren, and at a golf club event.

What time was it in Canada? Ellie would want to be told about her son-in-law's death. It always amused Susan to think that Ellie was Evan's mother-in-law, as he was about the same age. His marriage to the much younger Diana had been his fourth trip down the aisle.

Susan recalled that Evan had two surviving adult children from his earlier marriages. Ellie had said Evan took little notice of them. She'd also said he hadn't taken much notice of Little Evan or Jenny, either. Ellie had often helped to look after her grandchildren before she went off to Canada with Thomas. Perhaps they wouldn't miss their father much?

Rafael's smartphone rang again. This time Susan homed in on it quickly, only to have it go dead on her the moment she said, 'Hello?' Definitely a wrong number.

Fitting cutlery into the drawer next to the sink, Susan thought that Rafael might well know something of Evan's dealings, since they were both involved in the housing market. Evan, through his estate agency, had tried his hand at buying and selling properties to develop, and Rafael because he'd inherited a rundown block of flats which he'd brought up to date, doing most of the work himself.

A third time Rafael's phone rang, and then clicked off as soon as Susan answered it. She laid it down on the table, wondering if perhaps someone had been trying to ring Rafael but didn't want to speak to her.

Susan also wondered how Ellie would react to Evan's death if she were back in Britain. Presumably she'd rush to help Diana, and would offer to look after the children?

What would Ellie want Rafael and Susan to do in this situation?

Shortly before Ellie and Thomas had left, Rafael had been invited to join the board of Ellie's charitable trust. Ellie had told Susan that Rafael's corkscrew way of thinking was a great asset when dealing with some of their less-than-perfect tenants. Would Ellie expect Rafael and Susan to act as her deputy in these difficult circumstances? Yes, probably.

Susan was restless. What of Evan's two older, grown-up children. Susan wondered if they'd been informed of his death. Presumably Diana would do that? Or would she?

Susan put the last of the crockery away and fished the kitchen clock out of its box. Where should it go?

The doorbell went, and Susan jumped. Oh, that would be their food delivery. Was it still raining? Yes, it was.

Only, it wasn't who she expected on the doorstep.

A youngish man with a beard and a middle-aged woman with prominent front teeth stood there, brandishing a form. Lanyards round their necks. Solid figures, pleased with themselves. Officialdom, here we come.

'Is this the correct address for Mrs Ellie Quicke? We've come to collect the children.'

Susan called back to Rafael. 'Social Services.' And to the newcomers, she said, 'Mrs Quicke is still away. Her daughter Diana asked us to look after the children. Can't you leave them with us? Jenny is badly upset. Poor kids. It must be hard to lose their father and then be whisked away from their home and everything they know.'

'I'm afraid you don't have any choice. They will be well looked after.'

'What does that mean? Will they be dumped on a paid foster-carer somewhere miles from home?'

'Please, no arguments,' said the woman, showing her teeth in what she must have imagined was a smile but which produced the unpleasant impression of her being a rodent in disguise. She flourished her form. 'This is our authority to take the children. One boy, named Evan, and one girl, Jennifer. We are taking them to a safe place where they can be looked after by people who have been appointed to do so. They cannot be left with anyone who has not been vetted. I'm sure you understand that.'

The young man with the weedy beard added, 'We have to be careful, you see. Child Protection Agency and all that. You might well be someone, well, someone who abuses children in your care.'

Susan said, 'What!'

The two newcomers pushed past Susan into the hall. The young man spotted the baby buggy and homed in on that. 'There's one!' He pushed back the hood and woke Jenny, who had been asleep till then.

Finding a stranger undoing the straps of the buggy, Jenny reacted with alarm. She had a good yell on her.

'Oh, please!' Susan reached out to take Jenny, but the young man evaded her.

The woman thrust past Susan into the living room and scooped up Fifi from her playpen. 'And here's the other.'

Susan screamed. 'No! That's Fifi! She's mine!'

Fifi looked up at the woman who'd so unceremoniously plucked her from her playpen, decided she didn't like her smell or the way she was being held, and opened her mouth to protest. She had a good scream on her and exercised it.

'What's the matter?' Rafael erupted from his study. 'What are you doing with Fifi? Here, give her to me.'

The young man with the weedy beard believed he was in the right of it. 'Leave off! We are taking them to a safe place and there's nothing you can do about it, unless you want to be arrested for interfering with us in the exercise of our duty!'

'What!' said Rafael, darkening.

Susan wrung her hands, reached out to Fifi and was thrust aside. Both children continued to scream. Their faces flushed bright red as they wriggled and fought to be free. Jenny almost made it at one point, till the young man took a firmer hold of her.

Rafael snaked through the chaos and put his back to the front door. 'Show me your paperwork.'

The woman bared her teeth at him. 'This is an official—'

'Show me your paperwork!'

Shifting Fifi from one arm to the other, the woman with the teeth presented him with her papers.

Susan bit her fingers. She was in agony. Her baby was screaming and she couldn't do anything to soothe her.

Rafael flicked through the papers. 'You are authorized to collect two children. One is called Evan and the other is called Jennifer. There's been some mistake. Neither of these children is a boy.'

'What!' The woman recoiled. She looked down at Fifi, doubt in her face.

Fifi was wearing a T-shirt and dungarees over her nappy. Jenny was wearing a pink dress and white socks with pink bows on them.

Susan snatched Fifi from the woman's arms. Fifi stopped crying and looked up at her mother. She huffed and kicked and waved her arms. Almost, she smiled.

'What? What, what?' The woman took her paperwork back. 'Someone has made a mistake.'

Susan took Jenny off the young man and for a wonder Jenny stopped weeping and clung to her.

Rafael stood away from the front door. 'Someone certainly has made a mistake. It might have led to your being charged with kidnapping the wrong child. If the person who made out that order of protection, or whatever it is, could make a mistake about the sex of one of the children you were sent to collect, then what other mistakes might they have made? I suggest you go back to your office and consult the legal authorities about this matter.

'And, before you leave, I think you owe us an apology for your high-handed behaviour. We understand you were misled, and fortunately no great harm has been done, but—'

'But—'

'Would you like to see these children's birth certificates? Neither of them is called Evan, I can assure you.' He opened the front door. A chill wind entered and swept around the hall. 'Bother! I should have listened to the architect when he said we'd need to add a porch. The north wind is the very devil to keep out. Penny saving, pound foolish, that's me.'

The two incomers dropped their eyes to the floor and slunk away.

Rafael closed the front door behind them, gently. Very controlled.

Susan burst into tears of relief. She covered both children's faces with kisses and tears. Both children reacted with smiles.

Jenny bounced in Susan's arms.

Fifi looked up at her mother with a look of mild anxiety.

Rafael collapsed on to a kitchen stool. 'Here's another fine mess you've got me into. How many laws have I managed to break today? Won't they come back with the police to take Jenny? We ought to have handed her over and told them where to find Evan, but we didn't. All because you have a heart made of butter.'

Susan bent over to kiss the top of his head. 'My hero!'

Rafael took Jenny from Susan and sat her on his lap. Jenny settled into the curve of his arm. He dried her tears and she put up one hand to rest against him. Her eyelids drooped.

'Cuckoo! Cuckoo,' said Rafael, in a soft tone at odds with the sentiment.

Jenny mouthed, 'Uh-oo. Uh-oo.'

Susan said, in a hushed voice, 'She'll drop off to sleep again with any luck. But Rafael, what are we going to do? Did you locate Little Evan's nursery?'

'Yes. They said he was collected as usual.'

'What? But Diana couldn't—'

'I don't suppose Diana ever does. It would have been his nanny who collected him.'

'But surely Diana would have known that. Why involve Social Services? And where's the little boy now? Oh, I suppose the nanny took him back home with her.'

'In which case, the police would have known where she could be found and wouldn't have sent Social Services looking for him. I've tried Evan's home number. It went to voicemail. If Evan's died, then . . . I'm not sure what will have happened to the house. Wouldn't the police have closed it off as a crime scene while they interviewed Diana?'

Susan kissed the top of her baby's head. 'Normally I'd take Fifi out for a walk now. It's raining, though that doesn't bother us now, does it? But . . . what do we do with the Cuckoo? We've only got one baby buggy and one highchair.'

'Which reminds me,' said Rafael. 'Diana did bring those bags of stuff. Perhaps there's a soft toy or two which the Cuckoo likes to hold to give her a sense of security or whatever. Come on, Cuckoo, let's investigate, shall we?'

No sooner had he sat Jenny on the floor and torn open the first bag, than the child reached out for a somewhat grimy lop-eared pink and white soft toy which might originally have been meant to resemble a rabbit of the Disney variety . . . and at that very moment the front doorbell rang.

This time it was the expected food delivery, so the two children were dumped in the playpen and left to their own devices while the goods were sorted and stowed.

As they did so, Susan told Rafael about the missed calls on his smartphone. He frowned. He said he got a lot of cold calls and put the phone in his pocket. But he whistled through his teeth as he got rid of the empty bags. Susan knew Rafael didn't make that noise unless he was seriously disturbed about something.

She said, 'You're all right?'

He snapped at her. 'Of course I am.' And then softened to a

smile. 'Yes, of course I am.' He gave her a hug and went to disembowel the rest of the bags Diana had dumped on them.

He was not telling her whatever it was that he was worried about. Susan shrugged. His business was his business. Babies were hers.

Babies, babies. Where was the nanny? Jenny didn't seem to have many words yet. There was no point in asking her.

Susan had been afraid that the two babes might fight, even though they were probably too young to take much notice of one another, but as soon as the Cuckoo had clasped the floppy-eared rabbit to herself, she'd been content, crooning to herself. Fifi watched, wide-eyed and open-mouthed. Fifi had never bothered with soft toys with the exception of the Gonk which slept in her cot beside her.

Fifi decided that their visitor wasn't particularly interesting and could be ignored. Instead, she practised pulling herself up and standing still, looking at the room from a different perspective.

As Susan put the last of the food delivery away, Rafael started his brand-new coffee machine, and announced, 'I've looked through the stuff Diana has brought for the children. We have nightwear and a change of day clothes. There are shoes for Little Evan, but none for the Cuckoo. There's a plastic toy train set and a pack of nappies. Whoever packed this lot up didn't do a particularly good job of it. I think it's time to confess that we have been obstructing justice and let Lesley sort this mess out.'

'Hold on a mo.' Susan looked around wildly. 'I think I know how to contact the nanny. The latest one is . . . Now, what's her name? Italian, Balkan? I suppose I've seen all the nannies who worked for Diana from time to time, when they dropped the children off for Ellie to look after. They've never lasted long, pour souls. Now, the nursery must have details of whoever is to deliver and collect Diana's children, so we could ask them to . . .'

'Got it!' Rafael was off down the corridor before she finished speaking. She followed him. There was no blind at the window here, and it was getting dark outside.

He checked a note he'd left on his desk and attacked his mobile. 'If the worst comes to the worst, I suppose we could phone Ellie, who's sure to have the nanny's details somewhere. What's the time on the East Coast of America now? Ah, here's the nursery's number.' He pressed digits. 'What's the girl's name?'

'She's Italian, I think. Lucy? Lucia? Something like that. I only saw her once. Diana took her on just before Ellie left. Hopefully, it's still the same one. Italian? No, maybe Scandinavian?'

'They're slow answering the phone. Pray God they're not closed for the day. What was the girl like?'

'Drippy. Long straight blonde hair that could have done with a wash. Rather sweet and gentle.'

'I suppose it suited Diana to have a nanny she could boss around, someone who wasn't pretty enough to appeal to her husband.' A voice answered the phone at the other end, and he said, 'Oh, hello. It's Rafael again. You remember I rang this morning to see if . . .'

Susan shot back to check on the children in the living room. They were fine. Rafael followed her, clicking off his mobile. 'Got it. Her name is Lucia, and they had her number on file. I'll ring her direct, shall I?' He pressed digits.

The phone rang and rang. At long last, a faint voice said, 'Hello?'

Rafael handed his phone to Susan, saying, 'You'd better speak to her. At least she'll know who you are.'

Susan said, 'Lucia, this is Susan here. We moved in with Ellie and Thomas, you remember?'

'Yes. Please, what is happening?'

'We're not sure. Diana asked us to look after the children. We have Jenny safe and sound but—'

Lucia was crying. 'She says to go! But it rains and we walk and walk and we are so wet and tired.'

'Ah, you have Little Evan with you?'

'I try to take him home but policeman say to go away and I not know what to do.'

'Get a taxi,' said Susan. 'Come here, to Ellie's old house. You know where that is?'

'I can't. I have no money.'

THREE

Friday afternoon

Susan said, 'Tell the taxi driver we'll pay. Give him our phone number if he argues.'

The phone clicked off. Rafael chanted, 'Now what have you done? Here's another fine mess you've got me into!'

Susan was counting on her fingers. 'We'll put Lucia in the guestroom at the front. There is a bed in there, though it isn't made up, but that won't take long. Little Evan is big enough to sleep in the bed in the nursery at the back with the girls. The Cuckoo can sleep in Fifi's cot, and Fifi can make do with the baby buggy for tonight.'

'Coo-oo!' That was Jenny, clutching her rabbit or whatever it was, and raising her free arm to Rafael. She wanted to be picked up and cuddled, didn't she?

'Oo-oo!' That was Fifi, mimicking Jenny.

Susan gave a little scream. 'Her first word! Yes, my darling. "Oo-oo!"'

'Oo-oo!' from both children.

Rafael picked Jenny up. 'Now look what you've done, Susan. The child will think my name is Cuckoo.'

Susan said, 'It was your idea.' She kissed the top of Fifi's head. 'Clever girl! We'll manage, somehow, won't we?'

'What are we going to say when the police come to arrest us for stealing Cuckoo?'

'Co-oo.' Jenny beamed at him, showing pretty new teeth.

Susan said, 'Lesley must be busy. I'll leave her a voicemail, saying we've now managed to find the two children, that Diana has asked us to look after them, and we assume that that's all right by Social Services.'

Rafael said, 'That might work. Depends on how much we've pissed off Madam Horsey Teeth as to whether she gives up or not. By the way, have you any cash to pay the taxi?'

'I doubt it.'

Rafael started back to his den. 'I'll get some from the safe.' Rafael believed in prevention rather than cure and had spent some considerable time building a safe into the foundations of his study and disguising it.

Prompt on cue, the doorbell rang.

Susan went to answer it, carrying Fifi.

At the last minute, she panicked, fearing it might be Social Services or the police, and not the taxi . . . but no, this time it was all right.

A limp-looking teenager with long straggly hair inched herself out of the cab. She had a hefty-looking rucksack on her back and looked as if she'd fall over if she weren't careful. She was followed by a small, fair-haired boy who didn't seem to know where he was or what was going on. Both were drenched to the skin. Both too tired to speak.

Taxi drivers don't usually help passengers out of their cab unless they're expecting a large tip, but this one took the girl's arm and helped her into the house. He was a stocky individual, with close-cropped, fawn-coloured hair and bright eyes in a brown face which had seen a lot of life.

Susan recognized him. She didn't have much call to take taxis, but Ellie did and this was her favourite driver. Being Ellie, she'd heard all about him and his family, information which she had passed on to Susan. So Susan was pleased to see him now. She said, 'Sorry to call you out on such a horrible day. Are you OK, and the family?'

He said, 'Fine, fine. Not so sure about these two. They've dripped all over my seats. Strictly speaking, I oughter have took them to hospital.'

Susan caught the boy as he tottered. She helped him in out of the rain, slamming the front door behind her. 'Oh dear. You're right. Except that a long wait in A&E wouldn't do them any good, would it? My husband's getting some money for you now.'

Little Evan was shivering. His chin quivered. He was wearing a soaked jacket and short trousers. He stood in the hall and dripped.

The girl stumbled forward. Eyelids at half mast, she made it to the bottom of the stairs and collapsed. She dripped, too.

Susan said, 'Can you tell us what's happened, Lucia?'

The girl didn't respond. She was sparrow thin, paper white and shivering.

A phone rang. Susan and Rafael ignored it.

One-handed, Susan dumped Fifi into her buggy, and managed to heave Little Evan astride on to her hip, while saying to the taxi driver, 'Thank you for bringing them here. Their mother asked us to look after the children for a while but she didn't say anything about their nanny and I don't know . . .' She cast a look of doubt at the girl who didn't look capable of looking after herself, never mind a child.

The taxi driver said, 'I don't like to leave you . . .'

Susan said, 'Their mother's bound to ring soon. We've only just moved in here and not everything works yet, but I think there should be enough hot water to give them each a bath. Then we'll feed them and put them to bed. We'll manage, somehow. I'm sorry to keep you waiting.'

Another phone rang. Susan's mobile? Where had she left it?

The taxi driver shifted from foot to foot. He wouldn't leave without his money.

Another ring at the doorbell. Who could that be? A van had drawn up behind the taxi. Susan managed to get the door open, one-handed. Was it the plumber? Alas, no.

A strange delivery man. 'Package for next door. Sign here.'

A stray gust of wind caught the front door and sent a blast of cold air through the house.

Fifi, who hadn't been properly buckled into the baby buggy, tried to stand up . . . and toppled over . . .

She was going to tumble, head-first on to the floor until . . .

Susan dropped Little Evan and caught Fifi as she fell. 'Oh, my love! There, there!' How could she have been so remiss! Fifi might have hurt herself seriously!

Little Evan collapsed on to the floor. He closed his eyes, opened his mouth and yelled. He had a good, penetrating yell on him. The tired yell of a child in despair.

Susan didn't know what to do. She cuddled Fifi, who had had a bad fright. She crouched down to pull Little Evan to her as well. Fifi took a deep breath and held it.

It was always a bad sign when a child falls silent after a fall.

'Just sign here,' said the delivery man, having no intention of getting involved.

'Oh, my love! It's all right, it's all right!' Susan rubbed Fifi's back. Fifi let fly with a scream which rose without effort above Little Evan's yell.

'Here!' insisted the delivery man, holding out his paperwork and ignoring the chaos around him. 'It's big. It'll take two of you to bring it in, maybe.' And he wasn't going to be one of them, was he?

The taxi driver scratched his neck. He wasn't going to offer, and he wasn't going to leave till he got his money.

Fifi gulped air, and wept.

Little Evan's yell subsided a notch. He wept into Susan's shoulder. 'Wa-wa-wa!'

The nanny also howled, but not very loudly. It seemed she hadn't any energy left for a good, long-drawn-out, wolf-like howl.

Rafael returned, bearing the Cuckoo on one arm, and talking on his phone. 'Yes, yes . . . No, we're not going anywhere!'

'Sign here!' said the delivery man, turning on Rafael.

Rafael handed the taxi driver a couple of notes. 'Thank you. We really appreciate that.'

Rafael then looked at the delivery note the van driver was holding out and said, 'Does this look like a hotel? Right number. Wrong street. Road, not Avenue. It's the first building round the corner in the next road.'

'You can take it in for them, can't you?'

'I regret. No.' Rafael held the front door open for the van driver to leave, which he did. Rain blew into the hall. Rafael shut the door, muttering about the non-existent porch.

Susan tried to stand. Didn't make it. She held her baby in one arm and a small-but-heavy boy in the other. Susan appealed to the nanny. 'Lucia, can you help me?'

Lucia had curled up into a ball. The rucksack on her back made her look as if she'd grown a hump. She was out of it, full stop.

Susan thought: If only Ellie had been here! Ellie always knew what to do in an emergency. Ellie said it was all a question of relying on the Man Upstairs. Or was it a woman nowadays? Susan wasn't at all sure she believed in All That, but in an emergency, she was prepared to give it a go.

So she drew the two children even closer to her, and muttered, 'Please, Lord! If you can spare a moment?'

The taxi driver stowed his money away with slow, deliberate movements. 'Mrs Quicke still away in Canada? I thought she'd be back by now.'

'That was the plan, but they got held up with this and that.'

He said, 'Looks like you could do with some help with those kids. My daughter Coralie, she's got her First Aid certificates. Scouts and Guides and stuff. She'll be home from school now. She's sixteen, good with kids, wants to work with them when she leaves school. Would you like her to give you a hand? I could get her round here in half an hour, maybe.'

Rafael produced another note. 'You fetch her and we'll be forever grateful.'

The taxi driver left, letting in another gust of cold air.

Susan wondered if they'd ever see him or their money again . . . but at least the phones had stopped ringing. Both of them.

Blessed silence! Small sniffles and sobs from the children. A steady drip of water on to the brand-new wooden floor . . . which Susan noted and told herself that when she'd got a minute, she must clean it up, because water marked wood.

She made another effort to stand. And failed. Evan was too heavy to lift from where she sat on the floor. She said, 'They need to go in a hot bath, to be dressed in warm clothes, fed and watered and put to bed.'

Rafael nodded. 'I'll take Little Evan, shall I?' He tried to unstick Jenny, who objected, screaming, 'No! Co-oh! Co-oh!' He detached her with some difficulty, held her out at arms' length and put her on the floor. She flung herself at one of his legs and buried her face in his jeans.

Somewhere a phone started up again. They ignored it.

With Jenny hanging on to one of his legs, Rafael shuffled over to Susan and lifted Little Evan into his arms. 'Bath? Upstairs?'

Little Evan's head lolled on to Rafael's shoulders. Jenny tugged on his jeans. He tried to walk across the hall. Failed.

Susan sighed with relief as one of her burdens was removed. Now she could stand. With some difficulty. 'Strip those wet clothes off him first.'

Still clutching Fifi, Susan leaned over the sopping wet bundle that was Lucia and shook the girl's shoulder. 'My dear, you must get out of those wet clothes. We have a downstairs shower and loo. It's just along the corridor here. Do you think you could manage to get that far?'

No reaction. Had the girl fainted, or fallen asleep? She was making dark marks on their beautiful new floor. Bother! And various other words!

Oh, that dratted phone!

Rafael, with Jenny still clinging to him, began to strip the wet clothes off Little Evan. That made another pool of water on the floor!

Susan took Fifi into the kitchen, found a biscuit and gave it to her, with a sip of juice. Fifi managed to stop sobbing long enough to ingest both.

When in doubt, feed them.

The landline in the kitchen started up.

Susan wrung out a clean tea towel, and washed Fifi's face. Checked to see if she needed another nappy. Fifi was fastidious and was never comfortable in a soiled nappy. Yes, the nappy needed changing.

Fifi calmed down. Lying on her back on the central island, Fifi tried to catch her foot in her mouth. She crooned to herself. Susan kissed her all over and gave her a cuddle.

Susan manoeuvred herself round Rafael and the now naked but still shivering Little Evan, to pop Fifi back into her playpen and thrust a couple of soft toys at her. Fifi frowned and murmured her displeasure, but didn't start screaming again. Perhaps her recent fright had tired her enough for her to drop off to sleep? But if she slept now, would she sleep the night through?

Susan, free to move without Fifi, got another biscuit and a cup of milk from the kitchen and held them out to Jenny, who first pretended she was not interested, but eventually allowed herself to be enticed away from Rafael's leg. Once Jenny was standing on her own two feet, Susan picked her up, noted that she was smelly, ignored the fact, told her she was a good girl, and dumped her in the playpen alongside Fifi.

Someone rang the doorbell, and one of the phones started up again.

Rafael picked up the naked, shivering boy, plucked his own

leather jacket from the hook on the wall behind the stairs, and wrapped him in it.

Susan answered the door to find the taxi driver and a teenager standing there. The girl was taller than Susan, well-built, with slightly podgy features. She was a lighter shade of brown than her father, with dark hair and eyes. Heavy duty anorak, jeans, sensible boots. No Clever Clogs but a down-to-earth, sensible girl who would stand no nonsense and therefore get none from her charges. She looked to be about the same age as Weeping Nanny, but Susan thought she'd be a hundred times more capable.

The girl said, 'I'm Coralie. My dad said you needed an extra hand.' She looked beyond Susan, took in the scope of the problem, shed her jacket and said, 'Which first?'

Rafael said, 'I'll bathe the boy upstairs.' And off he went.

Susan said, 'Many thanks. My name's Susan, and this' – she gestured to the dripping lump at the bottom of the stairs – 'is Lucia. She's Italian. Downstairs loo and shower. On the left past the kitchen. Strip, dunk and warm her up. She brought some of her belongings in her rucksack, hopefully containing a change of clothes. I'll find some towels.'

Coralie didn't wait for further instructions but bent over Lucia, coaxing and lifting her to her feet. Lucia's face was swollen with tears. She could hardly walk, but Coralie was strong and knew what she was doing.

'This way, Lucia,' said Coralie. 'That's the ticket.'

Susan followed Rafael up the stairs. Towels. They'd be in the linen chest which hopefully had come to rest on the landing? A warm dressing gown for Lucia, poor thing. Then beds must be made up for Lucia and for Evan and . . .

Drat that phone! Why can't people take the hint when we don't answer it?

There was an ominous swishing sound from the kitchen. Was that the dishwasher misbehaving? Well, towels first . . .

The phone stopped. Brilliant.

Susan found a couple of large bath sheets and dropped one in to Rafael, who had rolled up his sleeves and was holding a shivering small boy under the shower in their en suite.

She hastened back down the stairs – with caution as they were brand new and she wasn't accustomed to them as yet – and swivelled along the corridor, casting a quick eye to see that the two in the playpen were all right and not killing one another . . . No, they were ignoring one another, that's good . . . And registered in passing that there was water on the kitchen floor which there shouldn't be.

She tossed the spare towel into the downstairs cloakroom, where Lucia had been divested of her sodden clothes and helped to stand . . . and returned to the kitchen to find a man's bottom in front of her.

'Got a leaky hose,' said the bottom, which turned out to belong to the taxi driver, who was halfway under the sink at the side of the washing machine. 'You got any tools, like? Pliers, perhaps.'

'I'll ask my husband. He has tools.' Back up the stairs she went to deliver the bad news to Rafael, and to take his place rubbing down the little boy, who seemed half asleep but was warming up nicely. He'd need feeding before he was put to bed, wouldn't he? What did she have to give them?

That phone . . .!

Now, bedrooms. Ellie had said that Susan and Rafael should have the main pieces of furniture which had already been in these rooms before the renovation, so it was not impossible to put extra bodies up for the night.

The children would be fine all sleeping together and would be nearest to Susan and Rafael if anyone woke in the night. The smaller guestroom over the kitchen was sparsely furnished, but it would do for Lucia at a pinch.

Oh dear. Would Evan sleep in a double bed? Well, it wasn't huge, and they had nothing else for him. Sheets? Duvet covers? Pillows? She thought she knew where they were . . .

She rubbed the little boy dry. He was looking up at her. Tears welling. He didn't know his dad was dead and his mum being held down at the police station. Susan wasn't going to tell him. She asked him, 'Are you hungry? What about some porridge with honey in it?'

His mouth tried to smile and almost made it. 'Hippo?' he said. 'Jenny?'

'Jenny's fine. Downstairs with my baby. You remember my baby Fifi?'

A nod full of doubt. 'Hippo? Where my Hippo!'

He was too tired to yell. He was desolate. 'Hippo' must be his favourite toy. His safely blanket. Susan knew the importance of such things to children. Fifi had been given lots of soft toys but was really only interested in a repulsive-looking Gonk with enormous ears which she could either wave around or shove in her mouth. She also quite liked a rather strange pink teddy bear which bore an expression of mild anxiety. She wouldn't settle to sleep unless they were both in her cot with her.

Susan thought that finding something else for Little Evan to hold was probably even more important than getting him warmly dressed and fed.

Still wrapped in the towel, she carried him into the big bedroom at the back and dumped him on the unmade bed next to Fifi's cot. Her soft toys were ranged along the windowsill. Evan could have one of those, couldn't he?

Evan looked at the display without interest. Then he got off the bed and reached into the cot to grab the pink teddy bear with the anxious expression. He crushed that to him with both hands.

Oh dear. What was Fifi going to say about that?

But for the moment, the pink bear was comforting a small boy in trouble. And then it failed to comfort. Evan smelled it. It must smell of Fifi. Well, why not?

He threw it away from him. It wasn't his. It wasn't Hippo. He opened his mouth to give a mournful, tired cry.

Susan wrapped him in a dry towel and cuddled him. He wept. She held him fast and rocked him. Eventually his tears stopped although he still sobbed, soundlessly, now and then. Susan carried him, slowly with care, down the stairs to the hall to find something for him to wear and something to eat.

Oh dear. That phone . . .

Inside the kitchen she could see two men's behinds. Rafael's was lean and muscular and so-o-o tempting . . . but she knew better than to try to caress a man's behind when he was at work. Both men were kneeling in a sheen of water, with their heads in one of the cupboards, the contents of which were now strewn above and around them . . . and which would need washing and drying before they could be put away again.

Susan told herself that it didn't matter. It really didn't. Water leaks can be mended. Eventually. Her kitchen would be returned to her. Shortly.

She found the bag containing Little Evan's clothes and took him into the big living room to dress him in warm pyjamas and slippers with the heads of puppy dogs on them. He was docile under her hands, on the verge of sleep . . . which meant she could keep an eye on the two younger children, who were ignoring one another and, at least for the moment, not screaming the house down. Jenny had gathered together all the soft toys which lived in the playpen, leaving none for Fifi.

Fifi had hauled herself to her feet and was trying to work out how to walk sideways. It was a little early for her to walk, perhaps, but she was agile and determined. She concentrated, one foot wavering around, not sure where to put it next.

Coralie appeared. 'Have we anything for Lucia to wear? Everything in her rucksack is soaked.'

Nothing of Susan's would fit that poor drowned rat. She said, 'Take one of the towelling robes which are hanging up behind the door of the big bedroom on the right upstairs.'

Coralie disappeared.

A cheer arose from the kitchen. The men had fixed the problem. Well, bully for them. Susan would bet they wouldn't think of returning anything to the cupboard, or mopping up the floor. Urgh!

But of course she must thank them and smile. Well, they deserved to be thanked, of course. But oh . . . that dratted phone!

Once Evan was warmly dressed, she popped him into the playpen, too, explaining she was going to get some food for him and Jenny. The boy followed her with his eyes as she left them for the kitchen . . . where she found two men with soaked jeans, giving one another a high five. Pleased with themselves.

Well, of course they were pleased, having located and stopped a leak from the dishwasher. She ought to be pleased, too. Well, she was. Of course she was. She smiled and congratulated them, and they puffed out their chests and said that these things happened, didn't they?

At least the microwave was working. She shooed the men out of her domain to allow Rafael to pay off Sam, the taxi driver, and to thank him for dropping everything to help them out. Would he like to fetch Coralie when she was ready to go home? Brilliant. See you later, then.

Coralie brought Lucia in and dumped her on a chair. She looked more dead than alive.

Rafael didn't want to deal with her. 'I must change my jeans. They're wringing wet.'

Of course they were. And so was her floor.

Rafael left.

Susan said to Lucia, 'Would you like a cuppa?'

No reaction. Susan sighed. She said to Coralie, 'Could you make up the beds for me while I clear up here? Back bedroom. Fifi's cot is in there already. Make up the double bed. Then do the single bed in the front bedroom, the one over the kitchen. There should be pillows and duvets in the chest that's on the landing. If not, try the largest of the cardboard boxes that's landed up in the main bedroom.'

Coralie said, 'Sure,' and disappeared. She was a treasure!

Susan mopped the floor around Lucia – who didn't offer to help – and dried and stowed away the pots and pans which had landed up on the floor. She considered the next problem on the list. They had no highchair for Jenny. They had one for Fifi, of course, but it was a starter chair for a small child and wouldn't accommodate Jenny's robust frame. They'd been planning to get a larger one for Fifi as soon as they moved in, but hadn't thought they needed it yet.

Ah well. Susan fancied she was turning into a machine to look after her enlarged family, with Coralie acting as First Lieutenant.

Can a machine have a deputy? Well, I don't see why not.

Susan found some packets of porridge for the older children, which she would microwave, adding honey and/or milk to taste.

She collected the children one by one. Fifi went into her highchair with a biscuit to gnaw on till she could be attended to properly. Jenny and Evan were seated, with care, on cushions on kitchen chairs.

Rafael returned to help. Rafael prepared a mug of hot milk for Lucia and laced it with something which Susan decided she was not going to enquire about. Perhaps it was better to give the girl a slug of something alcoholic than sleeping pills. Poor child; adrift in a foreign country . . . though what she was doing walking around in the rain with young Evan after collecting him from the nursery, heaven only knew!

'There now, Lucia,' said Rafael, 'Can you tell us yet what's happened?'

Lucia gazed into space with half-closed eyes, and didn't reply.

Rafael said, 'She's out of it. I'll carry her upstairs and put her . . . where?'

Susan signalled with her chin. 'Up above here. Coralie's making up the bed for her. Show her that her bathroom's next door.'

Rafael picked up Lucia and carried her off upstairs. Susan looked after him, thoughtfully. She could tell he was worried. Had he got himself involved in some slightly dodgy deal she wouldn't like to hear about? No, surely not! He'd promised her faithfully that he wouldn't do that again. And yet, and yet . . . he was definitely fretting about something. Perhaps he knew something about Evan's death that she didn't?

Susan gave Fifi another biscuit to crumble and put juice in her lidded cup. That would keep her quiet while she fed the others. The bowls of porridge were made and disappeared, plus half a banana each. Jenny was wide awake but Evan seemed only half aware of what was going on.

Susan foraged in the freezer for adult food. She'd baked and brought over quite a few things from their temporary quarters in the bachelor flat. There should be a large cottage pie in the freezer. Yes, that might do.

She made up her mind that Rafael was not going to tell her what was worrying him until the children were in bed. Yes, that would be it.

Rafael reappeared. 'I put Lucia into the bed and she crashed out, straight away. There's no curtains or blind at the window, but I don't suppose she cares.'

Susan reflected that there wasn't a bedside light, either. They had brought over some such bits and pieces from the flats with them, but they would still be in the packing cases, somewhere. And they'd thought of getting new curtains for that room, hadn't they? Well, Lucia needed sleep more than a bedside light.

More milk for the littlies. Bread with peanut butter on it for Jenny who, still attached to her long-eared rabbit, managed to get on to Rafael's knee to be fed. She was like a fledgling bird, opening her mouth to receive food and making no effort to feed herself.

Evan pushed his empty plate away from him and shook his head. He was done. And then, finally, so was Jenny.

Susan made an executive decision: Evan had just been bathed, and she wasn't going to bother giving Jenny a bath that night.

Coralie reappeared to help Susan disinter some pyjamas for Jenny from the bags Diana had left, give her a change of nappy and carry her upstairs to sleep in Fifi's cot in the back bedroom.

Meanwhile Susan checked on Evan. Mouth and hands were wiped clean. Bottom was checked. He was more or less out of it, moving like a rag doll. She handed him over to Coralie to take upstairs. The double bed would be far too big for the little boy, but Susan couldn't think where else to put him. He was too big to go in the cot, and anyway, Jenny would have to sleep in that even though she was getting too big for it.

Now to feed the adults, and perhaps there would be a moment to ask Rafael what was troubling him? Back to the freezer. Vegetables were needed and yes, an apple pie. The microwave pinged.

Susan put food in front of Rafael and Coralie. The latter said her father was off duty now, so she'd ask him to come and collect her in half an hour or so.

Susan's mind was on Fifi, who was overdue her last feed of the day, but she remembered her manners long enough to say, 'Coralie, you're wonderful. I couldn't have managed without you. How long is it before you leave school? You know just how to handle children.'

'You want me to help tomorrow? It's Saturday. I'm free.' She tucked into her cottage pie with zest.

Susan plucked Fifi from her highchair and found herself saying, 'Praise the Lord,' just as dear Ellie would have done.

At last, at last: Susan could feed Fifi. She lifted her baby on to her breast, and sat down, closing her eyes. Susan was worn out. Her kitchen was a war zone. When had she eaten last?

But what was this? Fifi was flailing away, not sucking.

Oh. My. Had her milk dried up?

Oh, no!

It was not surprising under the circumstances, but Susan felt bereft. It was as if her only reason for being in this world had suddenly been removed. She wanted to cry.

She scolded herself. *Pull yourself together, girl!* She tried for a smile as she cuddled Fifi for a moment before handing her over to Rafael, who continued to eat, one-handed. She said, 'Looks like little one is growing up. I'll have to find something else suitable for her now. She can sleep in the baby buggy. We can take it off its frame and carry it up to the nursery later.'

Susan felt dizzy. She tried to stand and failed to do so.

And the phone rang.

And the doorbell. Susan turned to look out of the kitchen window, which didn't have a blind on yet. Even from where she sat, she recognized a visitor who was not going to go away.

It was her aunt Lesley – Detective Inspector Millburn, to give her her full name – at the door. Fair-haired, late thirties, solid-boned. She was alone. Not backed by Social Services. And, she was flaming mad!

Coralie said, round a mouthful of pie, 'Shall I answer it?'

Susan shook her head. She forced herself off her stool to let Lesley into the hall.

It was still raining, though slackening off. Lesley shook out her umbrella as she stepped into the hall and looked into the kitchen. 'Don't you ever answer the phone?' Then spotting Coralie, she said, 'Ah, there she is! Why didn't you let me know that you'd got the girl here? Well, at last I can take her statement!'

FOUR

Friday evening

Susan said, 'I'm hearing things. Coralie, this is Inspector Millburn from the local police station. Lesley, what do you want with Coralie?'

'She needs to answer some questions about Evan's death.'

Coralie's mouth dropped open.

Susan worked it out. 'You want to question Diana's nanny, Lucia, about Evan's death? Yes, I can see that you would, but this isn't her. Would you like something to eat? Cottage pie? Orange juice, tea or coffee to go with it?'

Clunk! Susan realized that even the thought of coffee was nauseating. This was all Too Much! Fifi was fussing on Rafael's arm. She wanted food and now her mother had failed her! This was terrible!

Coralie didn't stop eating. 'What am I supposed to have done now?'

'Nothing,' said Susan, foraging in the fridge for something – anything – to give Fifi. Ah, some yoghurt. Fifi liked yoghurt. She handed it to Rafael, and turned aside to blow her nose.

Lesley seated herself beside Coralie. Lesley had not taken in what Susan had told her. She said, 'Forget food. I'll start with Lucia. Where have you been all day, eh?'

Coralie grinned. 'At school. I like this cottage pie. It's better than the one Mum makes. She's got this thing about using soya instead of meat.'

Lesley said, 'What!' And then: 'You know something, Susan? I *could* do with something to eat. I've been on the go all day and . . . What! You say this is not Lucia?'

Susan said, 'Lesley, this is Coralie, the daughter of Sam, who is Ellie's favourite taxi driver and coming round to take her home in a minute. Coralie is still at school. The first she heard about us was when her father roped her in to help us with the three children after school today. She's been wonderful, but she doesn't know anything about Diana, apart from the fact that it was someone called Diana who dumped her kids on us.'

Curiosity emboldened Coralie to ask, 'This Diana's in trouble with the police? She's not here, is she?'

Rafael said, 'Coralie, you don't need to get involved in this. Can you ask your father to collect you straight away?'

Coralie had no intention of being excluded from something so exciting. 'Dad said he'd collect me as soon as he could.'

Lesley pounced. 'Susan, you referred to "children" in the plural. Social Services are in a tizz, unable to find Diana's children. Have they been here all the time? Have you been telling porkies—?'

'Calm down,' said Rafael, spooning yoghurt into Fifi. 'We didn't lie. We didn't have Little Evan when they arrived looking for him. They thought Fifi was the boy they were looking for and would have taken her away if we hadn't proved that she was the wrong sex. They backed off then, realizing something was wrong with their paperwork. We *were* looking after Jenny at that time, but not Little Evan, though we did manage to locate him later.'

'As for the nanny,' Susan said, 'she's upstairs, fast asleep. Worn out. I doubt if you'll get any sense out of her till the morning. Now, Lesley, there's some cottage pie left, and one of my apple pies has survived the move. Why don't you relax and eat with us? It's been a long and tiring day. And Rafael, when you've got a minute, can you see if you can find Little Evan's Hippo in the stuff Diana left with us? It's his special soft toy and he's missing it.'

Lesley unzipped her jacket, but didn't take it off. She was sticking to her remit. 'Social Services are blazing mad. They don't like being given the run around. Cottage pie, you say?'

Susan's mind was on what else to give Fifi to eat. 'Diana asked us to look after her children, and that's what we've done. Coralie has offered to help us with them over the weekend. We're coping so far, and if we can't cope in future we'll yell for help. I'll microwave some cottage pie for you, Lesley. And there should be some cream in the fridge to go with the apple pie.'

Fifi finished the yoghurt. Rafael burped her. She obliged, but continued to fuss. Fifi was still hungry.

Coralie said, 'Give her to me. Does she have a bottle yet?'

Rafael, misreading the 'no' signals from Susan, handed her over, to resume ingesting his share of the cottage pie.

Susan was filled with such jealousy of Coralie that she felt faint. She didn't like the idea of Fifi getting comfortable in Coralie's arms. Susan wanted to snatch her baby away and feed her, herself. Only, she had no milk.

Worse still, Fifi had assessed Coralie and decided she was a bit of all right. Treachery! How could her baby smile at a stranger!

Susan told herself she was being unreasonable. That worked, a bit. She poured some juice into a cup that Fifi occasionally permitted herself to use, and handed it over, saying, 'I've always had enough milk before now . . .' She tried to be brave, but her voice wobbled. 'We don't have any formula in the house. I'll have to get some tomorrow.'

A taxi's headlights strobed into the kitchen – the sooner they got a blind up there, the better – and the driver tooted his horn.

'That's Dad.' Coralie rose, with some reluctance. 'I could tell him you need me a bit longer?'

'No, my dear,' said Susan, retrieving her child and the cup from Coralie with alacrity. 'We'll be delighted to see you tomorrow morning and we'll work out how much to pay you then. Now, off you go.'

Coralie reclaimed her jacket, saying, 'I'll be back early in the morning. I'll bring you some formula, shall I?'

Rafael suspended operations on his plate to say, 'Hang on. Can you give us a number where we can reach you?'

Coralie recited a long list of numbers and left. Rafael nodded. 'Got it.'

Susan closed her eyes for a second. Truth to tell, she couldn't remember any series of numbers longer than three, but Rafael was exceptional that way. She sat down in Coralie's place and fed Fifi the rest of the juice.

'Rafael, can you see if there's any of my homemade soup in the fridge, and pass me a banana?' The microwave pinged.

Lesley rapped on the table. 'Forgive me for dragging you back to the present!' She'd gone all sarcastic. 'I didn't come here to talk about who eats bananas and who has baby formula. This is a murder enquiry. Now, this girl, Coralie. She's going to go home and spread alarm and despondency all round the neighbourhood, isn't she? And, if she's that young, her family won't let her come back tomorrow, will they?'

'I don't think wild horses would keep her away,' said Rafael, dishing up some cottage pie for Lesley. 'Are you able to tell us exactly what has happened? We know Evan was taken to hospital and that he died. That's all we do know.'

'He was attacked by intruders in the night and left to die.'

Rafael said, 'Burglary gone wrong? You hear of it now and then. Bad luck.'

Susan shivered. 'That's awful. He's got grown-up children by earlier wives, hasn't he? Have they been informed? I don't think they've had much to do with him recently. Ellie would know. I seem to remember one of his wives was French. Or did she just have a French name?'

Rafael was nodding. 'His first wife was called Monique. She died last year and I chauffeured Ellie to her funeral. Did you ever meet Monique? A formidable lady. Evan was furious when he found that she hadn't left him anything in her will. How he could have thought she would, I can't imagine, since he'd deserted her and had never paid any attention to his son by her – or to any of his other children, come to think of it. Monique left most of her estate to Ellie's trust fund because she knew how much good they could do with it.'

Lesley said, 'How many times was Evan married, and how many children did he have?'

'His earlier wives are all dead, and I don't think any of them would be of interest to you, Lesley. Two children survived to adulthood. Ellie approved of the eldest girl, who's called Freya. She seems sensible and well-adjusted, which is surprising considering her father's lack of interest in her. After her own mother died, Monique took Freya under her wing and the girl is now independent, working as an estate agent and doing better than Diana. There is a boy as well, but there was something wrong with him. He must be in his early twenties now, but he's in a secure unit and I can't think he'd have been allowed out.'

'I remember him,' said Lesley, grim-faced. 'No, I'm sure he's not allowed out, but I'll check all the same. Evan's death does look like a burglary gone wrong. Diana's only become a person of interest because she lied to us about her movements.'

Susan said, 'She didn't kill him, did she? How did she lie, and what do you think she's done?'

'She's obstructed the police in the course of their enquiries, that's what she's done. It's more than enough. I'd like to add everything from assault and battery to fraud and murder, but I've absolutely no proof that she's guilty of anything but being one of the nastiest pieces of . . .! Forget I said that. I mean, it shouldn't weigh with me in the slightest that she's always behaved appallingly to her mother. In my opinion, she's a gold-digger of the first water, but I'm not allowed to hold that against her in this case. Or am I?'

Rafael and Susan exchanged glances. Lesley was overtired, overwrought and on the verge of behaving unprofessionally. Why hadn't she gone home to her husband to relax?

Mm. Well, they knew the answer to that. Ellie had always worried about Lesley's marriage to a man who thought more of playing cricket and/or rugby than of his wife.

Rafael handed Susan a banana and rummaged in the freezer for soup. 'Well, Lesley. We do agree with you that Diana is a bully and not above cutting corners. Surely that is background information which you are entitled to hold and which must influence your thinking, even if she is innocent of anything else. You don't really think she killed her husband?'

'No.' Lesley gave a tired sigh. 'I wish I did because it would be so satisfying to do someone so dislikeable for murder. But to be honest, I don't. Only, she's not been straight with us and I want to know why. I want to know what she did from the moment she woke up this morning. I want to know why she's left the children with you and why she's failed to make a statement of what she knows. But, if you've got her here then I'll snatch a bite before asking her any more questions.'

Rafael met Susan's eyes. They didn't have Diana. An idea flickered into Susan's mind as to where the woman might be. Had Rafael thought of it, too? He looked troubled. He'd been worried about something ever since they'd first heard about the attack. What did he know and why was he keeping quiet about it? He broke eye contact to put a tub of Susan's home-made soup into the microwave.

Lesley said, 'Evan's children. I can only hope that Diana's been in touch with them, but . . .' Clearly, Lesley didn't think Diana had done so as her voice tailed off before she added, 'Someone will have to speak to them.'

Rafael said, 'We've got their details on file at the trust. I'll get them for you later.'

Lesley chucked off her jacket and tucked into her plateful.

Susan watched Rafael out of the corner of her eyes while he microwaved the soup and Fifi got through a third of a mashed-up banana, which Susan polished off.

Rafael gave Lesley some apple pie, and she ate that, too. Fifi moved on to the soup. She wasn't sure about it at first, but after a spoonful or two, got a taste for it.

'So,' said Lesley, clearing her plate. 'It's late, but before I pack it in for the day, I'd better talk to Diana and the nanny.'

'As Susan said, the nanny's fast asleep in our guest bedroom,' said Rafael, stacking the dishwasher with dirty plates, and setting it going. 'She's out of it, period. You can talk to her in the morning. What happened was this: Diana dumped Jenny on us this morning and—'

'Ah. Now, what time was this?' Sharply.

Susan kept an eye on the dishwasher. Was it going to leak again? She said, 'I don't know. Is it important?'

Lesley lost her composure. 'I don't know. I don't know anything, except that the picture is all wrong. It looks as if Evan disturbed some burglars last night, they attacked him and he was unfortunate enough to suffer serious injuries which led to his death. Diana says she'd taken a sleeping pill and slept through it all. She told me she'd got the children up, dressed and fed and took Little Evan to the nursery. On her return she left Jenny playing by herself upstairs before going down to get Evan's breakfast, only to find him in the hall lying in a pool of blood. She didn't mention having a nanny, and I only discovered there was one much later on. So I need the girl's story.'

Susan looked at Rafael for a lead.

He was frowning. Unsure of himself for once. He shook his head – at himself or at her? He collected all the wet clothing that had landed in the hall and set it in the tumble dryer. He said, 'Look, this may take some time. We'll tell you everything we know but first let's make ourselves a cuppa and take it into the big room where we can spread ourselves out and relax.'

Lesley looked as if she were going to object, but finally nodded. 'You're right. I'm too tired to think straight. Let's do that.'

Rafael made coffee for himself and tea for the women. Susan carried Fifi through into the big room, switching on the sidelights and drawing the heavy curtains over the French windows at the back.

Then she collapsed on to the big settee with the squashy cushions, and allowed herself a little playtime with her baby, who giggled and gurgled and made it clear that Susan was her favourite person in all the world. Very shortly Susan knew that she must give Fifi her bath and put her to bed, but under the circumstances she could stay up a little longer than usual, couldn't she?

Lesley subsided into a roomy armchair and closed her eyes. 'What a day! My beloved husband wanted me to join him this evening at some "do" at the cricket club.' She shuddered slightly. She was not a fan of the game or of her husband's friends.

Susan recalled again that Ellie had had no great opinion of the man Lesley had married.

Lesley said, 'Let me recap. At five past nine this morning Diana reported a burglary at her house in which her husband had been badly beaten. She said he was still breathing but unconscious. Two detective constables attended the scene. They found Diana sitting on the floor beside her husband, holding his hand. He was alive, just. There were spatters of blood and evidence of a struggle throughout the ground floor. One constable accompanied Evan in the ambulance to the hospital, while the other stayed behind to secure the scene.

'Diana was informed that, because of the state the place was in, the family would have to move out for a while. Accompanied by the remaining constable, she went upstairs to wash her hands, change her bloodied skirt and pick up a couple of things from her bedroom. She collected little Jenny and some bags of the children's belongings from the top floor, with help carried them downstairs and put them into her car. She drove away at a quarter to ten saying she'd drop Jenny off with her grandmother Ellie before going on to the hospital.

'Meanwhile, Evan was rushed into the operating theatre at the hospital. The detective constable who'd gone with him, hung around, hoping he'd pull through and be able to tell them who'd done it. The clock ticked on. No Diana. An hour went by. Still no Diana.

'The detective constable at the hospital became alarmed. Suppose some accident had befallen Diana on her way to hospital? She phoned the station for instructions and I was detailed to take over. I understood immediately why the case was given to me. It amuses my boss to give me anything which might possibly cast a bad light on Ellie or her family.'

Susan and Rafael ironed out smiles. In a senior moment, Ellie had referred to Lesley's boss as 'Ears' because those appendages of his turned bright red when his blood pressure rose. The nickname had become common knowledge, and 'Ears' had vowed that some time or other he'd put Ellie behind bars. So far he'd failed to do so, but he wasn't going to stop trying, was he?

Lesley continued, 'So I set out for the hospital, reviewing what I knew about Evan. It has always amused Ellie that she was Evan's mother-in-law, since they were roughly the same age. I knew of his reputation as a local businessman with a finger in many pies. I arrived at the hospital at ten forty-five. Evan was still in the operating theatre but there was no sign of Diana, who eventually appeared at the hospital at four minutes past eleven. She explained her late arrival by saying she'd had to leave her child at her mother's house, and when she arrived at the hospital she hadn't been able to find a parking space. At eleven ten the surgeon came out of theatre to say Evan had died and Diana turned to stone. Shock, yes.

'She was neatly dressed for work in a black suit and medium high heels, not a hair out of place. She was the very picture of a successful businesswoman. I asked if there was anyone she'd like to be with her. I was thinking of Ellie, of course. She just stared at me. I asked if she'd like a cuppa, and she blinked a couple of times and said she would, as she hadn't had any breakfast. We got her something to eat and drink. I got the impression that she was thinking very hard.

'When she'd finished eating, she asked me what would happen next, about the body and so on. I told her there'd have to be an autopsy, that Forensics would be looking for evidence of the perpetrators at the house, and so on. She seemed to be taking it all in.

'I asked her if she felt able to tell me what happened. She said she'd taken a sleeping pill last night and overslept. She said she and her husband didn't sleep in the same room or even on the same floor. His increasing frailty meant he'd been sleeping downstairs on the ground floor. She was on the first floor and the children in their nursery at the top of the house.

'I asked if the children had slept through the night, too. She said they wouldn't have heard anything at the top of the house with the door shut. She said she'd woken early, gone upstairs to get them washed, dressed and fed, before taking her little boy to the nursery. She said there was a servants' staircase which came out by the kitchen at the back of the house and she'd taken them up and down that way so as not to disturb Evan, because he always slept late. She said on her return she'd left her little daughter playing upstairs in her playpen in the nursery and gone down to make Evan his breakfast before she went off to work, and that's when she'd found him.

'I asked if she'd touched anything. She shook her head and said she'd held his hand for a while. I asked if he'd managed to tell her who had done that to him. She shook her head. She said she'd seen that he was badly injured and had phoned nine-nine-nine for an ambulance and the police. She said Evan must have disturbed burglars and tried to defend himself.'

Susan said, 'Well, that hangs together. She brought Jenny here, not knowing Ellie hadn't yet returned. Which reminds me that we must look for Little Evan's toy Hippo. It's his security blanket, his favourite soft toy, and he's missing it. Diana must have packed it up. It'll be in the bags she brought, somewhere.'

Rafael frowned. 'I don't think so. I've been through those bags. Clothing and shoes. That raggedy rabbit which Jenny's got. That's all.'

Susan said, 'Oh dear. Perhaps the nanny knows where it's gone. I hope he hasn't lost it somewhere.'

Rafael said, 'Agreed, Diana did take her time getting to the hospital, but I can't see anything sinister in that.'

Lesley insisted, 'She left home with Jenny at nine forty-five. She arrived at the hospital at four minutes past eleven. Yes, she had to drop Jenny off here, but . . . does it really take one hour and twenty minutes to do that and find a parking place at the hospital? I *know* that something's wrong with that timetable. I *know* she did something else in that time. Something she doesn't want us to know about.'

Susan said, 'If I'd been in her place and Rafael had been injured, I'd have picked up Fifi and a nappy and jumped into the ambulance with him. I know Diana's a cold fish, and I realize she did have to move herself and the children out of the house for a bit, but did she really have to pack up so much before she left? Look at the pile in the hall. There's bags and bags of stuff. Couldn't she have taken the very minimum with her then, and gone back later to pack up at her leisure? But then, what do I know? Sometimes in an emergency you get your priorities wrong.'

Lesley said, 'The constable says Diana left her house at a quarter to ten. Suppose she then took ten minutes to get here, ten minutes to explain what had happened and to leave Jenny . . . and another ten to get to the hospital. That leaves just over three quarters of an hour of her time unaccounted for – unless you know otherwise? What time did she get to you?'

Susan thought it through. 'We overslept, tired after moving in yesterday. We haven't got the kitchen clock up on the wall yet, and I'm not sure what time we had breakfast. Then Rafael went in to work. I was sorting the kitchen out. Fifi had gone down for her mid-morning nap. I'd say it was about ten, maybe a bit before?'

Rafael got out his smartphone. 'I can get it closer than that. The plumber phoned me to say he wasn't coming today at . . . yes, here it is. He phoned at nine forty. I rang Susan to tell her, got no answer—'

'I had to let the phone ring while I was dealing with Diana.'

'I was on my way to an appointment – I never got there, I must contact them to apologize – but I rang Susan a couple of times and she didn't pick up. I was concerned that she might have some domestic emergency or other and couldn't get to the phone, so I dropped back here . . . about ten fifteen? Diana had just left.'

Susan said, 'She arrived here demanding the keys to next door. She expected her mother to be in and to take care of Jenny. She didn't know Ellie had delayed her return or that her house wasn't ready for occupation. She dumped Jenny and some bags of stuff on me, ordered me to fetch Little Evan from his nursery later on, and left.'

Fifi had fallen asleep, spread-eagled on Susan's stomach. With an effort, Susan got to her feet. 'Fifi needs her bath and bedtime.'

'Hang on a minute,' said Rafael. 'Lesley, who set the child protection police on us, and can you stop them storming the house tomorrow?'

Lesley fidgeted. 'It wasn't me. What happened was that when Diana had told her tale, she said she had to get back into the house to collect some papers she needed from the safe. I said we couldn't allow that, but we'd be on site and make sure nothing was touched. She persisted, saying she needed these documents including her passport. And at that, I'm afraid I blew up. What did she need her passport for? Was she planning to ditch her children and sneak out of the country? Didn't she see how suspicious it was that she should want it now?

'She said she needed it for a conference she'd been booked to go to abroad, which was essential for work purpose. She lost control. I'd never seen her lose control before. She went scarlet. She wept tears of sheer rage. She swore at me, said she was going to see her solicitor that very minute, that I had no right to detain her and she was leaving to go about her business there and then. I said we should continue this discussion down at the station, and she said she'd told us all she knew and needed to go to the loo.

'She disappeared down the corridor, and at that point Ears rang, wanting to know if I'd arrested Diana yet. I had to admit to my boss that I wasn't happy about Diana's story and that she was demanding access to the safe at home in order to collect her passport. You can see how it looked, can't you? My detective constable had gone after Diana but lost her in the car park. Ears said he'd put out an all-points bulletin to arrest her. It was he who organized a visit from Social Services. Yes, I do think it was over the top, but he's my boss. I'm only sorry you had to get involved.'

Rafael said, 'His reaction was over the top, but so was Diana's.'

Lesley stretched and sighed. 'I know she lied about something, even if I don't know what it was. Someone killed Evan. I really don't think it was Diana because whoever did it must be carrying traces of blood all over them, not just on one hand and her skirt. There was no way she could have been involved in the hand-to-hand struggle that must have taken place there. I'll ring Ellie and give her the bad news – not that she can do anything about it while she's in Canada – and then I'm going to call it a day. I'll be round first thing in the morning to have a word with the sleeping beauties. Don't let either of them go till I've spoken to them, right?'

FIVE

Late Friday evening

Rafael saw Lesley out, while Susan laboured with Fifi up the stairs and into their big bedroom. She was too tired to get out the baby bath but dunked Fifi in one of the matching pair of washbasins in the en suite. Fifi woke up and splashed merrily. She loved water. Normally Susan would have let Fifi have a lengthy play but tonight she skipped that, hoping the child would have been so tired out by the events of the day that she'd sleep the night through.

Rafael came up with the top off the baby buggy. 'Where do you want it? Here, or in the nursery next door?'

'In here, I think.'

'That cat of Ellie's is pressing itself against the windows. I thought it had transferred its affections to the staff at the hotel nearby. I didn't let it in. Shall I bring up my laptop so that we can Skype Ellie up here, before we go to bed?'

'Are you going to tell her what you didn't want to tell me?'

'Ah.' He went to the window and looked out at the night. 'You know me so well. All right. I was asked to take part in a dodgy deal a while back. I was told that Evan was in it up to his neck. I declined. I heard later that there'd been a massive falling-out among those who had put money into the venture and that umbrage had been taken in large quantities by all and sundry. It did cross my mind at first that Evan might have been stupid enough to short-change a certain businessman in their dealings in that matter. It took a while but I eventually ran my contact to earth and told him what had happened to Evan. He laughed himself silly. Said it served the old fool right. He said Evan thought of himself as a shark but that in reality he was just a tadpole in a village pond. End of story.'

Susan laid Fifi down in the buggy and put her Gonk into her hands. Fifi gazed up at her mother with a slightly anxious expression. Something wasn't right. There was a change in her routine. No milk. Strange children invading her space. And surely she'd been sleeping in a cot recently?

Susan whispered a prayer over her baby, pulled up the hood and dimmed the bedside lights. 'And the rest of it?' she said. She went to stand beside him at the window.

He put his arm around her. 'Well, it's the plumbers. They undercut everyone else to get the contract from the trust to do the plumbing here and next door. The trust thought we should give them a try but as you know, it's been a disaster. In here it's not been too bad, apart from the leaky hose to our dishwasher, but next door . . .! One excuse after the other. Their office systems are archaic and their foreman inefficient. Either the workmen don't turn up or the parts they've ordered fail to arrive and what does arrive, doesn't fit.

'Next door should have been finished three weeks ago. Last week they started angling for more work from the trust. I had to say I wouldn't recommend it. That's when the pressure started. They ring me night and day. They offered to install wet rooms in my block of flats at cost, if I'll swing another contract from the trust their way.'

Susan put her arm around his waist. 'And you refused.' It was a statement and not a question.

'I was tempted. But yes, I did refuse.' He attempted a laugh. 'Anyway, their incompetence would have driven me mad.'

He made as if to draw the curtains and froze. He was looking down into the garden. Susan looked, too. She saw a square of light, interrupted by their silhouettes, thrown down on to the lawn below. They switched their eyes to the left to see that there was a similar shape of light thrown on to the garden below from another window, not next door – which was the nursery – but further along in the next house, from Ellie's bedroom.

The silhouette of a woman appeared in the square of light and then curtains were pulled across. Rafael drew their curtains, too.

Susan said, 'That's Diana, isn't it? Do you think Lesley guessed that Diana might move in next door, in spite of there being no water there?'

Rafael shook his head. 'Lesley thought we were looking after her.'

Susan said, 'When Diana came this morning she demanded the keys to her mother's part of the house and I refused to give them to her. I told her Ellie and Thomas were still away and that their house wasn't ready. I'm not sure if I told her there was no water available or not. I'm pretty sure Ellie took Diana's keys off her some time ago, but she's still got in.'

'Smashed a window in the kitchen door and got in that way, no doubt. I suppose there's some water in the tank but there can't be much, which is why the plumber was supposed to be coming back today. She'll use the bathroom, won't she? I wonder if there's enough water in the tank to let her use the toilet?'

'Or boil herself a kettle to make some tea?' Susan giggled, and then was serious. 'You could argue that she didn't lie to the police when she said she was taking refuge in Ellie's house.'

'Shall we Skype Ellie now?'

There was a mournful cry from the nursery. Rafael had left on the landing light, so Susan could see one unhappy, disorientated little boy, who'd lost his security toy, standing by the bed. She gave him a cuddle. He wept unrestrainedly. She reminded herself that though Dreadful Di was his mother, and Autocratic Evan his father, there must be something of Ellie in him. She whispered soft words to him so as not to wake Jenny, who was fast asleep in Fifi's cot.

'Hippo,' he murmured. 'Nanny got Hippo?'

'Nanny's fast asleep. You can see her in the morning.' Susan noted that he didn't ask for his mother or father. She promised him, 'We'll find your Hippo tomorrow. Can you remember where you left him?'

He thought about that. 'Under Nanny's bed. I wanted to take him to nursery, but she said I could have an extra biccy for being a brave boy and managing without Hippo.' He hiccupped a bit and said, 'Biccy?'

He was wide awake now. Susan led him down the stairs, warmed some milk for him and found the biscuit tin which, for some reason, had migrated to a high shelf, almost out of her reach. She found one of his picture books in the muddle of boxes and bags in the hall and read it to him. When he began to droop, she escorted him to the loo and finally coaxed him back up the stairs and into bed. She piled up all the soft toys she could find around him, saying that they were feeling lonely, and could he look after them for her that night?

She tucked him in with a firm hand and heard his breathing soften and become regular. Oh dear, would Lesley allow her to look for Hippo tomorrow?

Treading softly, she returned to the bedroom to find Rafael sitting up in bed, in the act of closing up his laptop. He said, 'I've spoken to Ellie. She agrees with me that if Diana had wanted to kill Evan, she'd have done it by arranging an accidental overdose. What's more, Ellie says Diana would have checked that he wasn't breathing before she called an ambulance. She has a very clear idea of Diana's capabilities, hasn't she?'

Susan sank on to the bed and eased off her shoes. Was she too tired to have a shower before getting into bed? 'Are they coming back early?'

'She says that since the house isn't ready and they've had this very prestigious invitation for Thomas to speak at the conference, they'll return next week as planned, and would we – she means you – organize that the cleaning agency sets everything to rights before they get back. She says that we – that is, you and I – have all the right qualifications to work out what happened to Evan, and she's sure everything will have been sorted by the time they get back.'

Susan flexed her toes. 'She'll want me to order in some food, as well. When will the plumber finish, do you know?'

'That plumber! I'll light a fire under him tomorrow. By the way, Ellie went on to make some "suggestions" which I interpret as "instructions". She hopes someone will remember to tell Evan's grown-up children about his death. I told her you'd already thought of that and yes, I've just sent Lesley the details so that she can check what they were doing.'

Susan decided to forgo a shower. She performed a quick lick and a promise and slid into bed beside Rafael. 'Ellie was fond of Evan's daughter, Freya, wasn't she? I can't see any reason why she'd want to kill her father. There was something wrong with the boy, wasn't there? Wasn't he sectioned after he killed someone?'

'I doubt if he was let out, not even for half a day. Now, Ellie reminded me that Evan's house is actually owned by the trust, and that he was supposed to be paying rent on it. She asked me to check, and I have. Evan was way behind with the rent.'

Susan stifled a giggle. 'Which means the trust can evict Diana? Oh, dear, I shouldn't laugh, but it couldn't happen to a nicer person.'

Rafael ironed out a smile. 'Yes, but it does raise another problem. What's going to happen to the children? Ellie is concerned about them. I said she can trust you to look after them till Diana is ready to take them on again. She sends you her love and says she's looking forward to some of your apple pie when she gets back.'

He turned out his bedside light and hunkered down. 'Ellie told me something else in confidence. She thinks Diana may have a toy boy. Knowing Ellie, she won't know why she thinks this, but somewhere or other in that peculiar brain of hers, she'll have noted something which has led her to that conclusion. So now I'm wondering who I know who might throw some light on the matter.'

Susan couldn't deal with any more problems. She turned out her own light. Rafael put his arm around her and she put her head on his shoulder.

He said, 'You know, Ellie said she thought of her house as offering a refuge from the world. She used to take in waifs and strays, didn't she?'

'Mm,' said Susan, who had been one of them. 'You think it will go on being that, even though it's been cut in two?'

Rafael kissed her forehead. 'It seems the baton has been passed to you, my dear.'

Through Friday night to Saturday morning

Jenny woke at two in the morning. She wept copiously till soothed with milk and a biccy by her 'Cuckoo'.

Fifi woke at three and wept until her soiled nappy had been changed.

Little Evan woke at five, crying for his Hippo. He'd wet the bed.

Susan and Rafael took it in turns to attend to the children, staggering back to bed between calls for attention.

The children all woke early, of course.

Bleary-eyed, Rafael and Susan climbed into some clothes, washed and dressed the children and took them downstairs to feed their faces.

Rafael observed, 'Ellie seems to think Diana will reclaim the children at some point. A consummation devoutly to be wished.'

Breakfast was a messy affair, but at least the skies had cleared and there was a promise of a fine day for a change.

Susan had always wanted a big kitchen like Ellie's. She felt it was the natural heart of a house, where everyone could sit around a table and eat before they went their separate ways out into the world. She accepted that in a family, some members would have better table manners than others. Some would make a lot of noise and others would concentrate on food and drink.

Fifi was a tidy little person, neat in all her ways. She'd never seen anything like the chaos which ruled at this particular breakfast table. She sat upright and wide-eyed in her highchair watching Jenny scream and squirm, refusing to sit on a chair by herself. Jenny was a splasher: food and drink went everywhere but in her mouth. Eventually Rafael put her on his knee, held her securely in one arm and fed her as if she were a hungry sparrow. That worked better.

Little Evan was silent. Perched on a cushion on a chair, he ignored Jenny to hoover up everything within reach before anyone else had taken more than two mouthfuls.

Coralie arrived at the house on the dot of half past eight. She shed her coat in the hall, picked up a spoon which Jenny had dropped, put on the kettle and measured some formula out for Fifi's bottle while greeting everyone with a beaming smile. Little Evan and Jenny watched her, withholding judgement, but accepted her when she shifted Evan higher on to the cushion on his chair, and wrapped a tea towel around Jenny's neck in lieu of a bib.

Susan observed the girl's kind but firm authority with the children and vowed to imitate it.

Susan and Coralie turned themselves into robots, serving eggs here, toast soldiers there, segmenting fruit, wiping mouths and sticky hands, gulping down a cuppa themselves when they could.

Lucia, the drippy nanny, wandered down, dressed in Rafael's

bath robe and with her long fair hair straggling over her shoulders. Little Evan and the Cuckoo ignored her. Drippy Lucia said she could only manage a grapefruit, but Susan didn't have any. She made no effort to look after the children but accepted tea and dry toast for herself.

Susan suddenly felt a bit sick, but told herself she hadn't time to do anything about it. Jenny lashed out, sending her cup of milk over the bathrobe Lucia was wearing. Susan added that to the mental list of things that would have to go into the washing machine that morning. Evan's sheets for a start. How many extra pairs of bedding did she have?

Susan dived into the loo next door and threw up. Oh yes! How inconvenient was this! She gargled and went back to the fray.

Little Evan tried to get off his chair, clutching a segment of orange in one hand and a biccy in the other. How he had managed to get at the biscuit tin was a mystery. Surely she'd put it up on the high shelf last night, after she'd fed him his midnight feast? No, perhaps she'd forgotten to do so.

Coralie thrust a bottle into Susan's hand and told her to sit down and deal with Fifi, which she did. Fifi objected to the change in her routine at first, but soon got down to it, and then took some porridge as well.

Someone rang the doorbell. Lesley? Yes, it was Lesley. Oh dear.

A quarter to nine of a sunny morning and all was well. Sort of.

Actually, Lesley herself was looking rough round the edges and older than her actual age. She hadn't slept well, but she wasn't going to let that stop her carrying on with her job. She had a lot of the bull terrier in her, had Lesley.

'Ah,' she said. 'Happy families.' She was accompanied by a young man who was also in civvies.

Two detectives in one morning. One too many?

Lesley pointed at Lucia. 'You must be the nanny.' She recited her rank and gave the name of her colleague. They both held up badges. 'So now, Lucia, let's go into the other room and you can tell me all about it.'

Lucia reacted like a startled horse. 'No, no! You not arrest me, please?'

'No, I'm not going to arrest you,' said Lesley through her teeth. 'But I do need to hear what happened to you yesterday.'

Lucia grabbed the table and looked at Rafael. 'Please, you protect me? You not let her arrest me?'

Rafael hid irritation. 'Of course she won't arrest you unless you've done something wrong. Lesley, can't you leave her in here with us while she tells her story? We'd like to hear it, too.'

Lucia said, 'Yes, yes. I tell you, I do no wrong. Only she, that horrible woman, do me wrong. You make her give me my wages and money for my ticket home.'

'Oh, stay here if you wish,' said Lesley, investigating the teapot and grabbing the last slice of toast.

Lucia breathed through her mouth. Her resemblance to a hamster became even more marked. She pushed her chair nearer to Rafael. 'I stay here, and you look after me, yes? Also, you get my locket back for me? Is in my bed, I think. I wish I had never come to this horrible country!' She wept. Unbeautifully.

Susan angled the bottle so that Fifi wouldn't suck in air. Susan had little patience with inefficient little girls who turned to the nearest man for help when they'd done something silly. She said, 'Coralie, do you think you could take Little Evan and Jenny into the big room and find them something to play with? Lucia, that's enough. There's a box of tissues just behind you. Blow your nose and tell us what happened.'

'Oh, oh!' Lucia wailed and rocked on her chair. 'You are so cold! Just like Mrs Diana!'

Little Evan and Jenny stared at Lucia with what looked like disgust. Coralie peeled Jenny off Rafael, saying, 'My mum says the best way to deal with a hysterical girl is to throw a jug of cold water over her.'

Lucia squeaked. 'I wanna go home!'

Little Evan objected to being led away by Coralie. 'Lucia! Where you put my Hippo?'

A tinge of colour came into Lucia's pale face. 'Oh, he so silly about his Hippo. He too old for it. Nursery say he must leave it behind. Is in my room, I think.'

Lesley rolled her eyes and tried to soften her approach. 'Now, Lucia. The sooner you tell us what happened, the sooner you'll be on your way. For a start, you slept with the children at the top of Diana's house, didn't you? Were you disturbed by any noise the night before last?'

Lucia sniffed and snuffled, used a tissue and managed to say, 'No. The children sleep through the night now. We shut the door to the stairs and all is quiet. But in the morning I saw that horrible woman, that Mrs Diana, with a man in the road outside the house. She so mad that I see her. She tell me to go!'

She looked around at their interested expressions and gained enough confidence to continue. 'The children get up as usual. Half past six. I wash and dress them. I make breakfast. I take them down the back stairs: quiet, quiet, must not wake Mr Evan. I put Jenny in buggy. Little Evan, he want take his bicycle but he not safe with it so I say he must take his scooter. He say scooter is for baby, so he walk beside me. He not happy.

'He is fine when we get to nursery. He run straight in. Jenny and I, back we go and we are coming near the house when we see Mrs Diana get out of big black car in the road. I think what any good girl would think. She is bad woman. I am sorry for poor Mr Evan!'

'You saw Diana with a man? She realized you'd seen her?'

A nod. 'I take Jenny in back way as always. Mrs Diana, she follow me in. I leave buggy in the little hall and I carry Jenny up the stairs. Mrs Diana, she follow me. She hisses, like this, "Ssss!" Like snake. But she say nothing till we are at top of house and I put Jenny in playpen.

'I think maybe she give me money to keep quiet but no, she say I am bad girl, making eyes at Mr Evan! Me? No! Never! I say, he like grandfather and not nice to me that way, ever. Mrs Diana, she shout at me, on and on. I think she will hit me. She say I must pack and go, straight away, that minute! I say I not know where to go, and she say to sleep on street for all she care. So I pack up my things quick, quick. I say, "Where is my money?" but she say I not deserve one penny and to go, out! Now!

'I think maybe I go to my friend who live in Acton but I ring and he not answer and I walk and walk and I cry and cry. Then it is time to collect Little Evan from nursery. I think I say goodbye to him. I go to nursery and he run out and he say he is hungry and he must have food, now! I say to him, "No, you must go home to Mummy". But he say again, "No! I hungry!" He always hungry and tired after nursery.

'We go to McDonald's and he eats. Then he wants go to park and it starts to rain and I think I must take him home, so we walk, oh so slowly, because he is tired and I am tired. All the way home we walk. But there is policeman at door. I say, "What is happening?" And he say, "Go go away! No visitors!" I ask for Mrs Diana and say I did live there, but he say she not there, and not to waste his time. So we go to tea shop and eat cake and that is last of my money. I find bench out of the rain. Little Evan, he so tired he fall asleep and I not know what to do.'

Rafael nodded. 'We can corroborate some of that. Diana asked Susan to fetch Little Evan from his nursery but didn't tell us where it was. We tried to reach Diana and failed. Eventually we found Lucia by contacting Little Evan's nursery and asking for Diana's nanny's details. They gave us her mobile phone number and we got through to her on that. Heaven only knows what would have happened to her and the boy if we hadn't finally managed to track them down and paid for a taxi to bring them back here. She wasn't capable of standing up straight when she arrived, never mind answering questions. Everything she had with her was soaking wet, including shoes. We put her stuff overnight in the drier and hopefully it's fit to wear again now. Diana had no right to turn her out like that, and to refuse her her money, but . . .' He shrugged. 'If there was another man involved, I suppose she was trying to save her reputation.'

Lesley said, 'That makes sense. Now, Lucia, we're very interested to hear about the man you say was with Diana yesterday morning. What time was that?'

'The nursery open half past seven. We come a bit later. Then I take Jenny back and I see Diana getting out of big, black car in the road outside the house. New car. Shiny.'

'Number plate? Make?'

Lucia shrugged. 'Very new. Very big. I not know make.'

'Tell me exactly what you saw.'

Lucia tried to look vicious but really it wasn't in her. Susan thought she looked like a hamster who'd found its water bowl empty.

Lucia said, 'She, Mrs Diana, I see her get out of car and stand on pavement. Then she reach back into car. I think she drop something on her seat.'

Susan asked, 'Her handbag? Large or small? Was it an overnight bag?'

'Is with gold chain, over her shoulder, like so.' She held up her hands to show it had been on the small side. 'No overnight bag. She look inside car for something. Big man get out of driver's seat. Dark suit. He go round car to help her find it. Keys, I think? He gives them to her. He grab her and he kiss her, and they laugh and he get back in car and drive off. She turn and see me. I look at her. She look at me. I not know what to do. I go into house by back door and upstairs as always. She follow me into house and upstairs and tell me to go.'

Tears welled. 'I say, "Give me my wages!" and she laugh, "Ha ha!". You will make her pay me, right?' She looked more than ever like a hamster whose food has been whisked away.

Rafael said, 'So she wasn't home the night her husband was killed.'

Lucia recoiled. 'What! What you say?' Her voice went up into a squeak. 'Mr Evan? He is dead? You not tell me that! Oh, oh! No, no, no, no!' She rocked to and fro, tears spurting. Full blown hysteria this time.

Susan swept up Fifi and made off to the sitting room, followed by shrieks from Lucia. 'She blame me! I know it! She blame me for everything! I am to go prison. Oh, no, no, no!'

Susan checked that Jenny was happy in the playpen with all of Fifi's toys around her, and that Evan was occupied with a book. She went to stand by the window overlooking the neglected garden. She checked that there was no light being thrown on to the lawn – which needed cutting – from Ellie's part of the house. Then she told herself that she needed a new head, since Diana wouldn't be needing artificial light at this time of the morning, would she?

Susan rocked from one foot to the other, holding Fifi in her arms and singing to her. Fifi loved being sung to but she wasn't easily distracted today. Fifi knew that something had gone very wrong in her little world. She screwed her head round to try to see what was going on behind them.

A small hand clutched Susan's jeans. Little Evan was unhappy, too.

Susan sat down in one of the big armchairs by the window, gestured the boy to stand close beside her, and sang to them both. First it was 'Twinkle, twinkle, little star' and then it was 'Pat-a-cake' with all the appropriate actions.

Fifi relaxed, gurgling her pleasure.

Little Evan leaned against Susan's leg. 'Where my Hippo?' And then: 'Silly Lucia! She cry all the time.'

A shriek disturbed them from behind, but it was a shriek of joy. 'U-oh! U-oh!' Rafael had collected Jenny and came to join them. Rafael threw the little girl up into the air and caught her again. She crowed. She loved it, and she loved him, and she didn't care about anything else in the whole wide world.

Evan put his hands behind his back in a gesture mimicking his father, and stared at Fifi, who was comfortably settled in the crook of Susan's arm. Fifi stared back.

Evan looked up at Susan with clear grey eyes which reminded her of Ellie, and said, 'Fifi?' He brought one hand round to his front and waggled his fingers at her.

Fifi looked back up at her mother, checking that it was all right to make friends with this stranger.

Susan smiled and nodded.

Fifi decided that she liked Evan. She waved her arms and gurgled her appreciation. She reached towards him. He caught her hand in his . . . and fell in love. Aged four and a bit. Headlong, desperately in love. He moved closer still, pressing against Susan, relishing the contact, the baby's warmth, the clasp of her hands, her unstinting approval.

Susan caught her breath. She told herself that there was nothing to worry about. A baby and a toddler expressed their liking for one another. A passing phase, surely. But her imagination projected the two of them forward down the years and suggested what might happen to these two if they continued to like one another in the years ahead. Susan foresaw trouble. Evan was a child damaged by his early years. He had received love from Ellie, but not from his father, and there was a query in Susan's mind as to how Diana felt about him.

Fifi had been blessed with love from many directions, all her life. She was a sunny, loving child but no fool. She showed signs of a quick intelligence. Apparently she approved of Evan. Well, she approved of lots of people. Her mother and father, Ellie and Thomas, and now Coralie.

Evan had inherited some characteristics from his parents which were perhaps not altogether desirable although both mother and father were clever in certain ways. Also selfish. Little Evan could be stubborn. On the other hand, he looked out on the world with Ellie's eyes. Perhaps he might turn out all right.

For a dizzying moment Susan wondered which of the two might be the stronger if it came to a conflict.

She told herself she was being absurd. She took a deep breath and let it out slowly. What on earth had come over her, imagining that the two children had bonded for life. What nonsense!

Rafael had collapsed on to the chair opposite, with Jenny rolling about all over him. Rafael sat up and wiped his forehead. 'I've got to go in to work. I have a man coming to look at the door of the lift in the flats, but I don't like to leave you like this. What do you suggest?'

SIX

Saturday mid-morning

Coralie came in, carrying the children's clothes which she'd sorted and folded into a neat pile. She said, 'I can help you out this weekend, but you need a bigger highchair for Jenny, a smaller bed for Evan and the children's toothbrushes and extra undies. Also their wellington boots and macs in case it rains again. Do we get some from the charity shop, or can we get hold of their own things?'

Lesley appeared behind Coralie to say, 'I'm done with that silly child, Lucia. Do you mean to keep her here? She's alternately weeping and wailing that she's got nowhere to go or swearing she's going to sue Diana for damages or go to the papers and tell all about the murdered man's wife being unfaithful to him. Which I'm sure she is perfectly capable of doing.'

Coralie had identified herself with Susan and Rafael. 'Lucia's not much use but I suppose she could help me look after the children for a bit. If she does what I tell her to do.'

Susan looked to Rafael for back-up. 'We can't turn Lucia out on to the streets, can we?'

Rafael sighed. 'No, I suppose not. Did she get the job with Diana through an agency? If Diana pays what she owes the girl, I suppose we could house her till she can get another post or can save up enough to go home.'

Lesley said, 'So, where did you put Diana last night? Isn't it time she got up and faced her responsibilities for a change?'

Susan and Rafael exchanged glances. Rafael said, 'We haven't put her anywhere. We haven't seen her since she dumped Jenny on us yesterday morning. But, we did see something last night that made us wonder if she might have taken refuge next door. We're almost sure there was a light on in Ellie's bedroom last night. The thing is, there's no water in that house. There was a leak in Ellie's en suite and the plumber turned the water off at the mains, so . . .' He raised his hands, feigning an uncharacteristic helplessness.

Lesley's mouth twitched. 'I must admit it did cross my mind that she might try to get in there, too. I rang Ellie last night and she agreed with me. She also said that Diana likes men who are physically well-built and have money. Oh, and she sent me a picture of a groundhog because I said once that I'd never seen one. It looks something like a big squirrel. I don't know what she meant by sending me that in the middle of an investigation. She can be infuriating that way.'

Rafael said, 'Susan's like that, too. She says something which sounds inconsequential but turns out to be true. Her brain makes what seems to be a giant leap into the blue, but she's actually observed a myriad of tiny things and come up with the right answer by some means known only to herself. She's always right. I've learned to listen to her when she says such things.'

Lesley shook her head in wonder. 'So what can you tell me about the groundhog, Susan?'

Susan said, 'I could swat both of you. How do I know what

Ellie meant? Well, perhaps . . . Is it something to do with Diana repeating a certain pattern of behaviour, as happens in the *Groundhog Day* film?' She shook herself out of the chair. 'And, if so . . . Back to basics. Rafael has to go to work, and I need to get these children sorted. Which reminds me: did you manage to get in touch with Evan's grown-up son and daughter?'

'I did. Son is in lockdown and daughter is at some course in Glasgow. I checked, and yes, she's definitely there and has been for three days. I spoke to her late last night. She was shocked to hear the news. She didn't pretend to care about Diana, but I gave her full marks for worrying about the little ones. They're her half-brother and sister, aren't they, even though she's hardly ever set eyes on them? She asked if there was anything she could do to help. She offered to fly back down today if there was a problem looking after the children. I said you were coping for the time being, so if there's no emergency she'll be returning to London on Monday afternoon as planned.'

Susan stared into space. 'Good. Yes, that's good. I was just thinking about what Diana did yesterday. She arrived here expecting to leave Jenny and a whole lot of stuff for the children with Ellie. When she heard Ellie was still away and I refused to give her a key to next door, she decided to leave Jenny and the children's things with me. She didn't leave any of her own things with me. What did you say she took from her bedroom? I got the impression it wasn't much. Surely she must have packed a bag of clothes for herself?'

Rafael said, 'I don't get it. Does it matter what she took?'

Susan reddened. 'Um, probably not. Forget I said anything.'

Lesley said, 'Ellie told me you had a good brain, Susan. She said you worked things out by thinking about how people are. So what's wrong with Diana not packing much for herself?'

'Because she's always perfectly dressed and made up. She's a businesswoman, always on parade. I would have expected her to pack not only toiletries and make-up but several changes of underwear, and at least one business suit, with shoes and jackets, another handbag, a whole lot of stuff. She'd need at least one good suitcase, if not more. She announced her intention of taking herself and the children to Ellie's but she knew the house had been uninhabitable for months and she hadn't kept any of her belongings there, had she? She packed up several bags of things for the children but what did she take for herself?'

Lesley looked annoyed. 'I'll check. She probably meant to return home later to collect some things for herself.' Lesley got through on the phone to the detective constable who'd been on duty at the house the previous day and exchanged a few sharp words. What she heard didn't improve her mood. 'The detective constable says Diana changed her skirt, washed her hands, picked up her jewellery box, and . . . that's all. And no, she didn't return home to collect anything else.'

Susan said, 'No toiletries? No business gear? I don't get it. Another thing – when she found out her mother couldn't take them in and dumped Jenny on us, why didn't she ask us to give her a bed? Had she, perhaps, some other venue in mind?'

Rafael snapped his fingers. 'She planned to move in with her lover?'

Susan frowned. 'Yes, maybe that's what she hoped to do, but it's not what she ended up doing, was it? She might have tried him, but in the end I think she did exactly what she said she'd do in the first place, which was to move into her mother's house . . . except she didn't pack any toiletries for herself. I don't get it.'

Lesley said, 'She didn't have keys to next door, and you didn't give her any. I suppose I'd better check to see if she broke in, and if she's still there. How frustrating. I really do need to speak to her again.'

She started to leave the room, but Susan called out after her. 'I need to get some more things for the children from their house. Is that all right? Will you tell whoever's guarding the premises to let me in?'

Lesley's voice floated back. 'I think Forensics have finished. I'll check. It should be all right if you only take stuff from the top floor. We'll need a receipt, of course. I'll check out next door first and I'll meet you there.'

Jenny hit Rafael in an effort to attract his attention. 'U-oh! U-oh! Play horsies!'

Rafael had had enough. He heaved himself to his feet and deposited the child into Coralie's arms. 'I'll leave you to the joys of domesticity while I get on with some real work. After I've dealt with the lift I'll work from my office at the flats to see if

I can find out who's been giving Diana a good time. Also, I know someone at the golf club who can tell me if Evan's been indulging in any hanky-panky recently. I don't really buy the "random intruders being disturbed" theory, do you?'

He slid out of the room leaving them, literally, holding the baby.

Susan and Coralie looked at one another, raised their eyes to heaven and said, 'Men!'

Susan said, 'Coralie, can you keep your mouth shut? If a story about cheating wives and slaughtered husbands hits the media, you might well find yourself offered money for information. Diana probably deserves everything that's coming to her, but I'd like to protect her children. If you feel it's going to make life awkward for you, then I'd understand if you wanted to follow my husband out of the door.'

'I'm like me dad. The things he's seen and heard . . .! But he don't talk about it none. I can keep me mouth shut if I think it's the right thing to do. These kids need me and so do you, by the look of it. How far gone are you?'

Susan was touched by Coralie's concern. So touched, in fact, that she had to brush tears from her cheeks. 'Three months, I think. I wasn't sure at first and I didn't bother to have a test because so much was going on, what with the move here and everything. Rafael doesn't know. He didn't want us to have another so soon. And now, all this . . .'

'No more picking up that great lump of a boy, then. You put your feet up when you feel like it, right? Now, I'll help you out over the weekend and as for next week, I'm sixteen and a half and I was going to leave school at the end of this term to train to be a nanny, anyway. So you'd be doing me a favour, like, giving me some practical experience.'

Susan said, weakly, 'You're an awful bossy boots, Coralie.'

'Just what you need at the moment. I said to my mum last night, I said that Susan needs to be careful or she'll drop the sprog early, and my mum, she's a midwife, she said as I oughter see you over this rough bit but she says she expects me back home every evening for a meal, so's she can check I'm not overdoing it. If that's all right with you?'

That was a very sensible suggestion. It had occurred to Susan the moment Coralie had walked in that morning, that it would be wonderful to have her full-time and able to stay overnight . . . until cold reason had intervened.

Coralie was too young to live in, and in any case, they had no spare bedroom in which to put her, unless . . . For all of five seconds Susan fantasized about offering Coralie one of the empty, unfurnished rooms in the attic at the top of the house, but then she recalled what they looked like. Putting a new water tank and electrics in had been a major project. Rafael had planned to fit the rooms out eventually to accommodate a lodger, or an expanded family . . . but not yet.

'You are amazing. Coralie, I accept with gratitude and we'll pay you the full rate for a nanny. Have you any idea what we do about young Lucia?'

'Hardly out of nappies herself, is she? Her clothes are dried nicely, and when she's washed her hair and got herself dressed, she'll feel a lot better. Now, I'll get Lucia to help me look after her two while you rescue a highchair and a small bed for Evan and some other stuff from their house. We could do with a second buggy as well. And see if Evan has a scooter. They all seem to have them nowadays and it makes walking with them a lot easier.'

'I think he has a scooter and a bike.' Susan busied herself making a list of what they needed.

'And don't you worry none about Lucia. I'll straighten her out and stop her making a fool of herself with the press. She needs to know she can't talk to them *and* expect to get another job in our line of business. Now you'd better get moving or we'll never get sorted by lunchtime.' She picked Jenny up. 'Pooh, you pong. Come along, now. Let's get you cleaned up. You're a big girl now, and should be in grown-up pants instead of nappies, don't you think?'

Coralie whisked Jenny off, talking to her about how nice it would be to wear pretty pants instead of nappies.

Fifi snuggled into Susan's arm. She was sleepy, due for her morning nap. She had curled her fingers round one of Evan's, and he was leaning close to her but looking back at Coralie with a speculative glint in his eye. Did he think he might play Coralie off against Lucia?

Susan said, 'Now, Evan. Coralie's a proper nanny, right? You do what she says and you'll be safe with her while I go to find Hippo, right?'

He thought about that. He was no fool, was Little Evan. Yes, he recognized that he'd be safe with Coralie. He nodded.

Susan hoisted herself to her feet with Fifi in her arms, feeling the awkwardness in her body for the first time. She was going to show her pregnancy this time earlier than she had with Fifi, wasn't she? 'Time for her morning nap. Evan, would you like to help me tuck her in?'

Susan imagined Ellie standing behind her, nodding and smiling. Ellie and Coralie would get on like a house on fire. Ellie would let Coralie get on with whatever she wanted to do, and Ellie would only have to put in a word now and then – as a suggestion and not an order – and Coralie would know instinctively not to overstep the mark.

Peace and joy would reign.

Susan also knew that Ellie would be giving thanks at this point for answered prayer. Susan said aloud, 'I don't know if I really believe, deep down. But . . . Well, thanks, anyway.'

Legally, Susan was able to drive their big car. She'd passed her test months ago and been added to Rafael's insurance, but she had hardly taken it out since. After Fifi had been born Susan had decided it was better for mother and child to go for a walk with the buggy round the park or to the shops, rather than be stuck in the back of a car in a traffic jam. In short, Susan had flunked it.

But needs must. Not without a qualm, Susan left Fifi and Diana's children in Coralie's hands and set off for Evan's house. She'd taken Fifi's baby seat out of the back of the car to provide more room for the equipment she planned to bring back, but now she wondered if she ought to have organized a removal van as well. How big was Evan's own bed? What did Jenny sleep in? A cot?

She missed Fifi's presence. Fifi was basking in Coralie's affection. Susan told herself she didn't hate Coralie. It was just that she, Susan, missed being away from Fifi. It was the first time they'd been parted. Susan knew it was a necessary part of Fifi's growing up process to have periods of separation. This was why mothers played 'Peep-bo!' with their children. Fifi would be perfectly all right with Coralie. Of course she would.

Susan drove sedately. Or that's what she told herself. She was only honked at twice for driving slowly.

When she got to Evan's house she drew up outside in the road, as there seemed to be a large number of cars in the drive. She recognized Lesley's car, but Diana's didn't appear to be there.

Susan got out of the car, explained to a PC on duty who she was and that she was expected, was told to wait there . . . until Lesley came out, saying, 'You're right. There's a pane missing from the kitchen door at Ellie's. Anyone could put their hand through and turn the key to let them in. Someone stayed overnight, but whoever it was had fled the coop before I arrived. I've put out an all-points bulletin for Diana. Meantime, you can come in. I'll go round with you to see what you'd like to take for the children.'

Lesley hesitated. 'Ellie did say I should let you have a look around, that you might notice something I haven't.' A light laugh. 'Ellie gets these ideas in her head. The house has been photographed from top to bottom. Forensics have been and gone. I'm taking you in through the front door because . . . I suppose you might see something which strikes you as not quite right. If you do, you're at liberty to say so. You don't mind a spot of blood here or there, do you?'

Susan shook her head and told her stomach to behave.

Lesley led the way into the house. 'The place is as the occupants left it, and at first sight it's telling me the same story that Diana gave us, that this was a break-in that went wrong. My instinct tells me it's nothing of the kind. I'm going to talk through what I think happened. Right?'

Susan nodded. She looked round the hall, and shuddered. There were dark splodges on the parquet floor and the panelled walls. There were drifts of grey powder where Forensics had been dusting for fingerprints. Evan's empty wheelchair lay at the foot of the stairs.

Lesley said, 'Yes, it looks exactly as it should if Evan was attacked when he interrupted a burglary. He fought, they whacked him about and left him for dead. Everything I see on the ground floor bears this out. Look, this is where Evan was sleeping when the action started.' She led the way into the big room on the left overlooking the drive.

No blood splotches, a few patches of grey powder. No signs of struggle. This was a room which had been occupied by an invalid. There was a hospital-type bed and all the paraphernalia of a sick room: an angled lamp and a hand bell; a paperback; some medication; spectacles; a box of tissues; a water jug and a couple of empty glasses on the bedside table. A huge television set sat smugly in the bay window. The remote control for the television was lying in the clutter on the bedside table. A man's clothing had been thrown carelessly over a chair nearby, and the previous day's newspapers lay in a heap on the floor.

Susan took a step to one side and accidentally disturbed the top layer of the newspapers, revealing the existence of a laptop.

Lesley picked it up, looking annoyed. 'That should have been taken in for examination with the one we found in the snug opposite. I suppose this was his, and she'd left hers next door. I'll put it in an evidence bag and leave it in the hall.'

Susan turned round, careful not to disturb anything else. There were venetian blinds at the window, and the floor was laid with a substance which would make it easy to move around in a wheelchair. All very clinical.

Lesley said, 'You see the bedclothes have been thrown back. It looks as though he undressed, got into bed, read for a while or watched the telly, turned off the light and settled down to sleep. Agreed?'

Susan said, 'Was he wearing pyjamas when the ambulance men found him? I mean, he hadn't got up and got dressed for the morning?'

'No, he hadn't. He was in his night gear when they found him. It looks as if something disturbed him in the night, he turned on his bedside light and threw back the duvet. Getting into his wheelchair he pushed back the bedside table, disturbing the papers so that they fell on the floor covering the laptop. He then went out into the hall to see what was going on.'

'This was during the night and not early morning? Were the venetian blinds closed or open? They're open now.'

'They were closed when the police arrived in response to Diana's call. They were reopened after the photographer had finished in here. Yes, his bedside light was on. The blinds were also closed in the snug opposite. Let's go across there now, shall we?'

Lesley led the way. 'We found a torch in the hall, left behind by the intruders. It had been covered with tape, won't take fingerprints. It looks as though the intruders brought torches with them in order to find their way around a darkened house in the middle of the night. They came and left by the kitchen quarters, by the way. Diana says she came down the stairs to make her husband's breakfast at nine o'clock, saw her husband lying on the floor in the hall and phoned it in. She says she didn't touch anything else, not even the light switches.'

Susan turned to look back into Evan's bedroom. 'Hang about. I believe Evan was something of a control freak. He wouldn't have gone to bed without having his smartphone within reach. He'd have felt naked without it. And I'll bet you anything you like that there was whisky in one of those cut-glass tumblers on his bedside table.'

'Correct on both counts. Ellie always said he drank too much. As for his smartphone, we found it under a chair in the hall. He'd taken it with him when he left the room, but hadn't been given a chance to use it.' She went on: 'His golf clubs are kept in the hall stand and it looks as if he armed himself with one of them on his way to the snug which is where we think he found the intruders. Now, come and look at this.'

The room on the opposite side of the hall contained a large TV, an expensive sound system, comfortable chairs, a low coffee table and a well-stocked bar.

Lesley said, 'It seems he pretty well lived in those two rooms with forays to the kitchen at the end of the hall and to the downstairs cloakroom.'

This room was a shambles, furniture had been overturned and bottles smashed. Broken glass glistened on the carpet. There were dark blood stains everywhere. Two pictures had been taken off the wall and left propped against a chair.

Susan looked at those two pictures. 'They took those off the wall and carefully laid them aside. Presumably they did that before Evan came upon the scene. They were looking for a safe?'

'The safe is actually behind some panelling in the hall and

they didn't find it. Diana is desperate to get into it. She says that she urgently needs her passport for work purposes.'

'Surely she's not serious about asking for her passport at the moment? Didn't you say she was after some documents as well? What would they be?'

'We'll find out as soon as we can get into the safe. She refused to give us the code but we'll get an expert to open it for us.' Lesley led the way back to the hall. 'We found Evan's wheelchair more or less where you see it at the bottom of the stairs. It had been overturned, with him still in it. One of his golf clubs was lying nearby. It was bloodstained, so he'd obviously used it on at least one of the intruders. He himself had been knifed *and* hit with a blunt instrument – possibly by his own golf club, though we won't be sure of that till later.

'Further along the hall . . .' She led the way. 'Dining room on the right, undisturbed. And then . . .' Lesley opened the door to a small room which had obviously been used as a study, with desktop computer, printer, et cetera. 'Diana's domain, we assume. Equally undisturbed. Then there's a toilet and shower . . . and finally we come to the kitchen quarters.'

An unobtrusive door let them into a small lobby leading to what had once been servants' quarters. On the right there was a glass-panelled door which allowed them to see into the kitchen. To the left was a narrow stair which led up and up, out of sight. Tucked to one side by the back stairs was a small bike with stabilizers, a scooter and a child's pushchair. Beyond was a substantial door which must lead to the outside world.

Lesley said, 'The kitchen quarters seem equally undisturbed. A smaller television's still there and a sink full of dirty dishes. A cleaner turned up yesterday at about half ten. She says she was supposed to clear up here, to give Evan some lunch and hoover around. She says she's not paid to clean up this mess and I don't blame her. Anyway, there's no blood, no destruction anywhere on the ground floor apart from the hall and the snug. Beyond the kitchen there's a utility room. Beyond that there's a conservatory and a pane of glass has been broken in the French windows that lead on to the garden. We think that's the way the intruders came and left.

'Putting it all together, it looked as if two or three people came in the back way. They were not looking for easily disposable electronic units or cash. They were looking for a safe. They didn't bother to take the televisions, or the laptops, or anything else that we can see. They made straight for the snug. Why? Because they had some reason to think there was a safe there? They took the pictures off the walls and set them aside. Some noise woke Evan, who got out of bed and into his wheelchair. He ought to have rung the police instead of trying to tackle them, but he didn't. He armed himself with a golf club and tackled the intruder or intruders in that front room. Judging by the destruction, there was a right ding dong.

'We think he got in a few blows himself which may be helpful when the labs have looked at the blood which has been liberally splashed around. He was driven back into the hall, the golf club taken off him, more blood was shed and finally, still in his wheelchair, he was thrown down on to the floor and left to die while the intruders retreated, probably by the way they had come.

'There were two sets of footprints in the blood on the hall floor. Trainers. Different sizes. That may be helpful. We think that two of the intruders wore gloves. There are imprints of a pair of leather gloves and of a woollen pair. We think one of the men wearing trainers slipped in the blood and saved himself from falling by putting his gloved hand down. There was also a bloody print of a woollen glove on the golf club which we think was used on Evan. Two intruders were careful to wear gloves.

'There was one fresh set of fingerprints on the door to the kitchen quarters. We don't know yet whose they were. Maybe they were made by someone unconnected with the break-in. A cleaner, perhaps. Or by Diana, even. So tell me, Susan, why am I not satisfied with Diana's story?'

Susan considered what had happened in that hall and felt sick. 'Evan put up quite a fight. Furniture was overturned. Glasses were smashed. All that must have made a lot of noise. This bears out Lucia's story that Diana spent the night elsewhere. If she'd been here, the noise must have woken her. I know she said she took a sleeping pill but no, I can't believe she was here.'

'You've put your finger on it. She wasn't here. Like you, I believe the nanny's story about seeing Diana canoodling with a man early the following morning. I agree it looks as if she hadn't slept in her own bed that night. She lied to us and we can get her for that when we find her.'

Susan said, with care, 'I can see her divorcing Evan to hitch her star to someone else, but I can't see her arranging to have him murdered when he was so frail and not expected to live long anyway. I mean, that's not clever.'

Lesley sighed. 'I agree. So why not tell the truth? She lied to us, and that's not clever, either. She's up to something, but what? Murder? I don't think so. I know "Ears", my beloved superior, would love to throw the book at her, but I simply can't believe it. If she was with her lover boy, then he'll give her an alibi, and there was no reason that I can see for her to arrange a break-in. I could swear that her shock when she heard of his death was genuine. I expect we'll find it was a random burglary by a couple of louts who had heard there were rich pickings to be found here.'

'And yet . . .?'

'Yes. I believe that she was in some way responsible for his death.'

Susan felt the same way. 'If she has an alibi, and if she can think up some story as to why she needs her passport now—'

'I know, I know. She's going to walk away smelling of roses. Well, I'm going to do what I can to prove that in some way she was involved, even though I can't think how. She's certainly going to have to explain the discrepancies in her story.'

SEVEN

Saturday mid-morning

Lesley led Susan back into the hall and up the front stairs. 'I'm not the only one who doesn't like the scenario that's been presented to us. The constable who'd been left on duty here yesterday morning and who oversaw Diana's leaving is an older woman, not easily impressed. She said she wasn't happy to write the situation off as a householder interrupting a burglary. She admitted she couldn't say why she wasn't happy, but she wasn't.

'When she arrived, Diana was sitting on the floor next to her dying husband and holding his hand. She said she'd come down to make him breakfast and found him there on the floor. She'd rung the police, opened the front door to let them in and returned to sit down on the floor next to her husband. When told she'd have to vacate the premises, Diana led the DC up the stairs to her bedroom. This way . . .'

The first-floor landing was spacious and well lit by a big, stained-glass window. Lesley flung open the first door they came to. 'At the DC's request, Diana shed the clothes she was wearing, washed her hands and found another outfit to wear. The DC bagged up her bloodstained clothing, including her shoes, and retained them for forensic examination. As you can see, the bed had been neatly made. Later, the DC volunteered the information that she herself had been trained to throw back bedclothes when she got up in the morning to let the bed air, and only made her bed after breakfast.'

Susan suppressed a smile. 'She was trying to tell you that she didn't think Diana had slept in her own bed. Well, we're pretty sure she didn't, aren't we? Lucia's testimony has put paid to that.'

Lesley agreed. 'Yes, I can get Diana for that lie. She told me at the hospital that she'd taken a sleeping pill, slept through the night and not been disturbed by any noise. She said she'd got up, dressed, went upstairs to get the children washed, dressed and to feed them breakfast. She said she'd taken both children down the back stairs, put Jenny in the buggy, had Little Evan walk beside her, delivered him to the nursery, brought Jenny back, took her upstairs and only then went down to cope with Evan . . . when she found him dying in the hall.'

'We know the nanny took Evan to the nursery. Not Diana. At least, I suppose that has to be checked with the nursery?'

'Yes, we'll have to check that. The detective constable said Diana had spent very little time in her bedroom. She changed her outfit, collected a small jewellery box from her dressing-table, and that was all.'

Susan queried, 'Handbag?'

'On the floor in the hall. She'd dropped it there when she

found her husband dying. She took it up to her bedroom with her when she went to change her clothes. Apart from the jewellery box, it was the only thing of hers she removed from the house.'

'Large or small? Not inspected at the time of leaving?'

'No. Diana then led the way upstairs to collect her daughter and to pack some things for the children.'

Susan said, 'She'd just spent a night away and should have had an overnight bag with her, or one of those large handbags into which you can stuff half the contents of your office. Lucia said Diana only had a small handbag over her shoulder when she got out of the car, so . . .'

Lesley frowned. 'Ah. You mean . . .?'

'She keeps some toiletries and a change of clothes somewhere else. She's an estate agent. Perhaps she has the keys to a flat nearby? Somewhere that she can take her lover to? Let's have a look at what's in the bathroom cabinet.'

Lesley said, 'It's all been photographed, so I don't see why not.'

In the bathroom, it didn't look as if anyone had used the shower for a while. There were tissues and shower gel at the side of the bath. The washbasin was slightly stained with the residue from when Diana had washed the blood off her hands, and a hand towel had been crumpled and left on the floor.

Susan said, 'What's inside the cabinet?' She prised the door open with her fingertips. 'Paracetamol, expired-date eye-drops, foot powder, indigestion tablets, shampoo and conditioner, an astringent eye solution, toothpaste. Electric toothbrush. A pack of sleeping pills, two missing. Question: why didn't she take any of this stuff with her?'

She went back to the bedroom. The dressing table boasted a full range of cosmetics and another box of tissues. It didn't look as if anything had been taken from there, either. Susan looked in the waste bin. 'Ah-ha, an empty packet of birth control pills.'

She showed these to Lesley and said, 'Diana's on the pill. I wouldn't have thought Evan was capable nowadays, would you? But perhaps she needs it for another reason?'

Lesley made notes. She was angry that she hadn't thought of this herself. 'We'll check on that.'

At that moment Susan remembered that she'd discussed going on the pill with Rafael and hadn't done anything about it. He didn't know she'd not been using contraception for some time. He didn't know she was pregnant again.

Oh dear. She retched and made it to the toilet just in time.

Lesley patted Susan's shoulder. 'Another one on the way? I keep thinking about having one myself but then Ellie said something about some men never growing up enough to be good fathers.' Her mouth twisted. 'My husband isn't ready for it yet.'

Susan nodded. She'd heard Ellie on the subject of the selfishness of Lesley's husband. It was best not to comment.

Susan washed her face with her hands, rinsed out her mouth, and patted herself dry with some hand tissues. 'Is there anything else on this floor that you want me to see?'

'No. The constable said she'd checked the other rooms on this level and none of them were in use. So, following in Diana's footsteps, let's go up upstairs to the children's quarters. As you can see, the top floor can be shut off from the rest of the house.'

At the top of the stairs they were faced with a landing which was only half the size of the one below. At some point a partition had been put up across the space to keep the nursery rooms as a separate flat which could only be reached through a stout door. Opening this let them into the other half of the landing from which various rooms could be accessed. A skylight showed the day had clouded over.

Lesley tried opening and closing the door to the top floor. 'It is just possible that anyone sleeping up here wouldn't hear any of the commotion downstairs, but we will have to test that. This way.'

Lesley ushered Susan into a large nursery, which took up most of the top floor. Here there were two small beds, unmade; a playpen and shelving full of toys large and small; small chairs round a table; an easel; a well-stocked bookcase. There was everything to amuse two small children, including a small television set. There were colourful posters on the walls, and a wall fitment holding clothes.

There were some signs of disarray. Diana had packed for the children in haste, hadn't she?

Susan thought she wasn't going to be able to get the two beds, the chest of toys and the easel into the car. She would have to ask Rafael to organize transport.

Lesley said, 'When the DC came up here with Diana, they found the little girl in her playpen watching a cartoon on a tablet.' Lesley stooped to pick up a tablet from the floor and handed it to Susan. 'You'd better take this. As you can see, there's nothing to show the intruders came up here. Next along . . .'

Lesley opened another door. A light came on automatically to reveal the first steps of the back staircase down to the ground floor.

Next came the bathroom. Towels in disarray, toothbrushes left out. Susan said, 'I'd better take their toiletries. I feel so guilty. They didn't get their teeth brushed last night, or this morning.'

Lesley moved her on. 'The kitchen. Small but practical. Fridge, cooker, microwave, sink and dishwasher but no washing machine or drier – they must use the ones in the kitchen area downstairs.'

Susan looked around. There was a large highchair for Jenny, a high stool for Evan, and an adult's chair, all ranged around a table set against the wall. There was evidence of breakfast for two children and an adult; three empty eggshells, toast crusts, half a bottle of milk, three banana skins, half a pot of tea; an adult mug contained the dregs of a cup of tea, beside two small plastic cups for the children.

This was the breakfast which had been prepared by Lucia and eaten by her and the children before they left to go to the nursery.

Lesley said, 'Diana told me she'd made breakfast for the children before taking her son to nursery. I tried to work out how long it would have taken her to get the children up, dressed, and fed, taken the little boy to nursery and returned. Then she had to take Jenny upstairs and put her in her playpen. And then – if you were Diana – you'd go down to make Evan his breakfast. How long would all that take? Two hours, perhaps?'

'Well, we know Diana didn't do that. She wasn't even in the house when Lucia got the children up, provided breakfast and took Evan to nursery. It was only when Lucia was on her way back to the house that she spotted Diana in the road, embracing a strange man who drove a big car. I suppose Diana hoped to hide her affair by following Lucia into the house and giving her the sack. If we believe the last part of her story, Diana didn't know that when she went down into the hall after giving Lucia the sack, she'd find Evan there, dying.'

Lesley bit back a laugh. 'It must have been quite a moment. In a way, I do admire her quick thinking. She might have got away with it . . . only . . . No, there's too many holes in her story. I feel almost sorry for her until I think that if she'd slept here on Friday night she could have heard the intruders, rung the police and got Evan to hospital in time to save him. Well, perhaps not. His injuries were extensive. But, she did treat young Lucia badly, didn't she? This is the nanny's room, next to the nursery.'

'Lucia thinks she left her cross and chain here. Mind if I look for it?'

The room was not large, but comfortably furnished with a single bed, armchair, desk, wardrobe, shelving and a chest of drawers. A small television was on the wall opposite the bed. A student's idea of digs?

Everything was in disarray, drawers pulled out, hangers left on the floor, a crumpled towel tossed into a corner, bedclothes thrown back.

Susan threw the duvet and pillows on to a chair, followed by the bottom sheet, but there was no trace of the jewellery. She pulled the bed away from the wall and there in the corner lay the chain, next to a bulky, pink soft toy with a silly smile on its face. The missing 'Hippo'?

Susan pocketed the chain and dandled Hippo. 'You'll let me take what I need for the children? It's silly to go out and buy stuff when it's all here. I really need the two small beds, Evan's scooter and bike, Jenny's highchair and buggy, as well as their other toys and clothes. I'll ask Rafael to organize some transport.'

'They now belong to Diana, but as she's gone AWOL . . .' A shrug. 'She asked you to take the children, so yes, I don't see why you can't take what you need, provided you give me a receipt for everything. Poor kids. How are they taking it?'

'They don't know their father's dead, and I don't know how to tell them. It's really up to Diana to break the news to them.' Susan started to make a pile of small items she could take in the car. 'Toiletries, a towel or two – I don't think I have enough. Their toys, books, that tablet. The children's outdoor clothes and wellies will be down in the lobby, I expect. I brought a couple of tote bags to take stuff away in, but they're not going to be enough, are they?'

There was a lot of noise from below.

Susan said, 'Was that someone in the hall because if so, I heard it from here?'

'But we didn't close that door at the top of the stairs, did we?' Lesley took the main stairs down at a lick.

Susan followed, more slowly.

A bright ray of sun from the window on the first-floor landing cast shadows over the hall, picking out the smears of grey fingerprint powder and the dark stains on the parquet floor.

Diana was there, having a shouting match with the detective constable in the hall. He was trying to tell her she couldn't come in, and she was screaming at him that he should get out of her way as it was *her* house.

Diana in a rage was quite a sight. She was not a big woman, but she dominated the constable, who looked both baffled and angry.

Lesley made her way down to the hall. 'Diana, where have you been? We need to talk—'

Susan hung back as the two women went nose to nose.

Diana was white with fury. 'My husband is killed by criminals and what are you doing about it, may I ask? Then I came to fetch my laptop, which I need for work and this . . . this cretin tried to refuse me entry! My laptop is on charge in the study. It's bad enough that you refuse to let me access the safe, but this . . . this is police harassment.'

'There's no laptop in the study.'

'Don't be ridiculous. Of course there is. Do you think I don't know where I left it? I use it every day for business. I brought it home with me on Thursday evening as usual, read some emails, paid a couple of bills and left it on charge in my study.'

'It's not there now. And if it's so necessary for everyday life, why did you not take it with you yesterday?'

'I was in shock, wasn't I? If it's not there now, then I suppose the burglars took it. You've got to get it back for me!'

Lesley said, 'Calm down. We found two laptops when we arrived, but neither was in your study. We've taken both to see—'

'How dare you! You have no right—'

'Actually, I have,' said Lesley. 'It is normal practice to inspect the emails and business details of persons of interest in a murder case, which is why we removed your laptop.'

By which Susan understood that Lesley thought there was something on Diana's laptop which was *not* business, and that if it had been found in Evan's bedroom then it followed that it was he who had taken it there. If Evan had been snooping on his wife's laptop, then maybe he had some reason to do so. What might that 'something' be? Emails to her staff and prospective buyers? Or perhaps some emails which were not of a business nature?

Diana was defiant. 'My laptop is password protected.'

'Then perhaps you will be so good as to give me your password. We have people who can always work it out, you know. But the sooner we can read your emails the sooner we can clear you of—'

'Of what?' Diana sneered.

'It's standard procedure. We have to clear you of any interest in your husband's death.'

Diana managed a harsh laugh, but her eyes switched to and fro.

Lesley produced her best imitation of a crocodile. 'I expect you wrote the password down in your diary, or on a calendar. People have to remember so many passwords nowadays that they have to keep a note of them somewhere.'

Diana blenched. Clearly, Lesley's words had hit home. She said, through her teeth, 'Look all you like. I have a business appointment in town at noon and can't hang around here watching you playing games.'

Susan suppressed a giggle, but Diana must have seen some movement on the stairs for she looked up to see who was watching her from above. Susan had been rather enjoying the scene until Diana turned on her, too.

'And what, may I ask, is Susan doing here? Who's looking after my children if she's running around, hanging on to your coat-tails?'

Susan gasped. 'You horrible woman! If you must know, I came to collect some things your children desperately need. They are being properly looked after, which is more than I can say for the way you handled them, dumping them on me without checking whether I had beds for Jenny and Evan, who's missing his Hippo. He wet the bed last night, and you haven't even asked how they are!'

Diana's eyes switched left and right. 'Of course I care about them. But I can't have them with me for the moment. You'll have to look after them for a while.'

Susan told herself to breathe deeply. 'Have I your permission to take their things from here and hold them till you are able to take the children again? I need all sorts of things, including Evan's bed and Jenny's highchair and buggy. Everything they might need. I'll give you a receipt for what I take.'

Diana bit her lip. 'I suppose that's reasonable. Yes, go ahead. I know where you live.'

Lesley leaped on this. 'Diana, you are officially giving Susan permission to take the children's belongings? Their beds, toys, everything that belongs to them?'

'I said so, didn't I? I suppose it's marginally better she looks after the kids than handing them over to Social Services.' In the tone of one choosing which filling she'd like on her pizza, she said, 'You can give them a kiss from me.'

Susan rolled her eyes, but kept quiet.

Lesley tried to resume control of the proceedings. 'Well, now that's settled, Diana, I'd like you to come down to the station and talk through one or two details of the statement you made yesterday. I must warn you that we have located and spoken to your nanny, who has told us an interesting story about you meeting a man—'

'Did she tell you that I'd sacked her for misconduct? No, she wouldn't tell you that, would she! She was always rubbing herself up against Evan and using baby talk! Ugh! And he? He ought to have known better. He was deteriorating from day to day but he still encouraged her to come on to him. She was such a lazy cow, she neglected the children and expected me not to notice their clothes were food-stained and their hair and teeth not brushed.

'I told her, oh yes! I warned her. Twice I told her she had to mend her ways, but would she listen? No way. She said I was a jealous cow and that Evan would stand up for her. I should have sacked her there and then, but I was booked to go to a conference overnight so I left it till my return.'

'What conference?' said Lesley. 'This is the first I've heard of—'

Diana ploughed straight on. 'And what happened? Did she listen out for the children? If she had been, she'd have phoned the police and they'd have arrested the burglars before Evan . . . No, it doesn't bear thinking about!'

'She says she saw—'

'You can't believe a word she says. She hasn't told you I'd given her a final warning to leave, has she? No, of course not. And you fell for it! Did she tell you she wanted me to pay her off in return for forgetting she'd seen me being dropped off by a friend after a conference out of town? No, she didn't, did she? He's a work colleague, by the way. He happened to offer me a lift to and from the conference. He's a useful contact, but nothing more than a friend. Well, that was the last straw. Yes, I gave her the sack. Of course I did. What would you have done in my place?'

Susan was shaken. Could it be that Diana was right about Lucia?

Diana sounded so convincing! But . . .

Lesley frowned. 'So you admit you weren't here last night. I'd like this friend's name and where I can contact him.'

'Certainly not. I won't have my friends treated as if they were criminals.' Diana clearly felt this was a winning move. Her colour returned to something resembling normal. 'I've heard of police brutality and this is the outside of enough. My husband is dead and I have to keep the show on the road. I need my laptop. I have work to do, even if you haven't.'

'I can always arrest you for obstructing police enquiries.' Lesley had begun to lose it.

'Instead of trying to track down the men who murdered my husband, you steal my property and intend to constrain my freedom of movement? I don't think so.'

Between gritted teeth, Lesley continued, 'Would you prefer to be taken down to the station in handcuffs?'

'Is that a threat? Well, you may force me to go with you to the station but I can tell you here and now that I'm not saying another word till my solicitor is with me. You know the man I mean, don't you? My mother's solicitor. He's the best.'

Lesley bit the words off. 'I know his reputation. Are you sure he'll act for you? Have you asked your mother if she'll foot the bill?'

'What's that to you?'

There was a ring on the doorbell, and the detective constable went to see who was calling. There was a whispered exchange with Lesley, and in strolled . . . Rafael, carrying an official-looking envelope.

Susan blinked. What was he doing here? He moved into the pool of light cast from the window on the floor above. It silhouetted him against the panelling. Rafael was wearing black leathers so he must have come on his motorbike. Susan thought he looked like an eagle. A handsome eagle, but one whose eyes had locked on to its prey. His prey was Diana, whom he'd never liked and whose treatment of her mother had frequently made him angry on her behalf.

His eyes flickered up to Susan, acknowledging her presence. For a second his expression relaxed only to harden as he turned on Diana. His manner was dispassionate. He was ice cold.

Susan shivered, deliciously. She knew of her husband's reputation as a shrewd business operator but she hadn't seen that side of him before. She was about to see him in action. Hooray!

Diana lost a fraction of her defiant attitude. 'You? What are you doing here?'

'Looking for you,' said Rafael. 'Your office said you'd been in but left to deal with some important matter. I hoped I'd find you here . . .' He handed her an envelope. 'This is a formal notice of eviction from this property.'

Diana gasped. 'You can't do that! Now Evan's dead this is my house!'

'No, it isn't. As you very well know, this house is owned by the trust fund which your mother founded. Evan rented it from the trust. No rent has been received for some five and a half months, so the trust has every right to serve you with a notice of eviction.'

Diana tore the papers into small pieces and threw them at Rafael. 'What nonsense! How dare you! My mother would never evict me.'

'She is not here. The general manager and the finance director of the trust convened a meeting of the trust this morning. They considered the records and decided that, as Evan had failed to respond to no less than four reminders about non-payment of rent, the trust needs to take steps to evict him.'

Diana lost none of her bravado. 'How dare you! With my husband not yet in his grave! How heartless is that! How could you possibly threaten a poor widow and her children with eviction at this time! I'll go to the newspapers! They'll take my side and your name will be mud!'

'The trust is giving you thirty days to get out. The courts might give you another thirty days, but in the end you will have to vacate the premises. Even you cannot expect to occupy a house without paying for it.'

'You haven't dared to run this by my mother. She'll not see me thrown out of my family home.'

Rafael suppressed a smile. 'Your mother is unlikely to oppose the wishes of her general manager.'

This was hitting below the belt. Diana had once been married to the man who was now the trust's general manager. During the course of their marriage Diana had systematically reduced a decent, hardworking man to a quivering wreck. With Ellie's help, he'd rebuilt his life. His second marriage had been happy and he was an outstandingly successful general manager of Ellie's trust. Although he had a reputation for fair-mindedness, Diana understood that in this matter he would not take her side.

Diana staggered. She clutched at the newel post at the bottom of the stairs. 'I'll give you a cheque now for half of whatever's owing. I'll give you the rest at the end of the month. You can't turn us out.'

'The trust will be happy to receive some back rent from you. But the eviction order stands.'

'You bastard! I'll have you for this! I know what you are!

A worm feeding off the carcass of the dead! A criminal who swindled his way into the property of a dead man! A womanizer who only married that fat slob Susan because she was Ellie's favourite! And little do you know what she's been up to behind your back!'

Susan yelled, 'How dare you!' She plunged down the stairs and would have attacked Diana if Rafael hadn't managed to step between them and envelop his wife in his arms. She struggled to release herself, but he lifted her off the floor and swung her away.

Lesley tried not to laugh. 'That's enough!'

Diana took a hasty step back. She teetered on high heels and fell to the ground. Awkwardly. She screeched. 'She assaulted me! I'll sue her for assault!'

'Steady!' said Rafael to a struggling Susan. 'Susan, don't give her the satisfaction of suing you for assault! I cherish your defence of me, my sweet, but I think you'd better calm down.'

Lesley said, 'She didn't push you, Diana, and the only slanderous words I heard were those you uttered about Rafael.'

'You!' Diana swung on the detective constable. 'You heard her defame me!'

'I heard you slander this man here,' said the DC, poker-faced. 'You said something nasty about his wife, too.'

Rafael set Susan on her own feet but retained his hold of her. He looked amused. 'Well, Susan. Have you really been playing away? Am I not man enough for you?'

Susan crumpled against him. 'Oh, of course you are. How could she even think . . .! And it's no use saying she didn't mean it, because she did. She spreads fear and hatred wherever she goes. She's horrible to Ellie, and she doesn't give a damn about her children, and she's going to walk away from this just like she always does, leaving someone else to clear up after her! And what she said about you is not true, either!'

Rafael looked at Susan with something like a guilty plea in his eyes. 'And you'll never bring my spotty past up against me again? I promised you I'd go straight and I have.'

'Yes, of course you have.' Susan wanted to kick him. Hard. She wanted to throw him down on the floor and have her wicked way with him. She was sulky and cross and weepy and she wanted reassurance that he didn't think she was a fat slob and that he'd only married her because Ellie was fond of her.

The landline phone rang. Or was it someone's mobile?

Susan dived for her pocket, as did Rafael . . . as did Lesley and the DC. It was Susan's phone which was ringing. And then Lesley's. Both answered.

EIGHT

Saturday late morning

Lesley said, 'What! Who . . .?' She strode up and down the hall, listening to somebody on the phone who was telling her something she didn't want to hear.

Susan's mobile said, 'It's Coralie here.'

Who was Coralie?

Oh, of course. Coralie. Back at the house. Looking after Lucia and the children. 'Yes, Coralie?'

There was a commotion in the hall. Lesley shouted, 'Stop her!'

Diana had taken advantage of the confusion to slip past the detective constable and disappear out of the front door. They heard her car rev up and thunder out on to the road before anyone could catch her.

Susan held her phone close to her ear. 'Can you repeat that, Coralie?'

Coralie did.

'Oh,' said Susan. 'Yes, I can see she would want her money but I'm at Diana's house now, collecting stuff for the children. I'll get back as soon as I can.' She switched off.

Rafael raised an eyebrow. 'We have another visitor?'

'Someone who wanted to ask Ellie for the money Diana owed her, but of course there's no one there so she knocked on our door and Coralie—'

'Coralie invited her in and pried all her secrets out of her. Coralie is enjoying this.'

'Yes,' said Susan, with doubt in her voice. 'This is getting messy and she's very young.'

Rafael turned Susan towards the stairs. 'Let's fetch the kids' stuff and get out of here.' When he saw what needed to be collected, he took charge. 'We'll put a few things in your car and I'll organize a van to get the rest.'

He helped Susan make a list for Lesley of everything they were taking and decided what could go in the car and what would have to wait for a removal van.

Susan quailed at the thought of driving such a heavily laden car home but Rafael couldn't do it as he'd come on his motorbike.

Susan had been badly shaken by the encounter with Diana. She told herself not to think about it for the moment. Concentrate, woman! It was good for her to have to drive the car. She could manage it if she kept calm. Of course she could. Even in bright sunshine which got into her eyes. And no, she hadn't her sunglasses with her.

She set off in sedate fashion. She told herself that millions of women drove large cars every day and managed it. Providing, of course, that they didn't have to park in a space too small for their juggernauts. All she had to do was to drive along a couple of quiet roads, turn left into their road, left again into their driveway, and park as near to their front door as was feasible . . . and if it was at an angle, well, she should be congratulated at having got there at all, right?

The plumber's van was parked at Ellie's front door. Well, hooray. At last he could fix that water leak in Ellie's en suite.

The sun shone brightly and there was a slight breeze. A perfect day for moving house.

Coralie and a strange woman with frizzy orange hair shot out of the house with Lucia and formed a chain to unload the children's things from the car.

Coralie plucked the first bag out, threw it to the stranger, who handed it to the drippy Lucia, who dumped it in the hall. Coralie would make an excellent policewoman on demo duty, or a sergeant in the army. Coralie was just too efficient for words while Susan felt like a squashed tomato, or something that been run over by a bus.

'Brilliant!' cried Coralie, extracting the last of the equipment – Jenny's buggy – from the boot of the car, and slamming the hood down. 'Now we can get organized. Lucia, tuck the buggy under the stairs out of the way. Marcy, this is Susan, the boss, who you wanted to talk to. Lucia, take that bag of children's clothes upstairs, will you? I'll help you sort it when we've fed our faces.'

The woman with the dyed frizzy hair was called Marcy? She looked as if she'd had a rough life and mostly come out on top. Supermarket till operator? Ah-ha! Cleaner to Diana?

Marcy nodded to Susan. 'Marcy. Short for Marcia. Dunno what Mum were thinking of to call me by that poncy name, but there, we all have our cross to bear, don't we?'

The children bounced around, hyper at having their bits and pieces restored to them. Susan plucked Fifi from her buggy and cradled her. How she'd missed her baby! Fifi crowed, delighted to be back in her mother's arms where she belonged. 'Um, um, um!' she said. Which was short for 'Mum'?

Coralie reported. 'Fifi would *not* go to sleep, so Evan kept her amused by playing with her. Jenny's been as good as gold, haven't you, my pet?'

'Cuckoo, cuckoo?' said Jenny, who had pressed herself to the glass front door, looking out for Rafael.

Susan fished the cross and chain out of her pocket and handed it to Lucia, who burst into tears and kissed it before hanging it around her neck. The girl was looking much better. She'd washed her hair and was wearing a decent T-shirt and jeans.

Susan gave Evan his horrible Hippo, which he immediately held up to Fifi . . . who smelled it and crowed. What those two bright children could see in that repulsive soft toy, Susan failed to understand.

Susan gave Jenny her tablet. This distracted her nicely. She stopped looking for Rafael and toddled off to play with it in a quiet corner of the big room.

Coralie and Marcy put Jenny's highchair together in the kitchen while Lucia hovered, trying and failing to lay the table for lunch. Coralie told Susan to sit down and give Fifi her bottle. Susan tried to resent this. Who was the boss in this house, pray? Her or Coralie?

'You look tired,' said Coralie to Susan. Naturally this made Susan feel more tired than ever. So she did as she was told.

Marcy laid about Lucia with a tea towel. 'Leave setting the table to me. Go and make yourself useful for once. Get those children to go to the loo and to wash their hands before they come to the table, right?'

Coralie bustled about. 'Pasta with cheese sauce, frozen peas and sweetcorn for the little ones. Pizza for us, and a nice hot cuppa for afters.'

Marcy rattled cutlery on to the table, 'Ellie said as you was a good mother, Susan, and I can see you are.'

Susan worked out the connection. 'You got work with Diana through a local domestic agency? You knew Ellie because you've cleaned for her at some point in the past. You thought she'd be back by now, so you came round to see if she'd get you the money Diana owed you?'

'I did, but she wasn't there and the plumber said I should try next door which is how I met young Coralie here, and she told me about Mrs Di dumping her kids and their nanny on you. That poor kid, Lucia, she didn't know nothing when she come to this country and she don't know much now. The little ones put up with her and she didn't make no trouble except she did make eyes at Mister, oh yes, she did that all right, thinking he'd stand up for her to Mrs Di, which was not going to happen. Anyone could see that but her. I tried to tell her but some people don't like being told, do they?'

Lucia led the two older children in. The children looked clean and were ready for food. Marcy and Coralie got them seated at the table, while Lucia hovered in helpless fashion. Two competent nannies and one learner.

Coralie served hot pizza for the grown-ups. She cut off a wedge and put it on a plate at Susan's elbow, while she and Marcy oversaw the children's lunch, wiped up stray bits of food and spills of juice, managing to eat themselves and to talk at the same time. Multitasking par excellence.

Marcy said, 'It's like this. I went to Mrs Di from the agency for a couple of hours a week at first. Then he, the Mister, got worse and she was working all hours – or out all hours, anyway – and she said she'd pay me direct if I left the agency and went to her every day because her husband needed everything doing for him and Lucia here was not going into a sick room, she wasn't paid for that, was she?'

Lucia bubbled with indignation. 'No, never!'

Marcy nodded. 'Well, you did have your hands full with the two children. So I said I didn't mind if I did and it was fine at first. I turned up about half nine, sometimes later, Monday to Friday, put in four hours most days, sometimes five. I did the shopping and the cooking and the laundry and seeing to Mister when he rang that dratted bell that he had in the front room. I left Mrs Di a note of what hours I'd put in, and she'd leave me my money in the kitchen every Friday. I didn't do weekends, not with my family needing me then, you see?'

'I do,' said Susan. 'I bet you charged less than agency staff and did a better job of it.'

Marcy patted her hair. 'That's not for me to say, but yes, that's about right. It was more convenient as I didn't have to use up time travelling to and fro between jobs, and I kept me mouth shut about what I saw and heard.'

'I'm fascinated,' said Susan, burping Fifi and then giving her some of the pureed goo which Coralie had warmed up for her. Whatever it was, Fifi liked it.

Marcy rolled her eyes at the children. 'Little pitchers have big ears. Let's send them into the big room to play, shall we? Lucia, you can put the telly on for a bit to keep them happy. We'll take them out to the park later on.' She wiped Evan's hands and mouth and set him down on the floor. 'Off you go, little man.'

Jenny said, 'Cuckoo?' and lurched towards the front door, but went willingly enough when Lucia took her hand and led her away.

Marcy switched the kettle on. Coralie swiped everything off the table and into the dishwasher. Fifi dozed off in Susan's arms.

Coralie said, 'Shall I put her in the buggy for a nap?'

Susan didn't really want to let go of Fifi, but she knew it was the right thing to do. Susan found a tissue, blew her nose and gratefully accepted a mug of tea laced with sugar. And a chocolate biscuit.

Marcy watched Susan, sipping her mug of tea as it went down. Susan realized she was being judged and tried not to squirm.

The sun had moved round and shone full into the kitchen. They really must get a blind for that window.

Marcy said, 'Ah, there's nothing like a good cup of Yorkshire tea.'

Coralie nodded, drew up a chair and crunched on a biscuit.

Marcy said, 'This is a nice, quiet house. Yon Fifi's a happy soul. Yours is a good man, Susan, I can tell. Same as Ellie's.' She drained her mug and looked into it.

Coralie grinned. 'Don't tell me you read the tea leaves.'

Marcy laughed. 'Not since they changed to tea bags, no.' She sat with her legs spread out, capable hands folded on the table before her. 'Well, Susan, the thing is, Coralie told me you'd see me right if I was straight with you, but I have to tell you, I won't go to the cops.'

Susan watched Marcy as Marcy watched her. Susan thought about the way Diana bulldozed her way through life. 'Diana threatened you with some lie or other to make you keep your mouth shut?'

Marcy nodded. 'Ah, Coralie said as you weren't as green as you looked.'

'Par for the course,' said Susan, who was still wincing about being called a fat slob, and worried about what Diana had alleged that Rafael had done. Yes, he had waltzed round the edges of the law a couple of times before he met her, but she'd believed him when he'd said he wouldn't do it again. Besides which, he was lily-white compared to some of the business deals Diana was said to have done! Wasn't he?

Susan said, 'Diana threatens people with some crime or other to undercut any attempt they might make to assert themselves. She made out that Lucia had flirted with Evan. What did she say you'd done? No, don't tell me. Let me guess. She said you'd stolen something?'

'Right on. What happened was this. I turned up yesterday a bit after my usual time, maybe nearer half ten than ten because I missed my bus and had to wait for the next. When I got there, it was to find coppers all over the place. They asked me what I was doing and I said wasn't it obvious, and then they told me Mr Evan had snuffed it. I didn't know what to think. I stood there, struck dumb.

'They asked when I was last there and I said everything had been all right the previous day and I'd made some liver and bacon for Mr Evan for his lunch which he liked but which Mrs didn't and I used to give it to him for a treat. I'd washed up as usual and made the beds, and no, I hadn't seen Lucia because I often didn't see her for days, and she sometimes takes the children to McDonalds and then to the park when she's collected Evan from nursery, so I didn't think nothing of it. Then I'd gone home. So I give them me details and they showed me out.

'Only when I was outside in the cold did I remember I hadn't been paid for the last two weeks, because Mrs had made some excuse and promised me the lot, with a bonus, that Friday. So I had to find her, didn't I? I rang her mobile but she wouldn't answer. So I went and had a small fish and chips at the pub which is on me way home, and I kept ringing her. And when she did pick up, she said she'd join me there. So I waited and had another half.

'When she came, she didn't even sit down but put something in my hand which I thought might be my money, but it wasn't. It was a pawnbroker's ticket. She said as she owed me nothing because I'd stolen a diamond ring which had belonged to Mr Evan's mother and pawned it. I was fair flummoxed, sat there with me mouth open. She whipped the ticket away and put it in an envelope in her handbag. She said there was no point my lying, that I'd needed the money for my daughter's wedding, which was a lie because she knew very well as I'd paid for that with my lucky Lotto win, right out of the blue and very handy that was, too.'

'A ring really had gone missing?' asked Susan.

A spread of hands. 'First I'd heard of it.'

'I suppose it was kept in the safe in the hall, so there'd be a limited number of people who had access to it?'

'That's what I said, once I'd recovered my wits. I said I couldn't have done it because I didn't know the combination to the safe. She said I'd been going through papers in her desk and found it that way. As if I could be bothered! There's not enough hours in the day to keep that place going *and* satisfy Mr Evan's whims. So no, I hadn't ever thought of trying to get in the safe. But she said she'd found the pawn ticket in the pocket of my apron and if I didn't make myself scarce and keep my mouth shut, she'd tell on me to the police.

'She went off in her car like a rocket, leaving me sitting there wondering what had hit me. So I had another half and thought about it, and it come to me that she was right and if I went to the police, I'd lose my reputation and never get another job, which we need with my husband not up to work nowadays. Back trouble, see, that they don't seem able to sort. So I came to ask if Ellie would see me right and that's how I landed up here.'

Susan put the pieces together. 'Diana must have been short of money. She looked around her for something to sell and settled on a diamond ring which had belonged to Evan's family and which was kept in the safe. She knew Evan would make a fuss when he discovered it had disappeared, so she decided to pawn it and accuse you of theft, which would keep you quiet while putting some cash into her own pocket. Is she really that short of money?'

Marcy said, 'She's laid off at least one of her staff at the agency recently. I got that from my friend that I see down the pub now and then, the one that cleans her office. Everyone says that the housing market is sluggish and the estate agencies are in trouble. And that's a big house to keep up, with staff to pay and all.'

Susan pushed her mug forward for a refill. 'She actually put the pawn ticket in your hand?'

'You know why she did that? To get my fingerprints on it.'

Coralie said, 'She set you up good and proper, Marcy.'

Susan took two chocolate digestive biscuits. She put the chocolate sides together so that she didn't get her fingers messy, and bit into the two together. Aaah, that hit the target. She said, 'Pawnbrokers have CCTV nowadays, don't they? They have to make a note of whoever brings something in to pawn. The police can find evidence that Diana pawned it herself or . . .' She realized the other two were ahead of her. 'No, she got someone else to pawn it for her. Who?'

'I been thinking of that,' said Marcy. 'I reckon it was the lad as does the lawns for them. Gardener, he calls himself. Odd job man, in my book. Smart arse. Baseball cap on backwards, sagging pants. You know the type?'

They did.

Marcy said, 'He'll have done it for a tenner, knowing it was dodgy and not giving a toss. All innocent looks and gift of the gab and got two girls in trouble already.'

All three shook their heads. That lad would be no help to them without thumbscrews or waterboarding. Or, perhaps, a hefty bribe? But he'd not be a reliable witness even if they were to take the matter to the police.

Susan patted crumbs off her top. 'So, we come back to Diana. Granted she was short of money, but I'm wondering if there was something else. She was furious that the police had taken her laptop away. She said she needed it for work, and maybe that's true. But surely, if it were just work stuff on it, then she'd have backed it up with a memory stick thingy, wouldn't she? So why did she get into such a state about it?'

Coralie's imagination soared. 'You think there's secret emails on her laptop that she doesn't want anyone to know about? Perhaps from another man? Would that be the man Lucia saw her with?'

Susan said, 'Ellie thought Diana actually had feelings for Evan.'

Marcy agreed. 'I suppose she did, in a way. She looked after him, saw to his medication. Kept her temper though he was not the easiest. Only once she come into the kitchen fit to burst. She said as he was driving her crazy, wanting this and that and then changing his mind. She said she felt like screaming the place down. Then she calmed down and said as everyone had their off days and she went back into his room and was all sweetness and light. Yes, for such a cold fish, she did have a soft spot for him. I couldn't help but admire that in her, because he was a real trial to live with, he really was.'

Coralie was impatient to get back to the real news. 'Marcy, tell Susan what you said about Diana having other men.'

'Well, it all started six months ago, maybe a bit more. Some mornings her bed was neatly made and her shower didn't need cleaning and every now and then there'd be some red satin undies in the wash, which was the sort she'd never worn before, nor me, neither. Mister Evan wasn't capable in bed no more, so I thought she was going out now and then to get it somewhere else. To tell the truth, I didn't blame her.'

Coralie nodded. 'A shop down West Ealing has them undies in the window. Can't think why they don't get more cars bumping into one another as they go by.'

Susan wondered whether she should investigate that shop. Even a 'fat slob' might raise interest when wearing red satin underwear. Or should it be black?

Marcy ticked off items on her fingers. 'She'd put the satin undies out to be washed every now and then, usually on a Monday morning. Then one day there was a new black dress in the wardrobe, showing far too much of everything, if you know what I mean. Not like her work clothes. The new dress was there one day, and never seen again. Likewise a bottle of expensive perfume and some dark red nail polish that she'd never used before. And to cap all, two pairs of high heels, the sort that you wonder how they keep them on. Expensive, too. One of them had the price tag still on underneath. They arrived in their carrier bags one day and then they disappeared, never to be seen again.'

Susan mused, 'She was definitely playing away. One man or two? And did you find out who?'

'One man only, I think. She wouldn't have had time for more. Of course it was wrong but with Mister being like he was, well, I could sort of understand it. She was careful, you know. There weren't no phone calls to the landline or jewellery she couldn't account for. She kept her smartphone with her all the time, and her laptop, too. Not that I could have done anything with her laptop, me not being gifted that way. I looked in the bin, to see if she'd discarded the bills from a restaurant or a hotel, but didn't find nothing. I reckon she only played away on Thursday or Friday nights.'

'According to Lucia, she was out this last Thursday night when her husband was killed. Diana said she'd been at an overnight conference.'

'Humph!' said Coralie.

Marcy didn't believe it, either. 'Chance would be a fine thing.'

Fifi woke up and grizzled. Susan took her into the kitchen and settled the child on her knee. How sweet it was to hold your child in your arms. Fifi knew she was loved. Did Diana ever cuddle her children like this?

Susan wondered, 'How was Diana with her children? Ellie said Diana was a good mother. I can't believe she's abandoned them, just like that.'

Marcy pulled a face, twisting strands of hair around her forefinger. 'She was OK with them. Not lovey-dovey, kissy-kissy. No sympathy for grazed knees. She was strict with them, not petting them or giving them treats, but . . . yes, I'd say she was decent enough that way . . . for a working mother. She preferred Jenny, who's more like her for all that the girl's so fair and Diana's so dark.'

Susan said, 'I'm worried about them. They both slept badly last night and Evan wet the bed, but that's perhaps to be expected after such an upheaval.'

Coralie said, 'They haven't asked after their parents at all, though you'd think they would. It doesn't sound as if their father had much to do with them so maybe that's only natural in his case. Considering they've been whipped away from their home and dumped in a strange house, they're not behaving too badly. Little Evan seems a nice child. Jenny? She can be a little madam, if I'm any judge. And she ought to be potty-trained by now.'

Marcy looked at the clock. 'I suppose I'd better be getting along. Can you give me a tinkle when Ellie gets back and I'll pop in to see her about the money Diana owes me? I'll go back to the agency tomorrow and ask if they can find me some more work somewhere.' She looked hopefully at Susan. 'You're not thinking of having some help here, are you?'

Susan's eyes widened. 'This situation is only temporary. Diana has to find somewhere else for them to live and then she'll collect them . . . won't she? Surely even she can't just abandon her children and swan off into the blue with her latest man? Can she?'

The other two gave her a steady look. Did they really think that was what Diana planned to do? Yes, they did. Oh.

Coralie lifted her eyebrow at Susan. 'Given your circumstances you might want to think about having some help in the house.'

Marcy nodded. 'Thought as much. Not far along though, are you?'

Susan blushed. Everyone except Rafael seemed to have cottoned on to the fact that she was pregnant again. 'I'll have to talk to my husband about it. But there is one job you could do, Marcy. Ellie wants someone to go in next door and make everything ready for when they get back next week. They've had floorboards up and ceilings down, new plumbing and wiring. The decorators have finished but there's dust everywhere. The carpets are down and their furniture has gone back in, but heaven knows what the bathrooms and kitchen look like. I should think there's a good week's work putting it to rights. If I guarantee you'll be paid, would you like the job of putting everything to rights? You could borrow my key and start tomorrow, couldn't you?'

'Now that's a job to get my teeth into. I think I can remember where everything used to be, but if in doubt I can ask you, can't I? Only, could you give me something in advance, seeing as I'm missing my wages from Diana, and the rent will need paying willy nilly?'

There was a muted roar outside, and down the corridor came the thump of little feet. 'Cuckoo! Cuckoo!' Jenny banged on the front door.

Susan looked out of the window to see Rafael on his motorbike drawing up outside, closely followed by a small furniture van. Hooray! The rest of the children's things had arrived!

NINE

Saturday lunchtime

Rafael cut off the engine, hauled his bike on to its stand and took off his helmet to open the front door . . . Whereupon a gale swept him, laughing, into the hall. 'All hands to the van. I suggest the two beds come in first, and the scooter last.'

He picked up Jenny, and said, 'Hello, you!' And then: 'Ugh, you pong!' He handed her on to Lucia, who had appeared, looking more waif-like than ever. Rafael said, 'Clean her up, will you?'

'Where you want this, love?' Two large men swept in on a gale force wind and dumped various articles into the hall for the women to sort out and despatch in different directions.

Susan stowed an indignant Fifi into her buggy and wheeled it into the big room so that the baby could, hopefully, have a nap in peace and quiet. Coralie directed traffic while Marcy, unasked, cleared the table and made tea in Susan's largest pot. Finally the contents of the van had been transferred to the hall, mugs of sugared tea had been drunk, and the thumping and bumping ceased.

Rafael paid off the men and closed the door firmly on the outside world, saying, 'I'm getting back to that builder today. We can't go through the winter without a porch.'

Lucia hovered, keeping Jenny out of the way but otherwise not helping. 'It's not my fault. Jenny will *not* use her potty, no matter how much I tell her.'

Rafael patted Jenny's cheek. 'You'll do it for me, won't you, Poppet!'

'Me, Cuckoo!' said Jenny. 'You, Cuckoo, too.'

Rafael said, 'Probably, yes, if you can get yourself into clean pants. Take her away and clean her up, Lucia.' Shedding his leathers, he went into the kitchen, took a seat at the table and accepted a mug of tea. 'Well, ladies! Council of war, yes? Hi, Coralie. And you are . . .?' He raised his eyebrows at Marcy. 'Let me guess, you're the cleaner who knows all Diana's little secrets.'

'Ex-cleaner,' said Marcy, 'and yes, I do know some.'

Susan subsided into a chair, wondering why Rafael hadn't kissed her when he came in. Was it because she really had become a fat slob? She told herself not to cry. That would be stupid, especially in front of the others.

Susan said, 'Yes, we've been exchanging information. Marcy confirms that Diana has acquired some provocative underwear and clothing. Marcy also says Diana didn't always sleep in her own bed on a Thursday or a Friday. According to the DC who oversaw Diana's packing, the bed hadn't been slept in the night that Evan was killed. Diana probably thought Evan didn't know, but I'm wondering . . . we found her computer in his bedroom after he was killed. She'd left it on charge in her study, so I'm thinking he might have taken it to see if there was anything suspicious on it.'

Marcy said, 'Aren't you the bright one, eh, Susan?'

Susan dimpled at the compliment. How nice it was to be appreciated. 'We know that Diana's short of money. We also know that if anyone gets in her way, she accuses them of something nasty. Look at the way she sacked Lucia, and she got rid of Marcy by saying she'd stolen and pawned a diamond ring! Diana likes to be the one in control. I'm wondering if she's the same with her lover. Has she perhaps got something on him, something he might find it inconvenient to be made public? Something she kept in the safe in the hall or on her laptop?'

Rafael said, 'She's certainly made enough fuss about both.'

'So now I'm wondering if her lover might have arranged for a "burglary" to take place in order to retrieve whatever it was she had on him. He wouldn't act himself, but if he's in a position to employ others, he might suggest that one or two layabouts might "do him a favour" by faking a burglary at Diana's. The intruders probably had no intention of waking Evan. They broke in at the back and started to look for the safe. It's interesting to note that they didn't know where the safe was because they began by taking the pictures off the wall in the front room.

'Then, disaster! Evan woke up and armed himself with a golf club. This changed the scene entirely. One or more of the intruders was carrying a knife and bingo, there was an unexpected and messy ending to what was supposed to be a quick in-and-out job. Does that sound right?'

Three nods from around the table.

Susan said, 'The only thing is, we don't know who her lover is.'

'I do,' said Rafael. 'The rumour mill threw up his name straight away. It's King Kong.'

Coralie wasn't into silent films. 'Who's "King Kong" when he's at home?'

'Where were you brung up, Coralie?' That was Marcy.

'The name's familiar,' said Susan, whose mother had rather liked to watch old films when they were repeated on the telly. 'But what's a great hairy ape from a silent film got to do with Diana?'

Rafael picked up Jenny who had presented herself at his knee, smelling sweet. She'd brought her tablet and was intent on showing him something on it. He told her to be quiet for a moment and, for a wonder, she was.

Rafael said, '"King Kong" is the nickname that people at the golf club gave to a man called Keith Cottrell because he's got extra-long arms and is somewhat hairy. He's a big brute of a man but light on his feet. My informant says Keith is managing director of a prosperous building business: modern houses on new estates in the Home Counties. Keith's rise in life is supposed to be due to his marrying an older, wealthy woman called Cynthia whose father started the business. He also says Cynthia wears killer heels and he wouldn't like to get on the wrong side of her.'

Without a change of tone, he said, 'Is there anything to eat in this house?'

'We've eaten,' said Coralie, investigating the freezer. 'Will a pizza do? All right by you, Susan?'

Susan nodded, Coralie popped the pizza in the oven and Marcy made another pot of tea.

Lucia drifted in, looking lost. Coralie gave her a mug of tea and told her to sit down, which she did. Someone or something bumped at the back of Susan's chair.

Evan had taken the brake off the buggy and pushed it into the kitchen. He said, 'Fifi's woken up. Can we take her to the park?'

'In a little while,' said Susan. Fifi was almost hidden under Evan's hideous Hippo but seemed happy about it. Susan rescued Fifi and gave her a cuddle. Evan reclaimed his Hippo and eyed the biscuit tin.

Coralie slid slices of hot pizza on to a plate for Rafael, who was encumbered by Jenny. 'No, Cuckoo. No. My turn to eat. No, you're not sitting on my knee, not till I've got some food down me.' Despite Jenny's protest, he slid the child down on to the floor, and turned to Lucia. 'Can you describe the man you saw with Diana yesterday morning?'

Lucia looked scared. 'No. Too quick.'

Susan sipped tea without looking at Lucia. 'We've heard he was ginger-haired and rather short. Almost like a dwarf. Was that the man you saw?'

'Oh, no. He was big, really big. And dark-haired.'

'Of course,' said Susan. 'With a beard.'

'No beard, no.'

'Ah, but his car was one of those long, low, expensive jobs in red, one that has seats for just two people.'

'No, no. It was black and had four doors and there was a sticker with a funny face on the back.'

'But the car was some years old. You could tell that from the registration number, couldn't you?'

Lucia shook her head. 'Too far away.'

Coralie and Marcy refilled everyone's mugs of tea. Evan managed to manoeuvre the biscuit tin near enough to help himself.

Rafael congratulated Lucia. 'Good for you, Lucia. That was most helpful.' And to the others, 'He drives an Audi, last year's model, black.'

'There's no proof that it was him,' said Susan.

'No. But you'll tell Lesley, won't you?'

'Park,' said Evan, who had his mother's single-mindedness about such important things as biscuits, favourite toys and playing in the park. 'I want to take Fifi to the park. I want to show her how I ride my bike.'

Coralie cleared the tea things away, saying, 'Well, why not? Yes, Evan; the park. Lucia, you can take Jenny in her buggy, I'll wheel Fifi and Evan can come alongside on his scooter. No, not on your bike yet, Evan. Bikes take a lot of getting used to. You should have a helmet when you ride your scooter, too. Susan, did you find—?'

Susan shook her head. 'I don't think there was one. Do you need a helmet to ride a scooter? I'm not sure.'

Evan thrust out his lower lip. 'Don't need helmet.'

'You do for the bike. Not sure about the scooter.'

Susan said, 'Show Fifi how fast you can go on your scooter.'

Evan scowled but didn't insist. Perhaps he really wasn't that sure of himself on the bike, anyway.

Rafael was amused. 'And what am I to do?'

Coralie knew the answer to that. 'Go back to work and find out more about King Kong. Susan's going to put her feet up for a bit.'

Rafael studied his wife with something in his eyes that she couldn't interpret. He looked hangdog, as if he'd done something wrong and expected her to call him to task about it. Almost beseeching. Or was he thinking that hc really had married a fat slob, because she did feel as if she were exactly that at the moment.

He got to his feet. 'Yes, of course. Someone has to earn a crust around here. Tell Lesley about King Kong, won't you?'

Susan tried to leap to her feet, but had to cling to the table to steady herself. 'Hang about. Rafael, have you got some money we can lend Lucia and Marcy? Diana's short-changed both of them. Coralie needs paying, too.'

He nodded and disappeared down the corridor to raid the safe in his study, returning with a bundle of notes, which he handed to Susan. 'Get receipts. Minimum wage OK, everyone?' He collected his jacket and helmet and departed, letting in a blast of cold air as he opened the front door.

'Cuckoo!' Jenny tried to follow him but Lucia managed to hold on to her long enough for him to escape.

Fifi dropped Hippo and wailed till Evan picked it up and gave it back to her. She chewed happily on one of his ears and Evan beamed!

Susan thought, Uh-oh. Is Fifi teething again?

Coralie produced a notebook and tore sheets off. 'Set me down for a day and half, if that's all right with you? That's how many hours?' She counted on her fingers.

Lucia put out a hand, rather as if expecting it to be slapped away. 'Two weeks wages, please?'

Marcy slapped dirty mugs and plates into the dishwasher. 'Two weeks for me, too. Tell you what, this place could do with a tidy up, and then I need to see what's going on next door. It's going to take more than a few hours to hoover up over there what with the dust the builders make. And don't talk to me about plumbers! There'll be dust an inch thick for weeks.'

Susan paid them all off, getting receipts detailing how much work they'd done for Diana and how much for Susan.

Coralie pointed to Evan and Jenny. 'We'll all go wee-wee before we go out, right? And does Fifi need changing? Lucia; see to her, will you? Marcy, let's haul the children's beds upstairs before we go walkies, and where we're to put the easel I do not know. Oh, and Susan, there was a delivery man came when you were out, wanted to leave something, said it had been wrongly addressed but now he's found out it's supposed to be for next door. He left a card. I said you'd have to get in touch for a convenient time to deliver as I hadn't got the keys, and that wretched plumber had gone off somewhere mid-morning, though I see his van's back now.'

Marcy set the dishwasher going. 'I'll clear up around here and help Coralie make the children's beds upstairs while you have a rest, Susan, and then you can take me next door and we'll see what's what there.'

So Susan handed Fifi over and wafted herself upstairs . . . or rather, hauled herself up, holding on to the banister, and collapsed on to her bed, with Jenny's thin cry of 'No potty, no potty!' in her ears.

She wondered if she should thank someone for sorting out her problems so neatly. Rafael was a brilliant provider and would probably stick to her even if he had only married her because she was a favourite of Ellie's. No, that wouldn't work. He'd married her because he'd liked her shape, and her cooking and . . . She'd make him a nice steak and kidney pudding for supper. She hadn't had a satisfactory oven while they'd been staying at his flat, and she ached to get her hands working on some pastry . . .

How about those two crazy, bossy women who'd moved into her life? Phew! But Coralie and Marcy had come just at the right time to help her, when she was feeling – let's face it – rather down and out. And Lucia could be trained to be helpful, perhaps.

Praise be! Susan wondered about making the sign of the cross but she wasn't a Catholic and believed everyone worshipped in their own way, and that way really wasn't her thing, so she didn't. She heard the front door open and even upstairs she felt a draught of cold air . . . then the door slammed shut and the house was silent, except for Marcy humming to herself as she went around putting the bedrooms to rights and . . .

Susan dropped into sleep, just . . . like . . . that.

Saturday afternoon

Susan woke when Marcy put a mug of tea on a coaster at her bedside, saying, 'They're all back and the plumber from next door is wanting a word.'

Ah. The plumber had discovered that Diana had been sleeping there last night and wanted to know what Susan was going to do about it?

The smell of bread being toasted drifted up to Susan as she drank her tea and put herself back together to meet this new challenge. She knew Rafael was dissatisfied with this particular firm of plumbers and didn't intend to use them again despite their having offered him a thinly disguised bribe. They wouldn't try anything like that on her, would they? Well, she'd be prepared for it if they did.

She went down to find the children all around the table – Fifi in her own highchair and Jenny in hers – being fed and watered by Coralie with Lucia acting as second-in-command, and Marcy ready to leave.

Coralie said, 'I've been looking in the freezer. Fish pie all right for you this evening, Susan? With steamed veg?'

Susan nodded. She would cook a steak and kidney pie tomorrow. She kissed Fifi, who seemed perfectly happy playing with whatever it was Coralie had found for her to eat. Where were the keys to next door? She found them, Marcy said they'd better put their coats on as if she knew anything next door would feel like the Arctic because builders and plumbers never shut doors, did they?

It felt strange to walk into Ellie's house. The hall was empty, echoing, redolent with fresh paint. The grandfather clock was silent. It probably hadn't liked being moved around while the decorators did their work. The parquet flooring was dull and dusty and might need professional attention. The telephone shelf still held an old-fashioned telephone, plus an untidy pile of junk adverts and papers.

Marcy ran her finger along the back of the one and only chair in the hall and said – yes, she actually said – 'Tut!'

The conservatory straight ahead looked desolate. When Ellie left, she'd taken all the plants out and left them on the patio outside to be watered by the gardener, who was supposed to have come regularly to look after them and to mow the lawn. Judging by what Susan could see of the meadow outside, he hadn't been round much. Most of Ellie's beloved plants looked dead.

Perhaps it would be a good idea to spend some money on

getting Ellie some new plants? Susan made a mental note to contact the gardener, override whatever excuses he'd come up with and get him moving again.

Marcy stood in the doorway to the living room and heaved a great sigh. The walls were freshly painted, yes. Good. The furniture had all been piled into the middle of the room and covered with a dust sheet or two. Also good. But the full-length velvet curtains had been taken down from the windows and dumped on the floor without any protective dust covers . . . as had some pictures.

The room opposite – which was a library-cum-study for Thomas – showed little signs of having been visited by painters, builders or plumbers. Except for the dust. There was a week's work here, wasn't there?

Susan put her hand on Marcy's shoulder. 'Courage! You can do it!'

Marcy raised her eyes to heaven. 'The hoover used to be kept in the scullery beyond the kitchen. Do you think it's still there?'

A rhetorical question.

Susan tried the light in the downstairs shower and cloakroom. It didn't work. She must ask Rafael to get the electrician to look at it. The next room along was to be Ellie's new study. Yes, there was new paint on the walls, but desk, chair, filing cabinets, everything that Ellie would need was stacked in an untidy mound in the middle of the floor.

The kitchen looked comparatively clean. Presumably the painters/plumbers/builders had been using it as their headquarters. Ellie had decided to retain the old cupboards and large wooden table but they'd been spruced up and a new floor laid. The room looked like a feature in an upmarket country kitchen magazine. All that needed doing here was setting crockery and cooking utensils back in their right places and stocking the fridge and freezer. An open door to the old utility room showed that brand-new appliances had been fitted there. And yes, the hoover was still in the scullery.

The plumber was having a break with a flask of tea and a sandwich from a plastic box. He took his feet off the table when they entered and choked on a large mouthful before managing to say, 'There's a bloke upstairs. Walked in through the back door bold as brass. Said he was a friend of the owner's. I looked, and someone's smashed the glass in the back door. You want to get that put right before night, don't you?'

Susan wanted to run away and hide. This was the sort of thing Rafael ought to be dealing with. She said, 'Oh dear. Do you know someone who can put the back door to rights?'

'I could mebbe tack some card over it till tomorrow, when I can get my mate to do a proper job on it. What about the bloke upstairs?'

Susan said, 'I'll go and see who it is in a minute. Is the water back on again?'

'This morning. I'm running the central heating now to check the new radiators aren't leaking. It would be best you leave it on for twenty-four hours, get the house up to temperature, right? And what do you want to do about the hot water, seeing as someone's sleeping here now?'

So Diana had moved in?

Susan said, 'I suppose I'd better see who our visitor is first.'

Marcy bristled. 'I'll come up with you, shall I?'

Susan drew in her breath. 'I've just realized who it might be. In which case . . . Yes, please, Marcy. I'd be grateful.'

Marcy was ready for battle. 'I need to see how bad it is upstairs, too.'

They went up the old mahogany staircase together. Susan said, 'He'll be in the main bedroom.'

The door to that room was open. More fresh paint.

A big man was standing by the window, looking down on the ruined garden. Dark hair, long arms, good suit. He turned round when he heard the two women. 'About time . . .!' His voice trailed away. 'Who the devil are you? And where's Diana? She said she's moved in here, but . . . Where the devil is she?' He was very large and in a shocking temper.

Yes, a duvet and a pillow had been unearthed from the linen closet on the landing and left on the bed in a straggle. The door to the en suite was open. Diana must have had a shock to find there was no water available in the sink, and that she couldn't use the toilet.

'Well?' said the large man, clenching his fists and jutting his jaw at them.

Marcy moved to stand at Susan's shoulder. Marcy was going to fight at Susan's side. Well, hurray for Marcy.

Susan said, 'Mr Cottrell, I presume?'

He started. 'What! How did you know . . .? Who are you, anyway? You're too old to be Diana's daughter.' He snapped his fingers. 'Ah, I get it. You're the girl who's been buttering up the old lady, the one who managed to wheedle her way into getting half the house. Diana's told me all about you. She's going to sue you for alienating her mother's affections and make you hand over your part of the house to her, the rightful heir.'

'I think,' said Susan, trying to speak calmly, 'that you have been misinformed. Ellie made over the whole of this big house to a trust fund which aims to provide affordable housing for those in need. The idea was to turn this whole building into two semi-detached houses, one for Ellie and Thomas to use for life, and one for my husband and I to rent. Incidentally, Diana and her husband Evan rented their own house from that trust, too.'

'What? What? You mean . . .! No, that's a lie.' He glared at her, then narrowed his eyes, thinking over what she'd said.

Susan kept quiet. Marcy shifted from one foot to the other at Susan's side.

Mr Cottrell began to pace the room. 'No, I can't believe that! Diana said her mother was going senile. You're lying.'

'Why would I?' said Susan.

'These things can be checked, you know.'

'Yes, you should do so. It's always worthwhile checking when people make claims about who owns what.' That was a trifle impudent but it did stop him pacing. Was he beginning to suspect that Diana had told him a whopper or two?

Susan said, 'Diana told you what happened to Evan? You arranged to meet her here?'

'Well, I . . . Yes, she did ring me yesterday morning to say he'd been taken to hospital. I had to cut her off. I was in the middle of . . . Then, when I rang her back, she said she'd had to move herself and the children out and was staying with her mother for the time being. She said she'd forgotten her keys and I was to use the back door when I was able to get away.'

'Yes, Diana did intend to stay here with her mother, but it didn't work out like that. She saw Evan off to the hospital and brought the children to me next door. That's when she discovered that her mother's return had been delayed and that this part of the house isn't yet fit for occupation. She knew her husband was badly injured and might not survive but she dropped everything to ring you. Why did she do that? To tell you that Evan had been attacked and to ask if you knew anything about it?'

'What! No, of course not! Why would I know . . .? Don't be ridiculous.'

I think Diana wanted reassurance that he'd had nothing to do with the events of the night. I think I believe him when he says he didn't. Or do I?

Susan pressed on. 'Whether she believed you or not, it left her wondering what to do next. She'd dumped the children on us which gave her freedom of action, so she decided to move into her mother's house anyway. She didn't realize there'd be no water here. That's only been turned on this morning.'

'Then she'll be coming back here.' It wasn't quite a question.

Susan shrugged. 'She doesn't know the water's been turned back on yet. I suppose she's out and about, consulting her solicitor, cancelling her husband's credit cards. Did you think she'd hang about here, waiting to see if you could manage to fit in a visit to her in your busy day? Do you realize how that looks?'

The skin around his nose went white as his temper rose. 'You . . .! How dare . . .! Let me tell you that . . .!' He took a quick turn around the room, calming himself down. Second by second, he turned himself back into a wily businessman, a man who could be trusted to come out best on any deal that was on offer, a man who knew how to deal with little people like Susan, who had dared to pass judgement on him.

He said, 'You really have no idea who you are talking to, have you?'

'The police know that a man answering your description was seen with Diana early on the morning Evan died. Her bed had not been slept in. It's known that you have been spending time with Diana. How long do you think it will be before the police come knocking on your door?'

She saw him decide how to handle the matter. 'I will tell the police – if they are interested – that yes, Diana and I have enjoyed one another's company now and then, and that I am truly shocked to hear that her husband died as a result of a break-in. My sympathies are with the grieving widow at this dreadful time.'

'Really?' Susan spurted into laughter, and then told herself that it wasn't wise to provoke the lion in his cage.

His mouth tightened but again he fought his temper down. 'I repeat, I admire Diana as I admired Evan. My wife and I have known them both for years and we have rejoiced in the birth of their children. They are the envy of all of us who have not been so blessed. And yes, when our friend Evan became housebound, we did treat Diana to a meal now and then. She is excellent company. My wife and I are happy to help her in whatever way we can in her present difficult situation.'

Susan clapped, once, twice. 'You should go in for politics.'

'Well, I *had* thought I might . . .' He gave her a sharp look. 'I have nothing more to say.'

'You don't want to explain why Diana felt it so important to take time out of her race to the hospital in order to ring you? You don't want to explain why you are here, looking for her, the day after her husband was murdered?'

'It wasn't murder, I tell you. It was a burglary that went wrong. And it was nothing to do with me.'

'The police think it was murder, and I am sure they'll want to ask you about your relationship with the grieving widow. Even as we speak, the police are investigating the contents of her laptop, and they are wondering why she doesn't want them to find out what is in the safe. Is there something that compromises you on the laptop, or in the safe?'

His eyes flicked to and fro. 'What you are suggesting is totally out of line.'

'Did your wife always accompany you when you were consoling Diana for her husband's deterioration?'

'My wife is happy to know that every now and again, I can find someone to have the odd drink with.'

'That,' said Susan, trying not to grin, 'is something that needs to be checked and I am sure the police will be doing so.'

Breathing hard, he took a couple of hasty steps in her direction. He was within her personal space, crowding her. 'Little girls like you shouldn't try to interfere with people like me.' He put his hand on her shoulder, dug his fingers in and twisted, then grabbed her bosom.

Hard.

Susan screamed. Tears squirted.

Marcy swiped at Mr Cottrell. He stepped back and she missed.

He laughed.

Susan fell to her knees, covering her breast with both hands.

TEN

Saturday afternoon, continued

'You bastard!' Marcy took another swipe at Mr Cottrell.

Again, he stepped back out of her reach, laughing.

A stir in the doorway, and there was the plumber, eyes and mouth wide open. He said, 'What's up?' And to Susan: 'Something wrong?'

Marcy yelled at him. 'Get that bastard out of here before I kill him!'

'I'm going! I'm going!' said Mr Cottrell. And to the plumber: 'I can call you as a witness that she hit me.'

'What!' said the plumber. He knew who was going to pay his bills, and it was the housing trust, and not this intruder. He flapped a hand towards Susan. 'You all right, missus?'

Susan gasped, 'He hurt me. Get him out of here!'

Mr Cottrell picked up a briefcase he'd left by the window. 'You're delusional, woman! Why would I want to touch you?'

Marcy faced Mr Cottrell down. 'I know your kind! You're a bully, but only with those that are smaller and weaker than you. And cleverer. Susan got you tied up in knots, didn't she? And I know where those scarlet undies came from and who paid the bill for them, too.'

Mr Cottrell looked as if he wanted to take a swipe at Marcy, too, but thought the better of it. He brushed past the plumber and thundered down the stairs and out of the house.

Marcy helped Susan to her feet.

Susan cried out. 'Oh, oh! Ouch!' The pain was intense. 'You saw? You heard?'

'I did,' said Marcy. 'You have witnesses to what he said and what he did. You've got to report this. Have you got your mobile phone on you, or shall I use mine? We'll take some photos, shall we? And get you checked out at the doctor's. That way, we've got him bang to rights. Now, let's see the damage.'

She helped Susan to the unmade bed, pulled up her T-shirt and undid her bra to reveal one reddened breast which was already darkening in colour and becoming swollen. The marks of Mr Cottrell's fingers were clearly to be seen.

The plumber gawped.

'Thank you, that's quite enough,' said Marcy, shooing him away. 'Go and bleed your radiators or whatever it was you were doing, while I attend to Susan.'

Susan managed to manoeuvre her mobile out of her back pocket but was trembling so hard she couldn't get her fingers to work. She handed it to Marcy, whispering, 'Call Lesley. On the contacts list.'

Marcy found Lesley on the list, got through to her, and handed the phone back to Susan.

Susan forced herself to sit upright. 'Lesley? I'm at Ellie's. Diana's lover was here. A man called Keith Cottrell. He's most unpleasant. He . . .' Here she broke down.

Marcy said, 'Tut!' and took the phone off Susan to speak to Lesley herself. 'Lesley, you don't know me, but I'm Mrs Diana's cleaner that was and I'm here with Susan at Ellie's looking at what needs to be done. It's all right, we chased him away, but he assaulted Susan and she's a bit shaken up. She got him to admit he was seeing Diana, and that he was the person she rang on her way to the hospital while her poor husband was dying. I'll take some photos of Susan's bruises and stick with her till her husband can get her to the doctor's, right?'

Marcy clicked off, saying, 'She'll be right round. Now, will you let me take some photos? Those bruises are coming up nicely.'

Susan sat and suffered while Marcy took photos, and then bathed her breast with cold water from the basin in the en suite, thanking the Lord that there was water there at last.

The pain died to a dull ache. Susan even managed to speak to Rafael, minimizing what had happened, but she did not object when Marcy took the phone off her to tell Rafael that he ought to get round there sharpish, as his wife was not fit to get to the doctor's by herself and that someone called Lesley was coming round, too, if he knew who Lesley was from Adam, because she, Marcy, did not.

At which Susan managed a weak sort of laugh.

'That's it,' said Marcy. 'You have to report it, otherwise that man will think he can do it again, if he hasn't already. He reminds me of my brother-in-law that was. Used to knock my sister around something rotten till I caught him at it, and laid about him with my husband's walking stick, the collapsible one, which did it no good at all, but made me feel a lot better. Ten to one, this Cottrell's wife feels the back of his hand every time the wind shifts to the east. I wish I'd had something heavy to hand when he hit you.'

Susan said, 'I'm glad you didn't. You might have killed him.' She pulled Marcy down on to the bed beside her. 'I need you to say, "There, there." Please? It will make me feel better.'

Marcy put her arm around Susan, tentatively, and then strongly. 'There, there. If there were more of your sort around, the world would be a better place.'

Susan sighed, closed her eyes, and rested against Marcy. 'Thank you. That's just what I needed.'

After a minute or so, Susan straightened up and looked around her. She felt as if her breast was aflame, but perhaps it wouldn't hurt so much if she concentrated on what needed to be done.

She said, 'I'll feel better if I keep moving. Now, before Lesley and Rafael arrive, shall we sort out what needs doing here? Putting this house straight is more than one person can do in a week. Marcy, do you think you can project manage the job? The trust will pay. If you agree, I'll get on to the agency. Oh dear, it's the weekend, and they won't want to work on a Sunday. I'll get them to send a couple here, preferably people who know how Ellie likes things to be, on Monday morning. I'll make it clear that you're in charge and that the bill goes to the trust.'

Marcy narrowed her eyes, considering the extent of the job. Then nodded.

'Can do. I'll stay on here now till someone comes to look

after you, and then I'll make a list of what needs to be done. I'll get rid of the dust and those windows need cleaning in and out, for a start. Before I leave today, I'll set about that no-good plumber, see what he's done about making the back door safe.'

Susan's fingers were working again now, thank goodness. She got through on her phone to the head of the cleaning agency and made the arrangements while Marcy straightened the bed and tutted over the state of the toilet.

Susan felt as if she were one great ball of hurt.

The doorbell rang below. Susan managed to get to her feet with a helping hand from Marcy and slowly made it down the stairs to find Rafael letting himself into the house with the trust's keys.

Lesley was at his elbow.

Susan dissolved into her husband's arms only to recoil for her breast was too sore to be touched. She collapsed on to the hall chair without bothering to dust it, and let Marcy tell them what had happened.

Rafael took charge, getting an appointment for her to see the practice nurse at the surgery, while Lesley took photographs and a statement from her.

Susan felt like a doll, pushed hither and yon.

She wanted Fifi. She was not going to cry. That was stupid. She wept.

Rafael handed her a handkerchief and whisked her into the car and away to the surgery while Susan tried to think of something, anything, but the pain in her breast and shoulder.

She told herself that she'd seen or heard something important, something that made sense of everything that had happened. Then she told herself that she was delusional, to use the word Mr Cottrell had thrown at her.

Pain engulfed her.

Rafael phoned Coralie and had a report back from that stout damsel to say that all was well back at the ranch. Susan didn't think it was, but couldn't do anything about it while the nurse attended to her shoulder and swollen breast. Painkillers were prescribed and she was told there was no great harm done and the 'discomfort' would probably last for a day or two. Rafael asked for, and received, a written report on the visit to the surgery which they would need in order to prosecute Mr Cottrell for the assault.

Susan tried to concentrate on something other than the pain. Mr Cottrell had said something or reacted to something important, but it slipped away from her. Well, it didn't matter for the time being, did it? The painkillers began to work.

Saturday teatime

Home again. Rafael decanted Susan from the car, with care. She could hear Fifi's thin wail as Rafael opened the front door. Coralie was walking up and down the corridor, with Fifi in her arms. Fifi wasn't a happy bunny.

Susan reached for her baby, who clung to her – never mind that it hurt – and sobbed and sobbed. 'Poor little one. Did you think I'd deserted you?'

Fifi gave a little hiccup, was put over Susan's shoulder to bring up her wind, and then subsided into Susan's arms with a pleased look, her colour returning to normal.

Susan felt a nudge at her knee. There was Evan, holding up his Hippo. 'I gave her my Hippo, but she wouldn't stop crying.'

Susan wanted to say that Fifi had needed her mummy but didn't, because Diana's poor children had possibly never been comforted by their mother as Fifi was now being comforted by Susan.

It was Coralie who said it. 'She needed her mummy. Evan, you are a very brave little boy, and thoughtful, too. Now, let's fetch Fifi her bottle and then you can help me find something for your tea.'

She nodded to Susan. 'We had a good walk in the fresh air and played in the park till it began to cloud over. There's some post. I put it on the kitchen table. Lucia put some money on her phone and has been texting someone ever since.' Having dumped the problem of Lucia upon Susan, Coralie led Evan away.

Susan carefully lowered herself on to the settee and made a fuss of Fifi until Coralie returned to hand her a bottle of milk, carefully warmed to the right temperature.

Susan settled herself with one cushion under her arm and gave the bottle to Fifi . . . who refused it until she remembered that it might be all right if her mummy was giving it to her, and settled down to suck.

Susan relaxed and looked around her.

Jenny was sitting, rapt, in front of the telly, while Lucia was in a corner texting away on her phone. Did Lucia have a boyfriend? Hadn't she mentioned someone she'd hoped to contact when she was turned out of house and home? Someone who hadn't been available to help her that day? Or was she texting her family? She was not looking after Jenny, that was clear.

Rafael appeared and Jenny scrambled to her feet and launched herself at him shouting, 'Cuckoo, cuckoo!'

Rafael picked her up, saying, 'Cuckoo to you, too!' He put his free arm round Susan and kissed the top of her head. 'Take it easy, and I'll bring you a cuppa.' He switched the television off, told Lucia that she was needed in the kitchen to help Coralie feed the five thousand, and managed to get the girl moving.

Fifi lay on her mother's uninjured side. Fifi sucked enthusiastically, and then rhythmically, and finally slowed down. Susan winded her and gave her the last inch of milk. Fifi fell away from the teat, her eyes closing. She'd had a tiring and difficult day and needed a nap. She was warm and comfortable and much loved.

Susan inched out her mobile and called Lesley. 'I've remembered what it was that Mr Cottrell said, or rather that he didn't say. I told you Diana called him on her way to the hospital, didn't I? He said he was busy and called her back. Why did she call him?'

'I agree that a phone call made by Diana at that time couldn't have been a casual one. He's next on my list for an interview. You do want to press charges, don't you?'

'I should. Marcy tells me he's the sort who'll go on lashing out at people until he's stopped and taught that assaulting people is a game that's not worth the candle. If you tell him that I am prepared to press charges, it might push him off balance.'

'But you will go through with it?'

'I quake at the thought of having to go to court and explain—'

'Someone has to stand up to a man who thinks he can assault a woman and get away with it.'

'I know. I know. It's probably partly my fault. He took one

look at me and thought I'd be a pushover.' She tried to laugh. 'I bet he never tried it on with Diana.'

They both thought about that and shook their heads.

Susan said, 'Diana said they were at a conference together. Did that check out?'

'I can't find that any such conference was held locally this week.'

'Diana must have thought that up on the spur of the moment to cover her absence that night. Unfortunately, if they did spend the night together it does give them both an alibi for the burglary.'

Lesley said, 'I've been looking him up. He married the daughter of a man who has made a fortune in the building trade before launching out into other areas. My information is that she's on the board of all her father's businesses and is the power behind the throne. Keith is her toy boy with responsibility for just one of the family's enterprises. I don't think Keith would want to risk his marriage by being too closely associated with Diana.'

Susan slid down on to her back. Fifi slept on. Susan said, 'His story is that his wife allows him considerable leeway, that she knew he was comforting Diana as a friend. Rafael thinks she's not the sort to relish her husband openly preferring another woman. I suspect that Mrs Cottrell might well overlook an occasional overnight absence, but wouldn't care for her husband's supplying Diana with an alibi for murder. Unless, of course, she welcomed the idea of his providing her with evidence for divorce? From what he said to me, he seemed happy enough to have his bit on the side *and* keep his marriage going. Evan was on his last legs, so why would Keith jeopardize his marriage by hastening Evan's death?'

'Why fiddle around with another woman if you don't want to risk divorce?'

'He's a powerfully built man and fit. Perhaps he isn't getting enough of a workout at home. He has a strong sense of personal worth. He thinks he's worth *it,* whatever *it* may be. He'd think a fling with Diana would be excellent value if all the parties concerned agreed the terms of engagement.'

Lesley agreed. 'On the surface, he's no reason to want Evan dead.'

'The fact remains that Diana took the trouble to ring him on the way to hospital. If both parties were happy with the status quo, then why did she need to contact Mr Cottrell at that point in time? Did she just want reassurance that he still loved her and would continue their liaison, or did she want to remind him that she had some hold on him? Something which would keep him tied to Diana in future? Something which, if it came out, would push his wife into divorcing him?'

'Blackmail?' Lesley was dubious.

'Not sure. I keep wondering why such an important, busy man turned up at Ellie's today, expecting to find Diana there. Why did he do that? Who's pulling the strings?'

Lesley poured cold water. 'You say she wasn't there when you arrived. She might well have stayed there overnight, but she didn't stick around to catch up with him this morning, did she? She wasn't expecting him or she'd have stayed to see him. He must have gone to see her of his own accord. I wonder why.'

'To retrieve something she's holding over him?' Susan shifted Fifi to lie more comfortably on her. 'There was something, a flicker of his eyelids perhaps, when I mentioned the laptop. Diana didn't want you to take her laptop, did she, and she refused to give you her password? Why? I suspect there are emails on it from her to Mr Cottrell and from him back to her? Compromising emails. Evan must have suspected something was going on, and that's why he went in search of her laptop while she was out. He was looking for evidence that she'd been playing around. However well she tried to delete those emails, you can still find them, can't you?'

'We can, and her laptop's already in the hands of an expert who is trying to break her password. But unless Diana and Keith went in for explicit messages, if they confined themselves to making arrangements to meet, the emails would hardly be considered sufficient evidence for a divorce.'

Susan said, 'All right. Is there anything else she could have had on him? Something which she's put in the safe at home? Bills that he paid for the scarlet underwear and the high-heeled shoes, for instance. Did he buy them for her, and if so, could she have managed to keep the receipts for them? If he was clever enough to have paid with cash it wouldn't matter, but if he paid by card then his details would be on the receipt and would lead any investigator directly to him.'

Lesley clicked her tongue, agreeing. 'Or the receipt from any expensive dinner or hotel room, provided he paid by card. I'm beginning to agree with you that she's holding something over him and that's why he went to Ellie's today. Perhaps it's just that he wants to be sure there's no paper trail to give his wife ideas about divorce. Perhaps he's tiring of Diana and wants to retrieve whatever it is she's holding over him.'

Susan sighed. 'If we believe Lucia, then Mr Cottrell and Diana parted on the best of terms yesterday morning and neither of them actually took part in the break-in. But, judging from Mr Cottrell's behaviour that morning and since, there's something still tying them together.'

'I agree. Whoever organized the break-in was not intending violence. They were looking for the safe. They didn't know the house well enough to know where it might be. Evan woke up, and there was a fight which caused his death. If Diana had organized the break-in for some reason, she'd have told the burglars where to look for the safe, so unless they forgot her instructions – which doesn't seem likely – then she didn't have anything to do with it. And I can't see why she would want anyone to break into her own safe, can you?'

'How about it being Mr Cottrell who organized it in order to retrieve any incriminating evidence against him?'

Lesley said, 'I like that. It's more important than ever that we get into that safe. We've got an expert coming in tomorrow to deal with it.' She clicked off.

Susan wriggled herself into a more comfortable position. The painkillers she'd been given were kicking in. She closed her eyes . . .

And woke to find someone giggling, and wriggling; something soft and warm against her arm. It was Fifi who was giggling and wriggling while Evan was leaning against Susan, holding on to one of the baby's tiny hands.

Evan loved Fifi. Fifi accepted his love.

No, that was ridiculous! They were far too young to even think of such things.

Evan was a sturdy, handsome, intelligent boy with many good

qualities. For one thing, he thought about others even in dire straits. And, Fifi smiled on him.

Fifi smiled on everyone.

No, she didn't. She was very particular about who she liked. She'd put up with Coralie. She'd ignored Jenny. She loved her father, who adored her in turn. She loved her mummy. She loved her granny Ellie, and her step-grandpa, Thomas. She loved Evan.

Evan had never been loved as Fifi was loved.

For the first time it struck Susan that while blonde Jenny didn't look in the least like Ellie, Little Evan had his grandmother's eyes. Grey blue and far-seeing. Perhaps he had more of Ellie in him than Susan had thought?

Susan felt Evan's pain, his longing for love.

She drew back. She could not, no, she could not, give him the love he needed. It would cost her too much.

Then she decided that she must try, however much it cost her.

She put her arm around him and hugged him.

The look he gave her! The hungry look! Had he never been hugged before? His eyes flashed silver. She could feel his need of her. He was reaching out to her, begging for love. She flinched. No, she couldn't love him like a mother, could she? She sat up, moving Fifi into a sitting position. 'Have we missed tea?'

The hours flew by, centring around the children and their needs. Coralie turned the older children out to play in the back garden but the wind was chilly and they clamoured to be let back in. Jenny only wanted to play with her tablet and watch television. Evan got out his books but couldn't concentrate. He quarrelled with Jenny about which programme to watch on the telly, and they had to be separated and the telly turned off. Within minutes Jenny had turned it on again and Evan was drifting around at Susan's heels.

Susan shuffled through the post and left most of it for Rafael to deal with. But there was one card, hand-delivered, no stamp, addressed to Evan and Jenny: 'With love from Mummy.'

What? Diana had dropped a card into the house for them? Well, wonders would never cease. Perhaps she did love her children, in her own way.

Susan left it on the kitchen table for them to see.

Rafael popped back to say he'd spoken to the plumber, who'd left before anything had been done about the broken window in the kitchen door. He said Marcy seemed to have everything else under control, so he'd promised to deal with the broken back door himself. And how was Susan feeling?

Susan felt worn out, but managed to smile and say she was just fine.

Hearing Rafael, Jenny tore herself away from the television, shouting, 'Cuckoo!' She clamoured to be lifted up and played with but Rafael put her off, saying, 'Later, later!'

Jenny threw a tantrum, at which Rafael cast a comical look of despair at Susan and made himself scarce.

Coralie signalled with her eyebrows to Susan. Should she leave the child to get over it by herself? Susan nodded. Jenny would soon stop when she realized no one was taking any notice.

Susan decided to cook. She'd been so looking forward to working in a kitchen again. She hadn't tried out the new oven yet. She couldn't wait!

She put Fifi in her highchair where she could see everything, and cooked. Ah, that was just what she needed. Fifi played with pieces of dough and sang to herself. Susan sang along with her. Evan brought his books to show Fifi, who graciously permitted herself to watch as he turned the pages for her.

Coralie tried to get Jenny to join them but the child refused, returning to the television set each time she was enticed away. Susan moved from making pies to throwing a sponge cake together. Coralie sorted clothes and toys, clearing the hall of a lot of the children's things, except for the easel, which they couldn't find a place for. Susan suggested Coralie stored the children's toys in one of the built-in cupboards in the living room.

Evan brought a colouring book to the kitchen table and showed Fifi how to use his crayons. Fifi got the idea at once. Her manual dexterity was excellent.

Susan showed Evan his mother's card. He said, 'Mummy's coming to take us home soon?'

'I hope so, my poppet. Now' – distraction needed – 'would you like to help me by licking out the bowl?' No child could resist that. Evan certainly didn't. It was a toss-up whether Fifi or Evan got most on their faces. That made them both laugh.

How peaceful! This was what a family afternoon should be like.

Susan felt guilty that she hadn't spent time with Jenny but . . . well, perhaps later.

At teatime, Lucia emerged from her room to demand Susan give her money to compensate her for her lost job and the wherewithal to buy a ticket back to Italy.

Susan took the two halves of sponge cake out of the oven and tested them with her forefinger. 'I understand why you wish to return home, Lucia, but you can't go till the police say so. Now, why don't you see if you can get Jenny interested in something other than the telly?'

'Devil child. She hit me. Why I bother with her?'

Susan noticed Coralie hiding a grin. Susan said, 'Lucia, you signed on to look after these two children. You were paid to do so. I do understand that you've not found it easy. Was this your first job, perhaps? And you haven't had any training for it? No? Well, if you want another job as a nanny in this country, it might be as well to learn how to do it.'

'My boyfriend say I must be paid lots and lots for being sent away, and I must not work any more for horrible woman and child who hit me. I am worth more than that.'

Really? Is the boyfriend as stupid as you?

Susan said, 'It's only natural that you want to put all this behind you and move on and I'm sure the police will be happy to let you go when they have sorted things out. But, if you try to leave without permission, they will come after you and you will be arrested. I'll see if I can get hold of Lesley when I've finished baking and ask her if she's any news for you.'

Lucia said, 'You cannot keep me here by force! Just because some stupid old man gets himself killed by burglars.' She flounced out of the kitchen and thundered up the stairs back to her room.

Little Evan echoed, 'Stupid old man?'

Susan had been careful not to mention his father's death in front of the boy, but Lucia had not been so thoughtful.

Little Evan was no fool. He looked up at Susan, his eyes darkening.

She washed her own hands, wiped Fifi's hands and face, and did the same for Evan. Then she sat down and hoisted him on to her knee. 'Your father was a very brave man. Even though he was in a wheelchair, he fought off some bad men who were trying to steal things from your home. He fought like a lion, but they were too many for him and he was badly hurt. Your mummy got him to the hospital, but they couldn't save his life. She's very upset.'

The intensity of his gaze almost knocked her off the chair.

Susan continued, 'Your mummy hoped that you could all move in next door because she thought your granny and grandpa would be back from their holidays by now. You remember Grandma Ellie and Grandpa Thomas?'

He frowned, shook his head and then nodded. He wasn't sure, was he? Six months was a long time for a small boy to remember his grandparents.

Susan continued again, 'What your mummy didn't know was that your granny and grandpa wouldn't be back home till next week and that their house is not yet ready for them. So she asked me to look after you for a while. She's out now looking for somewhere else to make a home for you all, but she slept next door last night, to be close to you and keep an eye on you . . .' And probably that was the truth, or enough of the truth to make the boy feel he hadn't been abandoned. 'And of course she sent you this card, to show you how much she loved you.'

Evan showed no sign of grief. He looked long and steadily at Susan. She tried to picture what his life had been like. He and his sister had been living at the top of the house in the care of an inadequate nanny, ignored by an elderly father who was sinking into dementia. His mother had worked long hours and had more than enough to do to keep the business going and look after everybody. Ellie had always said that Diana had been a good mother to her children, and although Susan had thought that sentiment was wishful thinking, yet perhaps, according to her lights, Diana had done what she could. She was not exactly the maternal type, was she?

Once or twice a week Evan had spent time with Ellie and Thomas, and there he'd been much loved and had learned what a family could be like. For the last six months, his grandparents had been absent from his life and he'd been handed over to Useless Lucia. A card with kisses on it was no substitute to a loving present. Evan was hurting, and what could Susan do about it?

ELEVEN

Saturday late afternoon

Susan held the little boy fast.

Fifi lunged forward in her highchair, trying to reach him.

Evan's eyes silvered, and then returned to grey. He said, 'Can Fifi get down? She wants to walk.' He slid off Susan's knee.

Coralie looked at Fifi. 'Isn't she a bit young to walk?'

Susan shrugged. 'She's been trying to stand by herself. We bought her some shoes last week. I think they're in the chest in the hall. Can you look?'

Coralie found the shoes, put them on and lifted Fifi out of her chair. Fifi suffered Coralie's hands on her, but squeaked and squealed until set down on the floor, pushing away hands which tried to steady her.

Fifi looked up at her mother, broke free of Coralie and plunged forward into Susan's arms. They both laughed.

'Come to me!' cried Evan, holding out his arms to Fifi, who steadied herself by clutching on to Susan's leg before she managed to totter towards Evan a couple of steps, concentrating like mad . . . only to crumple and fall . . . as Susan caught her up.

This time all four of them laughed.

'Again!' Fifi struggled to her feet and launched herself again . . . only she wasn't quite as steady on her feet this time and fell into Coralie's waiting arms.

'You can do it!' cried Evan. 'Come on, Fifi!' This time the girl managed to get herself properly balanced before making three little steps into the safety of his arms. She sat down. *Plump!* And clapped her hands.

The others clapped her, too.

Susan was between tears and laughter. Her little daughter was growing up fast. She said, 'Now I won't have a minute's peace. It was bad enough when she was crawling here and there but now . . . she'll be up the stairs or out of the front door before we can turn round.'

Evan said, 'I'll look after her.' He sat down on the floor beside Fifi and showed her his picture book again.

Susan and Coralie looked at one another, acknowledging what was happening.

Coralie said, 'He's a better nanny than Lucia.'

A car swished into the drive and parked. Susan looked out of the window to see a tall woman in black unfolding herself from the car. For a moment Susan thought it was Diana, coming back to retrieve her children.

But no. This woman was older and looked expensive. She hung on her heel to inspect the two houses. She went to Ellie's house first and tried the doorbell. Was Rafael still over there mending the back door and would he let her in? Probably not. In which case . . .

Susan shed her apron, rescued Fifi from the floor and took her into the big living room. Fifi struggled a bit, wanting to get down and walk. Evan trotted alongside, saying, 'Let me! Let me!'

Their own doorbell rang.

Susan's breast throbbed. She put Fifi down in her playpen, ignoring her roar of protest. Evan pushed his picture book through the bars of the playpen and sat down beside it. Susan turned the telly off and dumped Jenny into the playpen, too, giving her her tablet to play with.

There was a squawk of protest from Coralie as someone pushed their way past her into the house. A cold wind swept in with the newcomer. The sooner they had a porch put on the better.

Footsteps sounded on the wood flooring in the hall and the stranger appeared in the living room and looked about her. Oh dear, the big room had somehow become the children's nursery, with toys scattered everywhere and Evan's easel set up by the window.

The newcomer was a Diana clone, twenty years older. No, she was what Diana aspired to be. This woman had required very little cosmetic surgery to present herself as a slightly haggard beauty, black of hair, pale of skin, her body toned to perfection. The suit and high heels she was wearing must have cost a fortune, as had her handbag. And, she was wearing an expensive scent.

Keith Cottrell's wife, Cynthia?

Had she come to apologize for her husband's behaviour and beg Susan not to pursue charges against him? Er, no. She didn't look the apologizing sort.

Susan wondered whether this woman would wear the trousers in the marriage or not. Keith was a powerful-looking man, but this woman was something else. She was older than her husband, had probably selected him for his energy and drive and would be content enough for him to have the occasional one-night stand away from her, provided that he didn't threaten the life she'd arranged for them.

Keith would have married her not only because she was the boss's daughter and wealthy in her own right, but also for her stunning looks. Only, as she'd grown older, he'd been attracted to Diana, who had the same black and white looks and more energy than his ageing wife.

Diana, with a husband and children, was no threat to Cynthia. Diana without a husband might well prove to be a different matter.

Keith had been happy to keep Diana as his mistress, and she had been happy enough to satisfy her own basic needs while Evan lived.

The situation had changed with Evan's death. Hence this visit from Mrs Cottrell?

The newcomer priced everything in the room and decided it was junk. She cast a look over the children and noted various food stains on their clothes.

She gave Susan the once-over and made her feel uncouth, unlovely and totally incapable of dealing with the situation.

Coralie hovered, fingers fiddling with her hair. She wasn't happy about the visitor, either.

Susan straightened herself up with an effort and nodded to Coralie to indicate that everything was all right. Coralie rolled her eyes but disappeared. The children looked up at the newcomer with wide eyes.

The newcomer introduced herself to Susan. 'Mrs Cottrell. And you are the nanny, I assume?'

Susan coloured up. 'I'm looking after the children for the time being, yes. I'm Susan, Rafael's wife.'

'Oh. He's the workman who answered the door at the house

next door? I thought I'd seen him somewhere. He must have done some little electrical jobs for my husband.'

'I expect you saw him at the golf club. He runs his own business.'

'Does he?' Her tone dismissed him as a piece of dirt. She sniffed the air. 'You've been cooking? Is that what you do for a living? It smells quite good. You must give me your card. I do sometimes employ caterers for my dinner parties.'

Susan told herself to keep calm. 'I regret. I don't do outside catering.'

Cynthia ignored that. She swung around, looking for someone who wasn't there. 'I need a word with Diana. Would you fetch her for me? Please.' The 'please' was an afterthought.

'I'm afraid I can't help you. She isn't here.'

Evan scrambled to his feet and went to stand in front of Susan. Guarding her from the intruder? Brave boy! Fifi hauled herself to her feet, the better to inspect the newcomer.

Mrs Cottrell looked around. 'Then where is she?'

Susan said, 'We haven't seen her since yesterday morning. I believe she's out, looking for a new place to live.'

'Really? Is this Evan's little boy? How quaint.' She turned her attention back to Susan. 'So, when are you expecting her back?'

'She didn't say.' Susan began to be more annoyed than cowed by this woman. Susan didn't have red hair for nothing. She said, 'I thought you might have come to apologize for your husband's behaviour this morning.'

'My husband? Has he been here?'

She didn't know?

'He expected to meet Diana this morning, next door. She wasn't there. He took it out on me.'

A manufactured trill of laughter. 'How absurd! You'll be saying he raped you next.'

'No,' said Susan, blocking that one. 'I'm not his type. I don't know if he's lost his temper and assaulted other women in the past or not, but you need to know that the police have been informed and I am pressing charges. Perhaps they're interviewing him even as we speak.'

For a second, Cynthia Cottrell was taken aback. Then she lowered her eyelids and turned away. She had painted her eyelids silver. 'A good try, miss. But not good enough. We've had little people like you try to extort money from us before, and it's never worked.'

'Perhaps he was careful to avoid witnesses before.'

The dark eyes glinted malice. She asked the question without words.

Susan nodded. 'A witness. And photographs.'

'I don't believe it. Why would he bother to touch you?'

'Because he lost his temper. Are you going to let him carry on with Diana?'

'Impertinence!' Cynthia swung round and caught her foot on the side of the playpen, jarring it and toppling Fifi over on to her back.

Fifi let out a wail and Susan rushed to pick her up out of the playpen. 'There, there!'

Fifi had been frightened, but was not hurt. Evan took hold of Susan's leg and reached up to Fifi. Susan captured his hand with hers and held it tightly to reassure him.

Cynthia said, acid dripping from her tongue, 'What a charming picture you do make. The Earth Mother surrounded by infants. Perhaps you should give Diana lessons in childcare. Now, I really must go. We are dining out tonight and I don't wish to be late. Diana will no doubt return at some point, and when she does, I must ask you to give her a message from me. I have let her have her little fling with my husband for a while, but it is time for her to find herself another playmate. Understood?'

Susan said, 'I am not your messenger. If you have something to say to Diana, you should say it yourself.'

'As I thought, you are not very bright. Tell her that unless she leaves my husband alone, I shall reluctantly have to leak news of his unwise friendship with a murder victim's widow to the press, which would undoubtedly get her arrested for murder.'

'That is ridiculous!'

Cynthia smiled. 'What you don't appear to know is that early on the night in which he was murdered, my dear friend Evan had rung me to say he'd found evidence on his wife's laptop linking her with my husband in an inappropriate way. He asked me what I intended to do about it. I told him that my husband knew which side his bread was buttered and would never do anything to distress me.'

She gave a cat-like smile. 'My father handed the business over to me long before he retired officially. He retains the title of president for all the companies we control, but it is I who make the decisions. When we married, Keith signed a pre-nuptial agreement in exchange for the title of managing director of one of our companies, which allowed him a hefty salary and bonuses. He has been remarkably faithful for many years, more years perhaps than I had expected. If he is discreet, I am happy for him to visit another woman now and then, but I will not be the subject of media interest. If Diana threatens my position, I will have to remind him of the facts of life. Believe me, he doesn't want a divorce. What's more, Diana wouldn't want it, either. She wouldn't shack up with a penniless man, now, would she?'

'This is nothing to do with me. You must speak to Diana about it.'

Cynthia ignored that. 'On the night he died, I discussed the situation with dear Evan, who said he'd tell his wife the same thing, which leads me to the neat conclusion that Diana really did have a motive to have her husband die that night.'

Susan said, 'But she didn't know—'

Cynthia Cottrell wasn't listening. She swept out of the room, opened the front door – letting in the cold wind – slammed it behind her, and was gone.

Evan tugged on Susan's hand, looking anxious.

She reassured him. 'Mrs Cottrell isn't very happy about something, is she? I'm sure your mummy will be back soon.' She could feel her heart beating . . . and her breast hurting . . . and Fifi deciding to fill her pants . . .

Fifi relaxed, and then started to wriggle. She hated having dirty pants.

Susan felt stunned. She couldn't cope. That horrible woman! She took Fifi and Evan into the kitchen and changed her little one. She ignored the argument which Coralie was having with Jenny about sitting on the potty.

Evan watched Susan, leaning on her leg for comfort.

Susan thought, *This is all more than I can cope with. Dear Lord, if you're there and can be bothered with someone who hasn't thought much about you since she was a child, I could do with some advice. Ellie always said you came through for her when she was in trouble, and I'm daring to ask for your help, too.*

Fifi was a happy girl now. She squealed and wriggled to get down from the table. Susan caught her just in time, gave her a hug and a kiss and set her on the floor. She would have to be watched or she'd crawl away and get into trouble. Or, no. No, there was Evan, helping her to her feet. He walked backwards, very slowly.

Fifi concentrated. Three wobbling steps . . . four! She sat on her bottom and clapped her hands in joy. She got up again with Evan's help, and took two more steps . . . and then hesitated . . . before taking three more . . . into her father's arms as he swept into the hall with a gust of wind.

Rafael threw Fifi into the air and caught her again. 'You're walking! How about that!'

Fifi wriggled and laughed.

Evan clapped and laughed.

Susan did, too.

She thought, *Mrs Cottrell was lying! I must ask Lesley to check Evan's phone records to see if he really was speaking to Cynthia on the evening he died. Even if she is speaking the truth, I don't see how Diana could have done anything about it because she was out that night and Evan didn't get at her laptop till after she'd left. So she couldn't know that Evan was threatening to divorce her, and she had no reason to kill him.*

Mrs Cottrell is a dangerous woman. I suspect she's capable of telling any number of lies to get her own way. And, she has the money to back her, which Diana hasn't.

I feel almost sorry for Diana, married to a man sinking into senility and trying to keep the estate agency afloat in difficult times.

But, to start an affair with a man she fancied? No, that was wrong. Fiercely wrong. And stupid to let lust overcome common sense. Look what happens. Overnight, she is threatened with losing her husband, her home and, very likely, her lover as well.

Jenny swooped in, crying 'Cuckoo!' She clung to Rafael's leg, and he put down a hand to caress her, saying, 'Have you been a good girl?'

'Yes, yes! Up, up!' cried Jenny.

Fifi looked down at Jenny and turned her head away to rest against her father's shoulder. Fifi didn't think much of Jenny, did she?

Susan felt a pang of remorse for Jenny, who might well feel neglected, what with all that was going on.

Jenny reached up to Rafael, again. 'Up, up!'

Rafael, half laughing and half serious, said, 'I'm not having smelly girls sitting on my knee.'

Coralie picked Jenny up. 'Let's try again with the potty, shall we? And then you'll be nice and clean and smelling sweet for tea. Come along, Evan, time to wash our hands before we eat.' She swept the two away.

Susan looked across at Rafael, but his gaze was guarded, giving nothing away. Susan had seen herself with Diana's eyes, and with Cynthia's. She felt fat and uncomfortable. Unlovable. She wanted to talk about Cynthia, but now was not the time. She said, 'You mended the window next door? What if Diana comes back again tonight?'

'I put a note on the door saying trespassers would be prosecuted.' Also, I left a message on her phone to say I'd mended the door and the trust would bill her for repairs. She's an estate agent. She has the keys to innumerable properties. She must be able to find somewhere else to stay.' He put Fifi into her highchair, avoiding Susan's eye.

We're behaving like strangers.

Susan started laying the table, sorting out what the children would eat, what the adults would eat later, and what should go in the freezer. She condensed her report into a few words. 'I've just had the pleasure of a visit from Cynthia Cottrell. She wanted me to tell Diana to keep her hands off her husband, who knows which side his bread is buttered.'

'Cynthia. I'm told she's deadlier than Di.'

That seemed to be that. Susan sought for another topic of conversation. 'Did Marcy get away all right?'

'What a woman. What a blessing. Worth her weight in gold. She says to tell you it's going to cost an arm and a leg to put the house to rights but she'll be back first thing tomorrow to make a start. She watched me write the note for Diana and said I was within my rights and that Diana would be holed up in her love nest, wouldn't she? I asked how Marcy knew about that and she said it was because some scarlet underwear and other clothes that left nothing to the imagination had appeared in Diana's bedroom only to disappear the following day, never to be seen again. Marcy said it stood to reason that Diana had kept them in a little love nest somewhere.'

'Marcy thinks Diana's holed up somewhere now?'

'It sounds reasonable to me. I tried her office again. Closed for the afternoon. So yes, I'd say she's retreated to her burrow.'

Coralie had made up some bottles of formula and put them in the fridge. She was worth her weight in gold, too, wasn't she? Susan set one to warm and handed Rafael some carrot sticks to let Fifi chew on something while she put a high tea together.

Rafael said, 'Susan, I know you would take in a wounded bird, never mind two stray children and their nanny, but it's a lot of extra work and could become inconvenient. Should we consider handing the strays over to Social Services?'

Susan reacted without thinking. 'I'd be happy for Lucia to be taken away, although Social Services won't have her, but Evan? No way! He's a little soldier. Jenny? Not an easy child. I feel guilty that I haven't given her as much attention as I've given Evan.'

Prompt on cue, down the stairs came Useless Lucia, brandishing her smartphone. 'Is too much! More money I must have. I am cut off in middle of phone call. My friend say I must not stay to be treated so bad, ordered to do this and do that, and not even nice room to sleep in. No television, not even small one! No blind to window. No bedside light. I not care what police say. I have done nothing wrong. It is Diana who has done wrong to me. I want my air ticket home, and compensation. You hear me?'

Rafael was imperturbable. 'I hear you. We owe you nothing. On the contrary, you owe us for bed and board. You had nowhere to go and had no money. We took you in and advanced you money to tide you over. Otherwise you would be walking the streets, wouldn't you?'

Lucia was all powered up. 'You treat me like slave! I will not be treated like slave, and I will not wait for stupid police to ask more questions.'

Susan hit her forehead. 'Bother. I did say I'd ask Lesley if you could go home. I'll ring her now. Where's my phone?'

Where had she left it? Oh, couldn't this wait till after she'd given the children their tea?

Rafael said, 'Lucia, sit down and eat or go up to your room, just as you please. I'll see if I can get through to Lesley.' He took out his own phone and saw there were messages on it. 'Oh. What does he want . . .?'

Coralie arrived with two children with clean hands and faces. Both smelling sweet. Both hungry. Jenny climbed on to Rafael's knee. He ignored her as he took his messages.

Lucia seated herself, carefully coaxing tears on to her cheeks and pressing a tissue to her eyes. Susan served some pasta for the littlies and Lucia. Coralie said her mum wanted her back for supper, but she'd stay till they'd got the children bathed and tucked up in bed.

The children ignored Lucia. As usual.

Rafael shot up out of his chair. 'What? Say that again!' He tried to put Jenny down, but she resisted, wailing loudly.

Lucia said, 'Oh, shut up, you are horrible child!'

This stirred Evan to action. 'You're the horrible one. I hate you!'

Rafael handed Jenny over to Coralie, saying, 'I've got to take this,' and set off down the corridor to his study.

Jenny wailed, kicking and shouting. Her face turned bright red.

Susan took Jenny from Coralie, and held her tightly . . . oh, that hurt, but she could stand it, couldn't she? Poor little Jenny. Poor little mite. Susan didn't think the child had ever had much attention from her father even before he declined into a wheelchair. Diana had always been busy, and a series of nannies didn't seem to have tackled the problem. A child without love grew up to be an unloving adult.

'There, there,' said Susan, rocking Jenny in her arms. Jenny was heavy. Susan manoeuvred herself into a chair, ably helped by Coralie. At first Jenny fought Susan, and then gradually, as tears flowed, she accepted the love which Susan was offering, and relaxed. One-handed, Susan began to feed Jenny, while Coralie dealt with the others.

Rafael came back down the corridor, still on his phone. He beckoned to Susan to come out of the kitchen, but she was pinned to her chair by Jenny who refused to move, so he shrugged and returned to his study, leaving the women to clean everyone up. He didn't appear when the children were taken into the big room for playtime, and he didn't even surface when they were taken upstairs for a bath and bed. Fifi made herself keep awake as long as the others. Fifi was not going to miss anything, was she?

Lucia helped a bit with getting the children in and out of the big bath, moaning the while that she shouldn't be asked to look after children when she wasn't being paid for it. Neither Coralie nor Susan bothered to reply to that, as they had another problem to solve.

Rafael had brought back the two small beds which Evan and Jenny had been sleeping in at home, but fitting them into a room which already contained a largeish double bed and Fifi's cot was a problem. Perhaps it would be possible for Rafael to take down the double bed and store it somewhere else for the time being? But where?

Eventually it was decided to leave the two small beds on their sides on the landing and to put Evan and Jenny together into the big bed. Unfortunately Jenny refused to sleep in the big bed. She wanted her cot.

Susan checked with Lucia, who said Jenny had been promoted to a small bed recently and her old cot had been disposed of.

Jenny threw a tantrum. *She wanted her cot.*

Susan and Coralie gave in, thinking that the children had been through enough trauma recently. If Jenny wanted to revert to babyhood for a while, then so be it. Fifi could sleep in the top part of her baby buggy and let Jenny have her cot.

Fifi went out like a light. The other children were read to and persuaded to close their eyes and pretend to be asleep, until they actually did just that.

The adults tiptoed out, exhausted and more than ready for an evening meal.

Finally, it was grown-up time.

Coralie was collected by her father. Lucia announced she was going out for a walk as she didn't care to be with people who didn't appreciate her . . . and she left, taking Susan's umbrella without permission in case it rained, which it might well do.

Only then did Rafael emerge from his den to join Susan in the kitchen for a belated supper. But there was no time to talk, for he'd brought his laptop with him and was engrossed in whatever he was reading on it. He forked food into his mouth, and said, 'That was good,' without interest. He did remark that looking after three children under five was more tiring than running a marathon and he didn't know how Susan coped.

Susan wanted to hit him, particularly since he'd hardly done any of the childcare. He took his dessert back to his study. Susan cleared up after a fashion.

She was draggingly tired. She hurt. She thought of going to bed straight away but couldn't face climbing the stairs.

She wanted to subside into their big, squashy settee with Rafael beside her. She fantasized that she could put her feet up, perhaps have a chocolate or two, and find a non-worrying programme to watch on the telly. Nothing demanding. Politics were out, as were programmes about incest or murder. Definitely nothing about murder.

She sank on to the settee by herself and closed her eyes. It had been a long and tiring day. And, her milk had dried up. She dozed, until she felt a small body nudge her leg. She cracked open her eyes.

Evan was there, holding Hippo and looking up at her with eyes that seemed far older and wiser than his years. He wasn't smelly, thank goodness. He looked as if he'd been crying but wasn't going to admit it.

She said, 'Bad dream?'

He nodded.

She let him climb up beside her. She put her arm around him and felt his head burrow into her shoulder. Hippo didn't smell too bad, up close. She pronounced the magic formula, 'There, there.'

He didn't relax. The bad dream still had hold of him.

'There, there. Can you tell me about it?'

A long silence. Then: 'Daddy's crying. Hippo doesn't like it.'

It was Susan's turn to stiffen. How could the little boy have heard . . .? No, he was imagining it. That big door at the top of the stairs would have stifled sound from two floors below, unless . . .?

She said, carefully, 'It was a bad dream. Gone now. What do you do when you get a bad dream? Do you tell Lucia?'

'No. Lucia says, "Go back to bed and don't bother me!" She's always watching telly, or on her phone. She bangs her door shut and locks it.'

Lucia deserved to get the sack if she didn't comfort a child who'd had a nightmare!

'So what do you do next?'

Silence.

Oh. My goodness! Surely he hadn't wandered downstairs on the night his father was attacked! Pray God he didn't see what happened! Oh, dear Lord, no!

TWELVE

Saturday evening

Evan shifted to lie more comfortably against Susan. 'When Daddy cries in the night, Hippo says we can open the door on the landing and see if Mummy's light's on down below. If we see the light, we hold on tight to the banisters and we go down the stairs one at a time, and then we climb into bed with Mummy and the bad dream goes away.'

Good for Diana.

Susan stroked the little boy's back. He began to relax. She said, 'You're safe now.'

'Hippo doesn't feel safe exactly. He doesn't like it when Daddy cries.'

How terrible for a child to hear their parent cry!

'It was just a bad dream, poppet.'

He lifted his head. 'Not a dream. Mummy explained. Daddy's sad because he's poorly. Jenny and I must be quiet, not bother him. I asked Mummy why the doctor not make him better, and she said he takes his medicine when I close my eyes and go to sleep. So Hippo and I go to sleep in her bed.'

Now for the fifty-million-dollar question.

'What happened if you got a bad dream and Lucia wouldn't help you and your mummy wasn't in her room? Has that ever happened?'

He nodded, but didn't speak.

She said, 'Did it happen the other night? Were you brave enough to go right down the stairs to see if your daddy was all right?'

'Hippo was frightened. Men shouting.'

Susan shivered. 'You went down? How far?'

'To the top of the stairs by Mummy's room. Mummy's light wasn't on, but there were lights in the hall and lots of shouting. Daddy was shouting, too. And then it was quiet. I could hear man breathing like this, in and out, in and out.'

'You didn't see anyone?'

A wriggle. Silence.

Finally, he said, 'I hid behind Hippo, but he looked up and saw me. He said, "Go back to bed. Don't come down again!" So I went back upstairs. In the morning Lucia was there and we had breakfast and I told Hippo it was a bad dream. I went to nursery but Lucia made me leave Hippo behind and I missed him while we were there, and when we came out we went to McDonald's and then we walked and walked and we tried to go home but there were strange people there and it was another bad dream . . . and then we came here.'

'The man in the dream, the one who told you to go back to bed. Did you see his face?'

He shook his head. 'He was all in black. All over. Like a spider.'

'But you recognized his voice?'

A nod. 'And his smell. He smells funny.' He yawned hugely.

'Cigarettes? Coffee smell?'

He'd lost interest. 'Where's Mummy? Is she staying with friends? She often stays with friends.'

'She asked us to look after you for a bit, while she finds another place for you to live.'

'We're not going home, then?'

Susan shook her head.

He said, 'I like it here.'

Another long silence. Susan thought he'd dropped off to sleep until he said, 'Hippo doesn't like hearing Daddy cry in the night. He won't be crying where he is now, will he?'

'If he is, he'll soon stop and be happy again. When you think of him now, think of him smiling at you. Then the bad dreams will stop.'

His whole body shook in a deep sigh. 'You said a prayer to Fifi when you tucked her up in her cot. You didn't say one for me or Jenny. Granny always says a prayer when she tucks us up in bed.'

Susan had felt embarrassed about saying a prayer as she'd laid Fifi down to sleep. She didn't always do it. She wasn't all that sure she believed in prayer. But somehow, under the circumstances, it had seemed the right thing to do. She said, 'Let's take you back up to bed now, and we'll say a prayer for Jenny and another for you, and then you'll be able to sleep without any more bad dreams.'

He scrambled down, still holding Hippo and took her hand. 'All right. Hippo feels better now.'

She took him back upstairs, popped him into the big bed, gave him a cuddle, said a little prayer over him and Jenny, checked that both girls were fast asleep, and dragged herself back downstairs, thinking she would get a hot drink and tumble into bed herself.

Fat chance! As she reached the hall Rafael emerged from his study, holding up his laptop and shouting, 'I've cracked it!'

Rafael was pleased with himself. He didn't notice that Susan was flagging but gave her a whacking great kiss, twirled her round till she was dizzy and said, 'Shall we tell Lesley now or in the morning?'

Susan assumed that was a rhetorical question since he'd flung himself at full length on to the big settee and beamed at her. His attitude proclaimed that he was the One and Only, the Solver of Mysteries-which-had-proved-too-hard-for-ordinary-mortals, and he expected the little woman to provide him with an appropriate amount of praise.

Susan tried to oblige. 'Really? How did you crack it? And did you know that Little Evan used to—'

Rafael waved her words away. He wasn't listening, was he? 'On the internet. You can find out all sorts of things if you only know how. I realize it's a bit of a closed book to you and you don't—'

'I can text and take photos.'

'Ah, yes. Well, one of these days we'll sign you up for a couple of beginners' sessions on a laptop and lo and behold! A whole new world will open to you.'

'Yes,' said Susan, feeling worn out and trying not to show it. 'But sometimes people just tell me things. Evan has just—'

'Never mind about that. Look what I've found!' He turned his laptop towards her and opened the lid.

She looked. She couldn't make head nor tail of the names and numbers on the screen. 'What am I supposed to be seeing?'

Rafael was only too happy oblige. 'Paper trails. People try to hide them but there's always something, if you know how to look. Now here' – he honed in on something in small print – 'is where I started. Evan's Estate Agency, established et cetera, nice photo of him taken twenty years ago, looking as if he were born to the silver, member of the golf club, and so on. Here's another of Diana, not so successful, looking as if it pained her to smile. Premises, et cetera, recent sales, properties much in demand, terms and conditions, et cetera. Looks prosperous, doesn't it?'

'Yes,' said Susan, who didn't trust estate agents as a matter of principle and would never, ever, have put business Diana's way.

Rafael scrolled down till he came to 'Properties recently sold', saying, 'We don't need to look in detail at those houses but at a quick glance I can tell you that not much has been sold by them in recent months, except . . . Look at this one.' He pointed to a modern house in one of those new estates where the car rules OK, and there isn't a bus, a school, a doctor or a shop for miles. He said, 'Got it?'

Susan hadn't.

Rafael explained. 'All right. Let's make it easy for you. Let's look at the board outside this house which is for sale on Diana's website. See? "A Betterment Project for Winston Enterprises". Now, Winston Enterprises is a multinational concern, lots of companies reliant on importing cheap goods from the Far East and selling them here for high prices. The City reports they're doing well. Their chairman is a man called Charles Winston –

originally Weinstein – and the managing director is his daughter . . . see here? Yes, Cynthia Cottrell is his daughter. Their headquarters are in a tax haven and Cynthia lives with Keith in a gated mansion out in the country to the west of London.

'Let's scroll down through their various companies. In every case we find Cynthia's name lurking somewhere on the board of directors, but no Keith Cottrell until we come to . . . yes, here we are: "A Betterment Project, Homes for Today. Managing Director, Keith Cottrell: Chairman, Cynthia Cottrell". So let's look at Homes for Today in detail. Here they are . . . Nice picture of Keith Cottrell looking responsible and trustworthy. Here's one of Cynthia . . . professional photograph . . . straight from the beauty parlour . . . looks good for her age, doesn't she? A tough cookie.

'Now, let's look at their website. "Proud to present . . . Brand-new housing estate convenient to the A40 . . . Another out near Denham . . . Plans in preparation for . . . Sales through . . ." Get it?'

Susan got it. 'Keith appointed Diana's agency to sell the houses on an estate which is being built by Cynthia's firm. I wonder what Cynthia feels about that.'

'And how do you think Keith Cottrell will feel about being dragged into a murder enquiry? Is he going to stand by his dearest Diana and risk losing his nice lifestyle, or is he going to run for cover back to his wife?'

Susan shook her head. 'His anxiety to meet up with Diana seems fed by fear of the way the situation might work out, rather than by passion to fall into her arms again. He's not going to stand by her. But he did urgently need to see her. I'm sure she's got something on him. Something he sent his heavies to retrieve from her house the other night?'

Rafael said, 'Or that Cynthia sent? She put up with his behaving badly so long as it wasn't in the public eye, but she doesn't want to lose him. She wouldn't want him dragged into a murder enquiry any more than he would. So yes, why shouldn't it be her who sent the heavies in? Or, indeed, her father. Want to see what he looks like?'

Rafael tapped keys and the picture of a silver-haired man with a thick neck appeared on screen. Beautiful suit. Heavy-lidded eyes. Carrying too much weight for his height but you wouldn't want to bump into him in the street or you'd be sent flying.

Susan shivered. 'Mafia man?'

Rafael closed his laptop. 'Case solved. Ellie said we'd crack it, and we have. We can leave it to Lesley to arrest whichever one of the three she fancies. The police should give me a medal, right?'

She didn't want to rain on his parade. Well, she did, actually. His air of Superior-Man-solving-a-problem-too-difficult-for-his-Little-Woman grated on her. She said, 'Yes, you've discovered that each of these three might have a motive to search the house for Diana's secret, whatever it is, but where does that get us?'

That didn't faze him. 'Forensics will cope with that. They'll find out who the heavies were from DNA left at the scene. Lesley will call the heavies in for questioning. No doubt they'll be only too happy to divulge the name of whoever it was who employed them rather than face a charge of murder. Their employers can be prosecuted under the conspiracy label.'

'Unless the heavies have been so well paid that they refuse to talk. Can't the Winston-and-Cottrell lot afford their minions' silence?'

He looked wounded. 'Oh, come on! Why the sour face? Don't you want this whole nasty affair cleared up and Diana out of our lives?'

'Sorry. Yes, of course I do.'

Couldn't he see that everything had got on top of her? Moving in and finding out she was pregnant again? Then the children arriving, and Lucia, and everyone expecting her to cope, regardless?

At that point Susan had to stop and laugh at herself, because she'd observed this situation before from the outside. It was always happening to Ellie, wasn't it? People in trouble saw that she was strong and expected her to carry their burdens when in actual fact she often felt like dissolving into a puddle of tears, rather like Alice in Wonderland. Though Alice did manage to get out of the puddle, didn't she? And she, Susan, was not Ellie. No way! Oh dear, she really was so tired.

Rafael put his arm around her. 'You're worn out. Why don't you go on up? I'll tidy up down here and come up in a minute. I'd thought of having a cuddle . . .?' He read her expression correctly, and continued, 'But perhaps not tonight. Who knows when the children will need us in the night?'

Sunday morning

Well, they did have a more peaceful night. Rafael only had to get up once to the Cuckoo, and Susan slept solidly through till Fifi woke and cried for her at half past six. Susan changed the baby and took her into bed with them to doze off for another hour. And yes, she knew you weren't supposed to do that, but honestly! Their bed was enormous and if they drew back the curtains Fifi would lie beside them and happily watch the tops of the trees waving in the breeze in the garden outside.

Little Evan slept right through with no more bad dreams, and he didn't wet the bed.

Fifi insisted on wobbling along the corridor upstairs by herself, but did allow Susan to carry her down the stairs. Susan added childproof stair gates to her mental list of what they needed to get. And a helmet for Evan, on scooter or bike.

Coralie had announced her intention of turning up at half past seven in the morning and did so. Hurray for Coralie! She told Susan that her parents wanted her back that afternoon for a family 'do' but she'd stay till one, if that was all right with Susan, which it most definitely was.

But, oh, how was Susan going to manage that afternoon? She told herself Coralie deserved some time off and there were plenty of women who had to look after three young children at any one time. Susan would learn how to do it. Of course she would.

Coralie helped Susan sort the children's breakfast out, and then took them off – with Fifi teetering along beside her – into the garden to run about and work off some energy.

Rafael excused himself from clearing up the breakfast things by saying he wanted to ring Lesley and leave her a message about the links to the Cottrells which he'd uncovered the night before. He went off to his study to do so, which reminded Susan that, what with one thing and another and looking after the children, she hadn't reported Cynthia's visit to Lesley, and then there was the information Little Evan had given her about the night his father was killed. Oughtn't the police to hear about that?

Well, yes and no. Rafael would tell Lesley about Cynthia's involvement in the affair, Evan couldn't identify anyone, and it would probably be very bad for his psyche to remind him of that terrible event, so . . . let it lie.

Lucia drifted in, saying it was her day off and she was going to Mass that morning and would like another advance on her wages so she could go out with a friend afterwards.

That went down like a lead balloon with Susan as it meant she'd have no help at all with the children that afternoon. She tried bargaining with Lucia, who turned stubborn and accused Susan of wanting to keep her as a wage slave!

Fortunately Rafael emerged from his study at that point to tell Lucia she couldn't go anywhere as Lesley wanted to see her again.

'It's Sunday! I must go to church.'

'Lesley said it wouldn't take long.'

'Then you must give me money for taxi to church, and for collection and for meeting my friend after for a meal.'

Rafael shrugged. 'We'll ask Lesley what the position is.'

Lucia flounced off, declining to soil her fingers by helping Susan put the dishes into the dishwasher, which thankfully was now working properly.

As Lucia went up the stairs, Susan heard her talking on her phone, complaining how badly she was being treated.

Rafael said, as Lucia slammed the door of her room above, 'Can we get her famous friend to put her up? She's no help to you, is she?'

'Agreed. What about asking if Coralie can stay on? She says she wants to leave school and she was thinking of training as a nanny, anyway.'

'Her parents may want her to stay on at school, and she isn't a trained nanny yet. But yes, I'll have words, see what we can work out.'

Down the hall came the patter of tiny feet. Fifi had escaped from Coralie and was aiming for her daddy, only she didn't quite make it. She slipped and toppled over untidily . . . but Rafael managed to get to her in time. Fifi crowed with delight and beat at her father's shoulder. Rafael crowed back and then, still holding her, he got out his smartphone. 'How many childproof gates do we need? I must measure up.'

Coralie appeared, panting. 'Sorry, she got away from me.' She checked that Fifi was all right and disappeared back into the garden just as the doorbell rang.

And there was Lesley, accompanied by a second no-nonsense, solid policewoman in plain clothes. Another detective constable?

Lesley was also on her phone, saying, 'Yes, yes. I'll be . . . No, not long.' She clicked off.

Susan took one look at Lesley and inhaled sharply. Lesley had lost her 'edge'. Lesley had had a bad night, or a quarrel with that egotistic husband of hers? Or both. Yes, both. Best not to notice.

'You want Lucia?' said Susan. 'Take her with our blessing.'

Lucia called down from above. 'Is Lesley come? Tell her I am worked like a slave and they must put me in four-star hotel!'

Lesley raised her eyebrows at Susan, who shrugged and suggested coffee.

Lesley said, 'No time.' She called up the stairs, 'Just a few more questions, Lucia. Won't take a minute.'

Lucia took her time descending. She was already wearing her jacket and had put on some make-up. 'I am late for church. I go to Mass at the abbey.'

Susan took Fifi from Rafael, as she was fussing to be let down. Once Fifi was on the floor, she held on to Susan's hand to look around, observing the world from a different angle.

Lesley said, 'All right, Lucia. I'll see that you get a lift in a minute.'

That didn't suit Lucia. 'You pay for taxi to church, right?'

Lesley's expression said, Fat chance! She took Lucia into the kitchen, gestured to her to sit and took some photographs out of her bag. 'I want you to think back to that last morning before you were let go. You took the children to the nursery and were walking back to the house with Jenny in the pushchair, when you saw your employer get out of a car in the road ahead. I have four photos here to show you. Do you recognize the man you saw?'

Lesley laid down the photographs one after the other. Susan picked Fifi up and looked at the photographs, too. Number three in line was Keith Cottrell. Susan watched Lucia focusing on the photographs.

The girl kept her face expressionless and pushed the photos away from her. She sat back in her chair, teasing out her hair, eyes sliding left and right. She'd recognized someone, yes. But didn't want to play ball?' She said, 'I not sure. I see for one minute only.'

Lesley was not amused. 'I'm not playing games. Did you, or did you not recognize that man from one of these photographs?'

'You treat me bad. You want I be snake in grass, you treat me better. A four-star hotel, and more money. I am not something from the bottom of your shoe. I am worth more.'

'You are worth . . .!' Lesley stopped, took a deep breath, and made herself relax. 'The man you saw may have been responsible for the attack on your employer. If we fail to identify him, then he will be at liberty to commit other crimes.

'Perhaps you think that such a man might pay you to keep your mouth shut about seeing him that morning? That's called blackmail and it is a criminal offence. I would soon hear about it if you tried that, and would have to place you under arrest, which means you would not be going home for the foreseeable future. Also, if you try to protect a guilty man he might well come looking for you, not to give you money but to silence you for good. Remember this: Evan ended up dead. Do you want to end up the same way?'

Sulkily, Lucia pushed one photograph out of the pile and put her finger on it. 'That is the man I saw.'

Susan, still holding on to Fifi, nodded. 'That's Keith Cottrell, the man who was here yesterday, looking for Diana.'

'Good,' said Lesley, producing another photograph from her bag. 'Now, Lucia, you know that Evan was attacked by some people looking for your employer's safe. You know that he fought back. Forensics have discovered DNA from blood and hairs left behind by two of the intruders, one of whom was already in the system. It is possible you may have seen him hanging around the house before the attack. I want you to look at his photograph and tell me if you've seen him before.'

The photograph was of an awkward-looking, raw-boned youth. Close-cut, fairish hair, nondescript coloured eyes fringed with almost-invisible lashes, large nose, poor complexion. He was wearing a hooded T-shirt which was none too clean.

Lucia looked at it. She shook her head. 'No.'

'He was one of the men who attacked and killed Evan. His DNA was in the system because he'd been in and out of trouble since he was ten. You've never come across him?'

Lucia lifted her upper lip in a sneer. 'He look stupid, no?'

Lesley turned to Susan. 'Have you ever seen this lad before?'

Susan studied the mugshot. 'Don't think so.' Of course, if he'd been hanging around a street corner with a group of other youths, she might not have noticed him. She could imagine what the boy was like: single parent, absentee father, low IQ, dropped out of school and joined whatever gang would accept him. A follower, not a leader.

Just as Lucia was a follower and not a leader.

She passed the photo to Rafael who was, fortunately, off his phone for the moment. Rafael scrutinized the photo and shook his head. 'Local lad?'

'Lived in a tower block where Social Services dump people. He was found in an alley behind the shops this morning. Dead. Knife wounds. It was probably some gang-related activity which put him there, but it's a pity because if he'd lived we'd have been able to question him about Evan's death.'

Lucia wasn't interested. 'You take drugs, then you die.' She got to her feet. 'I need money for taxi and church and for meal with my friend. I need key for front door, because I am with my friend till late.'

Susan said, 'I don't think we've got a spare set, have we, Rafael? What time do you think you'll be back, Lucia? One of us will wait up for you if you can't make it by ten.'

Lucia didn't like that. 'I am not child, told what time to go to bed.'

Lesley wasn't amused. 'If you can't get back by ten, you must phone and tell Susan you can't make it and get one of your friends to put you up for the night. Now, sit down again and give your statement to my DS. I'll drop you off at the abbey afterwards. Meanwhile . . . Susan, a word?'

Lesley led the way into the sitting room, leaving her police sergeant with Lucia.

Rafael followed them, taking Fifi off Susan, and dumping her in her playpen. He said, 'You've arrested Diana?'

'We're looking for her. Any ideas?'

Rafael glanced at Susan and looked away. 'You think she's on the run because she's afraid she'll be accused of planning her husband's murder?'

'We need to question her further, to eliminate her from our enquiries.'

Rafael said, 'I believe you can find people's location by tracing their smartphones. Ah, you've tried that and haven't found her, which means she's stopped using that phone. But she'll need to keep in touch with people somehow, so she's probably bought herself a cheap Pay As You Go phone which you can't track.'

Lesley shrugged. 'Been there. Done that. Any other ideas?'

'Susan and I thought she might have lifted the keys to one of the empty properties she's trying to sell, and moved in there but . . . No, you've checked that no keys are missing, haven't you? What about her bank account?'

Lesley allowed herself a small smile and shook her head.

Rafael narrowed his eyes. 'Of course you've already checked that, too. Diana knows you can trace where she's been from the use she makes of her bank card and there's been no activity on it? Hm. Well, either she withdrew a large sum of money in cash on the day Evan was killed, and is living off that or . . . No, she's set up another bank account with a different bank? Yes, of course that's just what she'd do. I'll bet she had one set up somewhere else, ages ago. Her own private account. She would have been squirrelling away what she could lay her hands on, money from kickbacks and what she got from pawning Evan's ring. She was making herself a rainy day fund.'

Lesley's mouth tightened. 'You know her much better than I do. We'll check that. Any other inspirations?'

Rafael shrugged. 'Why do you want her? You know she's got a foolproof alibi for the night Evan was attacked. What's more, she had no reason to wish a dying man dead.'

Lesley said, 'She lied to us, and I want to know why. Also, it occurs to me that if Evan had discovered she was having it off with Keith Cottrell, he might well have threatened to make her life miserable and she might have launched a pre-emptive strike to shut him up.'

Rafael was sceptical. 'She hadn't time to organize anything. Evan didn't investigate her laptop till after she'd left that evening.'

'So why did she lie to us? I agree it's more likely that it was Keith Cottrell who got someone to burgle the safe to recover whatever it was she'd got on him. We've managed to get into her laptop and there's evidence there to show that they were having an affair. Arrangements for meetings, and so on.'

Susan said, 'Yes, but Cynthia didn't want a divorce any more than Evan would. Rafael did tell you about her calling on me, didn't he?' She repeated the gist of what the woman had said the previous day, concluding with: 'Cynthia Cottrell was very sure that Keith would toe the line in future. She wasn't going to divorce him, not she! She did say she and Evan had discussed the matter on the evening before he died, and that they were going to take action to end the affair, but neither wanted a divorce.

'Evan certainly wouldn't have wanted one. Yes, he might have wanted to lash out, to scream and shout at her, and maybe even threaten this and that. But when he'd calmed down, practical considerations would have told him it wasn't in his best interests to divorce the woman who kept the agency and his house and the children going, not to mention looking after him in his increasing frailty. He certainly didn't need to set up a burglary of his own house because he could access the safe any time he wanted. Couldn't he?

THIRTEEN

Sunday noon and afternoon

Rafael said, 'I keep wondering what is in that safe? You've cracked the laptop and got confirmation that Keith and Diana were having an affair, but there's nothing to say either party was anxious to get a divorce. Right? Now, as to the safe. Let me guess, you found the usual stuff: passports, marriage certificates, some family jewellery, and they don't take you any further than the emails have done. And what else?'

Lesley almost laughed. And then shook her head. 'I can't say, yet. We're going through the contents of the safe now. There's some business papers which might be interesting but nothing to show where Diana might be hiding. I'm beginning to wonder if she has more papers in a bank vault somewhere.'

Rafael said, 'There's no bills for council tax or services paid for on another property somewhere? No? Which means that Keith was being careful not to let her hold them for him. There must be records somewhere of his bolthole, somewhere which has not gone through the books. Keith's in the building trade, isn't he? Couldn't he have kept a small furnished show flat for himself after the rest of the houses in his housing development had been sold off?'

'No, Rafael,' said Susan. 'If I read her correctly, I think it's *her* bolthole, not *his*. She wouldn't leave expensive shoes and toiletries in a love nest provided by Keith or any other man, in case they were used by someone else. Lesley, I'd look at recent contracts covering a small, central property rented out through her agency. A studio flat, perhaps? Something in one of the new builds down by the river? Or on the canal? Pricey, minimalist, and with a cleaning contract with an agency.'

Rafael nodded. 'Makes sense.'

Lesley said, 'I suppose it wouldn't do any harm to look. You will be amused to hear that when I went over to see Mr Cottrell, he refused to speak to me unless I had a warrant for his arrest, and even then he'd say nothing unless his solicitor were present. I mentioned that we'd had a complaint of assault and he just laughed and said it was always a certain type of woman who screamed "rape" when they'd been accused of having done something naughty!'

Susan closed her eyes and told herself to count down from ten. No, from a hundred. And made it to ninety . . .

Rafael put his hand over hers. 'Lesley, you're not letting him get away with that, are you?'

'No. We're getting a warrant and I'll tackle him again tomorrow.'

Coralie shot in from the garden through the French windows, carrying Jenny and leading Evan by the hand. 'It's started to rain. Potty time before milk and biscuits.'

'One moment.' Lesley stopped Coralie in mid-stride. 'I've got a couple of photos I'm showing everyone. Do you recognize one of these men?' She fanned out the photographs which included Keith Cottrell.

Coralie studied them with care, despite Jenny fidgeting in her arms. 'No. Sorry. Don't think so.'

'And this one?' The youth whose DNA had been found at the house.

'Mm. No . . . at least, sort of. Maybe it's just the sort of person . . . I remember someone like that at school, three years ahead? It looks like him, but I can't be certain. There was a whole group of them, always in trouble. To be avoided at all costs. The police were often at school wanting to question them about this and that. Vandalism, mostly, I think. They thought it was dead funny to tip the rubbish bins over or trip up the dinner ladies. They were suspended from school. Or maybe they just dropped out. What's this one done?'

Lesley said, 'His DNA was found at Evan's house following the burglary. There might be some perfectly good reason why, of course. Can you remember his name?'

Coralie's eyes were huge. She shook her head. 'Never knew him to speak to. That lot, they all had names taken from the telly. Ask the head.'

'What about his friends? You say he was in a gang?'

'Dunno. Not a solid group. Sort of shifted around, if I remember right.'

She screwed up her eyes, trying to remember. 'They said one of them carried a knife.' She shuddered.

'Have you seen them since you left school?'

'Don't think so. Thing is, we had this mantra: never meet their eyes. Never stand in their way. That's how you keep out of trouble.'

'But you'd have heard if they were banged up for anything?'

'I think,' Coralie said doubtfully, 'someone said they hung about in the multistorey car park at the back of the shopping centre, kicking balls about, probably dealing.' Jenny was squirming so Coralie swept her off to the toilet, closely followed by young Evan.

Lesley said, 'That's all very interesting. Now, if Lucia's signed her statement, I'll drop her at the abbey on my way to interview my young laddie's mother.'

'Remind Lucia,' said Susan, 'to be back before ten or to phone us if she's going to stay over with a friend.'

'Will do.' Lesley swept out, taking Lucia and her DC with her.

Susan didn't notice till Lesley had gone but another hand-delivered card was lying on the doormat. This time it was an invitation for Susan and Rafael to bring the children for tea and play at the Fun Factory about a mile away. Susan had heard of it. There was a sort of warehouse with activities for children, attached to a tearoom. Diana had chosen a good place to meet. Anonymous.

Susan took the card through to Rafael to show him. He said, 'Lesley didn't see this?'

'No. Should I call her back and tell her?'

Rafael thought about that. 'Diana may or may not have a bolthole down by the river, but I'm thinking she's much closer to hand because . . .'

'She's keeping an eye on the children.' Susan picked Fifi up and took her to the French windows. Rain spat at the glass. She could see where Evan and Jenny had beaten down the long grass, chasing one another around. Oh dear, the garden looked so unkempt. She really must get on to the gardener.

It had been Ellie's decision not to divide the garden into two – at least for the time being – so that there'd be plenty of room for her grandchildren and Fifi to run round and play. The high brick wall around it was masked by shrubs and some mature trees. Susan couldn't see even the roofs of the surrounding houses from where she stood, but she knew that if she climbed to the top of her house she could look over the wall into the grounds of the hotel in the next road.

Today it was too chilly to sit outside, but on a warm day some of the older, wealthy businessmen and women who frequented the hotel might be seen on the patio, taking their ease in chairs under bright umbrellas.

Rafael said, 'You think that Diana might well have gone to ground at the hotel? I wonder what name she's using.'

Susan said, 'Ellie always said Diana was a good mother. I

wasn't sure I agreed with her, but from the evidence of the cards and what little Evan tells me, I think she really does care about the children. She must be worried sick, knowing she's a person of interest and not having a secure base anywhere.'

Rafael checked that the French windows were properly shut and locked. 'She may be at the hotel temporarily, but I'm sure she does have a bolthole somewhere else. It will be a love nest, not big enough to take the children as well.'

Susan said, 'Coralie's off this afternoon and so is Lucia. Do we accept Diana's invitation? It would reassure her that the children are all right.'

Rafael barked out a laugh. 'Don't expect her to be grateful. Remember she will always be the self-centred, difficult woman we've always loved to hate. She sacked Lucia on the flimsiest of grounds—'

'Oh, come on! I'd have sacked her myself. Lucia did not look after the children properly.'

'She also accused Marcy of theft to make her keep her mouth shut. Diana is not a nice woman. I doubt if she will thank us for taking her children in and I'd lay odds she's only summoned us to meet her because she wants something. Any takers?'

Susan shook her head. No takers.

Sunday afternoon

WELCOME TO THE FUN FACTORY

The slogan was painted in huge letters across the wall of the building, but at the door it was made clear that children would not be allowed in without a responsible adult to look after them. In other words, if *your* child has an accident, *we* are not responsible. The entrance fee was not cheap but the place was well filled with families escaping from the drizzle outside.

The walls had been painted with bright colours, lively music was being pumped out though a speaker system and a small cafe area, decorated with fairy lights, twinkled a welcome.

Susan had taken Fifi to the children's playground in the park regularly, but the child's eyes were wide with wonder as she took in the slides and bouncy castles, the area for riding pedal cars and the rainbow heaps of balls to have fun with. 'Down!' she commanded, trying to escape from her buggy.

Evan and Jenny had been there before. Evan dumped his scooter and Hippo on Susan and headed for the bright red pedal cars, while Jenny tugged Rafael towards the slides.

'You're ten minutes late!' A sharp voice. Diana.

Susan freed Fifi from her harness and called out, 'Evan! Jenny! Look who's here!'

Evan froze on the point of getting into one of the cars. He cast a longing look back at the car, but he did run back to embrace his mother's leg and hide his face in her skirt. Yes, he was happy to see her.

Jenny was at the top of the slide, with Rafael waiting to catch her. 'Mummy! Look at me!' She slipped down in a flurry of arms and legs, to be rescued and set on her feet by Rafael . . . upon which she ran round to try the slide again. Jenny wasn't stopping her fun to greet her mother. No way!

Diana stooped to give Evan a hug and then pushed him away. 'Have you been a good boy? Go and play on the cars now.' So he did.

Fifi managed to wriggle her way out of Susan's arms and, once on the floor and hanging on to Susan's denim skirt with one hand, tugged her along to the glassed-in enclosure which held the brightly coloured balls. Susan said, 'Will you keep an eye on Evan, Diana?'

'He knows what he's doing. I want to talk to you and Rafael.'

Susan remembered Rafael saying that there would be no thanks for taking the children but hope springs eternal, et cetera, and she had hoped for at least some acknowledgement of what they'd done. 'You want to take the children back with you now, or this evening?'

'What! No, of course not! I shall have to leave them with you for the time being.'

Susan switched to Plan B. 'If we are to keep the children for a while, perhaps we should have something in writing from you to show Social Services? We've had trouble fending them off as it is.'

'Very well. I'll send you something, and I'll ring the nursery tomorrow to say you'll be bringing Evan in the morning and collecting him at lunchtime. They like to have it all noted down. I think Jenny should start there, too. Have you managed to get her potty-trained yet? I know Lucia was unable to manage it but she was so inefficient . . .' A shrug. 'A good thing she's gone.'

Susan held her tongue. *Poor Lucia. Yes, she wasn't much good, but she hadn't deserved to be thrown out on the street like that.*

Susan said, 'I have my hands full already, with Fifi' – who was almost horizontal, trying to pull Susan towards the bouncy ball area – 'and the house move. We're employing a local girl on a temporary basis to help out. How much longer do you expect us to keep the children?'

Diana looked away. 'I have no idea. Circumstances . . .' She waved the circumstances away. 'About the nursery, they'll want paying for the term. They've been on to me about it, but at the moment . . . Would you sort that for me? I'll repay you later, of course.'

Ugh. Now we're stuck with paying her bills, too. And we'll never see a penny in return.

Susan finally gave in to Fifi's tugging. She lifted the child into the heaps of shifting balls and held her there. Fifi kicked and waved her arms, sending the plastic globes high and wide. Fifi loved it. She crowed with pleasure. Susan's back began to ache and she had to lift her baby out to ease the pain.

Fifi fought to be put into the pen again. Her little chin was firm. Her eyes flashed fire. She was going to scream the place down in a minute.

Susan offered Fifi to Diana. 'Can you hold her a moment?'

Diana hissed her displeasure but took the baby in her arms.

Susan straightened up, rubbing her back. She was interested to see that Fifi took her time to work out if she liked Diana or not. Her nostrils whiffled. Fifi judged people by many criteria. Sometimes just by their smell.

Diana held the baby awkwardly at first, but then shifted her into the crook of her arm. She looked down into Fifi's eyes, and Fifi looked up at her.

One intelligent woman sizing up another.

Fifi's eyes flicked to her mother, and then back to Diana.

Diana's mouth curved into a smile. 'Nice little thing, isn't she? Very bright.'

Fifi blinked. She didn't scream but held out her arms to her mother to take her back. Judgement had been suspended.

Susan thought that was interesting. Perhaps there was some good in Diana, somewhere?

Susan laid down the terms of engagement. 'Let us have your new phone number, in case of emergencies.'

'So that you can give it to the police? No.'

Susan shrugged. 'You must understand that we need to be able to contact you in case of emergencies. As for the police, I don't understand why you want to avoid them. You didn't instigate the burglary at your house.'

'I'm not hiding from the police. Let's go and sit down. I need to put you and Rafael in the picture.'

The children were duly rounded up, given their choice of foods to eat – at which Susan started to worry about too much salt in the food on offer – and the adults ordered burgers and tea. Fifi sat on Susan's knee to eat a bit of this and that and had her first experience of drinking through a straw. The other two gobbled up everything in sight and ran off to play again. Rafael turned his chair so that he could keep an eye on them.

Diana took one sip of tea and one nibble of her burger and set them aside as inedible and undrinkable. She said, 'I suppose you think it was a bit "off" for me to have an affair with Keith Cottrell. It didn't affect my fondness for my husband, or how much it hurt to see such a strong man reduced to living in a wheelchair. Spending a few hours with Keith every now and then was a safety valve, something we both needed.'

'It was that way for Keith, too?'

'His wife's a cold fish and older than him. There were no children. We weren't hurting anyone.'

'Evan didn't object?'

'He may have suspected but he took care not to know. Cynthia knew but she didn't care so long as we observed the decencies. Right at the end, she did start to make noises about how long Keith thought it was going to go on, but she did nothing about it till Evan died.'

I wonder if that's quite true. Cynthia told me she'd discussed the matter with Evan the night he died. She said they'd discussed divorce and/or cracking the whip to end the affair. Both Evan and Cynthia had seemed to think they only had to shout 'Stop!' and the liaison would end. I wonder if it would have been that simple.

Diana said, 'I realized the situation would change as soon as Evan died. I got in touch with Keith. We both knew it was the end of the affair because he'd never leave his wife. He has far too much to lose. The problem was that . . . that . . .'

Rafael helped her out. 'You had managed to get something incriminating on him, something which you'd stashed in the safe at home?'

Diana reddened. 'It wasn't like that. Yes, there were some documents which refer to a venture which Keith and I had been discussing, nothing to do with the Cottrells. He didn't want to leave the paperwork lying around so I was holding it for the time being.'

Susan and Rafael exchanged glances.

What venture? Something which Diana and Keith had cooked up between them? Something to make them a little money on the side? A scam of some sort? Were those the documents which Lesley had mentioned finding in the safe? What would Lesley make of them?

Rafael said, 'You were setting up some kind of . . . business project . . . with Keith. His wife didn't know about it. Was it legal?'

'Yes, of course.' Diana was Mistress Indignation herself!

Was she lying? Yes. Diana had always been into dicey deals. Ellie had said that everything her daughter touched turned to fools' gold, and that she lost money quicker than she earned it.

Diana said, 'I know it would have been sensible to have destroyed the papers when I found Evan lying on the floor, but I didn't think of anything but that he was still alive. I think – I hope – he knew I was there, holding his hand.'

Momentarily she sagged in her chair. Then she straightened her back. 'There's nothing incriminating in those papers but Keith didn't want his wife to get hold of them. Now they're in the hands of the police and, well, it might look bad for him if the police chose to make them public. And quite unnecessary. The best thing to do for everyone concerned is for you to ask the police to let me have the papers back. They've nothing to do with my husband's death, but they could make trouble for Keith. I'd be grateful.'

She didn't sound grateful. She made it sound reasonable, which it wasn't.

Susan said, 'You know better than to ask us to interfere with evidence. So what is it you really want us to do?'

'Well, for a start, you can withdraw your absurd claim for assault. No one who knows Keith could possibly think he'd harm a woman and it adds to the stress he's under.'

Susan said, 'You should see the photographs of what he did to me.'

Diana swallowed. She abandoned a lost cause and instead tried to put on a wounded, innocent expression. She said, 'I thought you'd be more understanding. I'm in shock. Penniless, homeless, and dreading that my children might be taken from me.'

Three choruses of hearts and flowers. Remember how Diana treated Lucia and Marcy! Remember how she's dumped her children on us!

Diana tried another sip of tea and set the cup aside once more. She probably only enjoyed dragon's milk or viper's serum. She said, 'Well, the other thing is that, as you can see, I have a cash flow problem. Evan left a little life insurance and not much else. He put the estate agency in my name some time ago but under present conditions, it's hardly making ends meet. As we were renting our house, the agency is my only asset. I need a fresh start, to move away to a different neighbourhood. I have to find somewhere to live which is big enough for me, the children, and some live-in staff. Renting is a mug's game and there's not enough in the kitty to buy. You follow?'

Rafael and Susan did.

'I expected my mother to help, but she's being most unhelpful. She says she won't be back for a week or ten days and referred me to you, Rafael, to deal with any problems that might turn up before then. The thing is that the Cottrells have offered to buy my agency at a knock-down price, but if I accept I wouldn't have enough to buy a decent place hereabouts and I'd have lost any means of supporting myself and the children.'

Rafael said, 'Why would the Cottrells offer to buy you out?'

Diana twisted her hands in her lap. 'It's not Keith. No, it's Cynthia. She wants her pound of flesh. She went to her father, who's a right old tyrant straight out of Mafialand, and it's he who's calling the shots now. He's offering to buy the agency on condition that I hand over the handwritten notes that Keith and I made about a possible project. He wants them so that he has something to hold over Keith. And, he wants me to get out of Keith's life. He wrapped it up nicely, suggesting I could make a clean start with the money, buy a nice house in a cheaper area, find another job. He made it clear that he wanted me out of the area. He said' – she winced – 'what lovely children I had and how proud I must be of their good looks. His meaning was clear. He has a certain reputation. I am not easily intimidated, but . . .'

Was that true, or had she added the threat to get Susan and Rafael on her side? Susan shivered, imagining an attack on Evan or, worse, on Fifi!

Rafael put his hand on Susan's and held it. Susan calmed down. Rafael wouldn't let anything happen to Fifi.

Diana said, 'I'm not afraid of the police. *They* can't charge me with anything, but Cynthia's father is another matter. I've stopped using my smartphone so that he can't track me down. I've put my car in one garage and I'm renting a runabout from another. I'm sleeping in a different place every night. Keith can't help me. I tried my mother, naturally, but she doesn't seem to understand how real the danger is. I've tried to be patient, telling myself that she's out of touch, and that if she only realized . . . So I'm asking you to explain everything to her.

'I'm not asking for the moon; just a decent place for me and the kids to live. I know the trust has properties all over London. I realize that Evan was behind with the rent, but if my mother would guarantee say, three months occupancy free, that would allow me enough time to get back on my feet. I could look around for a better offer for the agency and set up somewhere else, perhaps in North London? It would solve all my problems. My mother wouldn't want her grandchildren put out on the street, would she?'

'Emotional blackmail,' said Rafael, in a soft voice. 'It won't work, Diana. As for asking the trust to help you out, I'd be against letting you move into any of our properties unless you could convince me you'd be able to pay three months in advance plus the money you owe for back rent of the big house. What about the money you got from pawning Evan's ring?'

Diana didn't bother to deny it. 'That went to pay some household bills, electricity, gas, the usual. I can't afford to come up with three months' rent at the moment. But I'm sure my mother will help me out when she understands the situation.'

'No, Diana. Your mother couldn't afford it. She has a decent income, but not enough to support you and the children as well.'

Diana's lips thinned. 'You are not being very helpful. The trust will make allowances for her.'

'I doubt it.'

Diana tried another tack. 'Very well. You do understand I have to move away. Suppose you get the trust to buy the agency from me at a decent price? With the money from that I could buy another agency in a less expensive neighbourhood. That way I would be able to earn a living and get a mortgage on a decent place to live.'

Rafael said, 'Put that proposal in writing to the trust, and I'll see it goes on the agenda for the next general meeting.'

'When will that be? You do understand that my problem is urgent?'

Rafael said, 'We'll schedule a meeting as soon as possible after Ellie's return. Let us have a phone number where we can reach you in case of an emergency.'

Diana said, 'I'll ring you as and when I am able to do so.'

Rafael got to his feet. 'You don't want to give us a number because you fear we'd give it to the police? Well, you're right about that. We will report this conversation as well. Now, I must go. Jenny's got stuck on the slide.'

And here came Little Evan, clutching Hippo. He pressed close to his mother's side. 'Are we going home now, Mummy?'

Diana tousled his hair. 'You're staying with Susan for a while. Be a good, brave boy, won't you?'

Jenny, released from the slide, came steaming up to them. 'Mummy, Mummy, did you see me? I was on the biggest slide.'

Diana took Jenny on her lap and gave her a cuddle. 'Clever girl!'

So Jenny is the favourite? Oh, poor Little Evan.

Evan looked up at his mother with such a mixture of pain and stoicism that Susan felt like crying.

And then, distraction! Fifi lunged forward, reaching out to Evan. Susan nearly dropped her but Evan came to the rescue, pushing Hippo into Fifi's face. Fifi took hold of Hippo and managed to manoeuvre one of his tiny ears into her mouth. She gurgled her satisfaction.

Evan looked up at Susan and said, 'I'll look after her.'

Diana had to spoil the moment. 'Oh, love at first sight, is it?' she said sarcastically. She shed Jenny, checked on her make-up and got to her feet, ready to leave.

Susan thought of various things she'd like to do to Diana, all of which were, regrettably, against the law. She put Fifi back into her baby buggy, Rafael strapped Jenny into her pushchair and Evan retrieved his scooter. They had quite a walk on them, but there was no alternative as Rafael only had one baby seat in his car.

Rafael said, 'Diana, while we have the children, we could do with the car seats from your car. Do you think you could drop them in to us tomorrow?'

Diana twitched her black skirt into place. 'Dear me! I thought the one thing in your favour, Rafael, was that you were a good provider. I have no idea where I'll be tomorrow but I'll keep in touch, right?'

Off she toddled, followed by angry thoughts from Susan, and wistful looks from Jenny.

Rafael said, 'She's right, you know. We have to report everything to Lesley. Those papers seem to be at the heart of the break-in. Which of the Cottrells do you think wanted them so badly that they'd arrange for someone to burgle the place? Cynthia or her father wanted them as ammunition for a divorce, and Keith needed them to keep him out of the divorce court. Eeny meeny miney mo. Whom do you fancy as murderer-in-chief?'

FOURTEEN

Sunday evening

Rafael and Susan were worn out by the children's bedtime. Jenny had a tantrum because she wanted to watch the telly instead of having supper. She filled her nappy twice and refused even to sit on the potty. To be fair, she had had a fateful encounter with a large ginger tomcat out in the garden. She'd chased it and been scratched for her pains. She'd screamed and screamed till soothed with a spoonful of ice cream from the freezer, a cuddle in Susan's arms and a smear of antiseptic cream on her poorly finger.

Fifi hadn't liked the screaming and had tottered off to find a quiet, dark place at the back of the settee in the big room. She was rapidly joined there by Evan in his new character of carer-in-chief. He laid all his toys out in front of her, and then entranced her by building a tower of bricks for her to knock over.

Rafael darted in and out; on the phone, reporting to Lesley, coaxing Jenny to sit on her potty, fidgeting because he'd missed so many appointments because of the descent of the children.

Susan threw some tea together while Rafael managed to talk to Coralie's parents on the phone. An agreement was reached that the girl should take a week off school to help Susan out. Well, half term was only a week away, and Coralie had said she'd truant if they didn't give her permission and she wasn't going back to school anyway as it was a dead bore . . . and so on.

Susan developed a headache.

Rafael's temper grew shorter.

Finally, the three children were bathed, put into night gear and settled down for the night, Evan in the big bed, Jenny in the cot and Fifi in the baby buggy.

Tomorrow, Susan promised herself, they'd reorganize

the nursery, get rid of the big bed and hopefully persuade Jenny to leave the cot to Fifi.

Susan dragged herself downstairs, flopped on to the settee and closed her eyes.

She must have dozed off. The landline phone woke her. She could hear Rafael was having an argument with someone on his smartphone in his den, so Susan had to totter into the kitchen to deal with it. It was Lesley, ringing to ask if Lucia were back yet as the police wanted another word with her. So up the stairs went Susan, to find Lucia hadn't yet returned. Ugh, didn't the girl ever open a window? Susan went down again to report Lucia's absence to Lesley and then to collapse in front of the telly.

Ten o'clock. Susan dragged herself upstairs to bed. Lucia's door was still ajar. Had the girl not returned? No, she hadn't, had she? Susan rubbed her forehead. What had the arrangement been? That if she didn't return by ten, she'd phone to say she was staying the night somewhere else? Oh well. Rafael could take the call as he was still downstairs in his study, arguing with someone about something. He'd have to let Lucia in when she returned.

At two o'clock, Susan woke. Rafael was breathing lightly, softly, beside her. Moonlight slid through a gap in the curtains. The children were quiet.

But something was wrong.

Susan made the rounds. Rafael had left a light burning on the landing, so they could see what was happening if anyone woke in the night. The children were fine. Susan pulled the blanket over Jenny. Evan had Fifi's Gonk in one hand, and his Hippo was in her buggy.

Lucia's door was still ajar. Susan pushed it open. There was no sign of the girl. The bed was as Lucia had left it, with the duvet thrown back and a pillow on the floor. Some clothes were on the bedside chair, and Lucia's rucksack was where she'd left it in the corner.

What was Susan to do?

Surely, nothing could have happened to the girl? She'd been told to ring and let them know if she were staying overnight with a friend. Perhaps she'd told Rafael?

Susan hesitated. Rafael was tired out. He would not be happy to be woken just to confirm that Lucia had phoned him.

Suppose she hadn't phoned, then . . .? Susan shook his shoulder. 'Sorry. Emergency. Did Lucia phone to say she was sleeping out?'

He blinked. Came awake. Sat upright. Thought.

Slapped his forehead. 'I knew there was something. I was so long on the phone, sorting out what didn't happen yesterday. Then I was tired and came up to bed and forgot about her. No, she didn't ring.' He thrust his long legs into slippers. 'I'd better check.'

'She's not in her room. Maybe she came in so late that she slept downstairs? No, we hadn't a key to give her, had we?'

'We made it clear that she must let us know if she wasn't coming back. If she was out of credit on her mobile, she could have got one of her friends to phone us.' He yawned mightily. 'I'm sure she's all right. She's a teenager. She wouldn't thank us for getting in a state about her staying out late.'

Susan disagreed. 'You mean we shouldn't ring the police and report her missing? She's a person of interest in a murder case and she's not where she said she'd be. I think we do need to report it. If she turns up safe and sound and gets a rollocking by the police for wasting their time, then perhaps that will teach her not to do it again. And yes, I know it's the middle of the night. Tell you what! We won't try to wake Lesley at this hour, but we'll phone a message into the station. Lucia might have met with an accident and have been taken to hospital.'

So Rafael phoned in the report and they both went back to bed, to sleep lightly, with one ear open, so to speak.

Monday breakfast

Lucia didn't return. The phone didn't ring, and neither did the doorbell, until they were all having breakfast in the kitchen and arguing whether Jenny should go to nursery with Evan or not. Did the Powers that Be need her to be potty-trained before she could be accepted there? What time did they open for business? Eight o'clock? Half past?

Fortunately the rain had cleared away. The sun shone, and there was a light wind which would dry everything nicely.

Here came Coralie, bright and cheerful and bubbling with

good cheer at taking time off school. She said she was ready to take on not two, but three children at a time!

Rafael rang the nursery to make sure Diana had told them of the children's change of circumstances and enquire how much the outstanding bill might be. The nursery softened its first, frosty tone to say a cheque would be most acceptable. At which Rafael sighed, and said he'd make one out for their new nanny to bring along with the two children. The new nanny was called Coralie, and yes, please make a note of her phone number. And yes, Evan had a little sister who was thinking of joining if they had room for her. They had? Good. Then Coralie would bring both that morning. And, er, yes, Jenny was in the process of being potty-trained.

Jenny looked less than impressed since it meant being put on the potty yet again. She tried for sympathy. She held up her finger to show the nicely-healing scratch. Coralie said she'd kiss it better and there was sure to be lots of big toys in the nursery garden for Jenny to play with, so she was reluctantly reconciled to the necessity for growing up.

Rafael wrote out a cheque, wincing at the cost because Diana owed not one but two terms for Evan. Coralie swept both children off to nursery saying she'd do any shopping on the way back if Susan gave her a list.

Susan couldn't think straight so said she was all right for the moment. Fifi had absorbed her breakfast while observing Jenny's shenanigans with a dispassionate eye, but she beamed with pleasure when the door closed behind their guests. Susan cleaned Fifi's face and hands and lifted her down to the floor, where she made for the nearest cupboard to explore.

Rafael said, 'Listen to the silence! Isn't it wonderful? And now, I really must get back to work.' He disappeared down the corridor, leaving Susan to start clearing the table, when . . .

The doorbell rang and here came Lesley, towing her silent sidekick. Lesley's expression told Susan two things: that she'd had another bad night and/or quarrelled with that selfish husband of hers and that there was no good news on the Diana front.

'A word?' said Lesley, taking a seat, sagging and then forcing herself upright. 'Is Rafael still here? Can you get him? I don't want to have to repeat myself.'

Rafael was on the phone, but cut the call short to join them.

Lesley said, 'Early this morning a shopkeeper arrived to open up and found a girl lying in the alley at the back of the greengrocers in the Avenue. The girl had been assaulted and was unresponsive. The shopkeeper rang for the police and an ambulance. She's been taken to hospital, but she's in a coma and the doctors are not sure if she'll make it or not. You put in a report that Lucia didn't come home last night? She hasn't reappeared, has she?'

Susan drew in a deep breath. 'She hasn't. You think it's her?'

'The girl in the alley is about the same height and has the same hair colour as Lucia. No handbag, no mobile phone, no ID. You don't know who she was meeting yesterday?'

'"Friends", she said. No names given.'

Lesley said, 'We'll have to search her room. Yesterday we dropped her off at the abbey. There were quite a few people hanging around outside, waiting for the next Mass to begin. Lucia ran up the steps to join them but I didn't see who she met. She didn't tell you where she planned to go yesterday?'

Rafael said, 'She didn't. That girl has no sense! What on earth was she doing in the Avenue late at night when she knew she had to be back here by ten? She might have been to the pub with one of her friends, I suppose. Or, she might have had the bad fortune to attract the attention of a drug user who was aching for a fix. She didn't have that much money on her, but I suppose a drug user could sell her mobile phone.'

Lesley said, 'Yes, it could be just that.'

Rafael said, 'The man was on the prowl. He saw she was alone and vulnerable. He asked her for money, she resisted, so he knocked her down and fled with her handbag.'

Susan said, 'Sorry to destroy the picture you're painting. I don't believe in coincidences. The assault on Lucia must be linked to Evan's death.'

Lesley put her hands to her head. The shadows under her eyes deepened. 'No, no, no, no. I can't bear it. The two cases can't be connected. You haven't any proof that they are, have you?'

Susan shook her head. 'No. Sorry. Shouldn't have spoken.'

Lesley tried to smile. 'Well, no harm done.' Offering an olive branch, she said, 'I must go to the hospital, see if I can identify the girl. But before that, I could murder a coffee.'

Rafael primed and started the coffee machine. 'Suppose we play around with what Susan said? What could Lucia possibly know that might make her a target? True, the girl's an idiot, but surely she's no threat to anyone? Do you really think the Cottrells, for instance, would send a thug to steal Lucia's handbag? Why on earth would they do that? They wouldn't.'

'Of course they wouldn't.' Lesley yawned and tried to hide it. 'You told me you'd seen Diana yesterday and she's trying to put the blame for everything on the Cottrells, right? Let's go over that again.'

Rafael said. 'You found some incriminating papers in the safe, didn't you? Something about a business venture which Diana was setting up with Keith, something which didn't include his wife or his father-in-law?'

Lesley almost smiled. 'Yes, we did. Handwritten notes of a scheme to set up a separate company. Diana wrote some of it. We're checking to see if Keith wrote the rest.'

'Surely the very existence of those papers is sufficient to set the Cottrells slavering at the mouth. Any one of the three might regard them as a weapon to use against the others: Keith, to save his marriage; his wife, as ammo for a divorce, and her father, ditto.'

'You're forgetting something,' said Susan. 'Neither Cynthia nor her father knew anything about the projected venture. The only ones who knew were Diana and Keith, and there was no reason for him to want them destroyed, was there?'

Coffee brewed, Rafael served it up as Susan cleared the table and wiped it down. Now, where had Fifi gone? Ah, she'd managed to open the door of the cupboard, found it empty and crawled inside. Susan rescued her and put her down on the floor with one of Evan's books to look at. Fifi waited till she thought her mother's back was turned and crawled back inside the cupboard. Susan let her be.

Lesley drank her coffee black. 'I need to look at Lucia's room and speak to Diana again. She gave you a phone number?'

'She didn't. She says she's afraid of Cynthia's father. She says he's threatened her and the children and wants to buy the agency off her at a knock-down price. He wants her to move out of the area so that she loses all contact with Keith. She believes he means her harm and is moving around from place to place, using a burner phone.'

Lesley said, 'She has nothing to be afraid of. We can give her protection . . .' She didn't sound convincing.

Fifi crawled out of the cupboard and hoisted herself to her feet, wobbled, and sat down – *plump!*

Susan said, 'I'll never have a minute's peace now she's walking.' She picked Fifi up and set her on her own knee.

A phone rang somewhere. Their landline? No, Susan's smartphone. Ah, where had she put it? Got it!

A breathy voice gabbled something in her ear. Panicking!

Susan said, 'Slow down, Coralie. It is Coralie?'

A gulp at the other end. 'Yes. Sorry. Deep breaths. Under control. Can you come, please? Quick as you can. Yes, the children are all right. I should have said that first, shouldn't I? No, really, not to worry, not a hair of their heads. I've barricaded myself into the playhouse with Evan, and they're searching for him right now!'

Susan said, 'Coralie . . .?' She shouted to Rafael. 'Coralie's in trouble!' And to the girl on the phone: 'What's happened?'

Coralie took a deep breath. 'I gave the woman who runs the nursery your cheque and that was fine because I think they'd lost all hope of getting the money from Diana. Evan went off to play in the garden at the back and I was being shown around with Jenny when this woman arrived and said she was their granny and was removing them from the nursery.'

'What!' Susan couldn't believe her ears.

Another deep breath, subduing panic. 'The manager didn't know who to believe, because she'd only just met me this morning and she called me into the hall to say the children's granny had come for them, and I looked outside into the back garden and there was Evan with some of his friends, and this woman said, '"So, where's Evan?" and she was looking right at the group he was in, and I thought if she didn't even recognize him . . . and hadn't Marcy said his granny was abroad?

'I didn't like the look of her, though of course I may be quite wrong, and she may be perfectly all right. So I said we should call the police, and she said I was a stupid little girl and ought to be reported to the authorities and the manager said they needed a signature and they went into the office, so I ran outside and picked up Evan and looked for somewhere to hide him while I phoned you. And I couldn't see anywhere except for this plastic Wendy house at the end of the garden, and we've scrunched into it, hiding and I can hear them searching the garden and calling for Evan, and he's so frightened! And so am I! Can you come and get us, please! And . . . oh dear, I'd better keep quiet or she'll hear me.'

Susan screamed down the phone. 'Coralie! Hold on! Don't let her take the children!'

Rafael said, 'What's wrong?'

Susan was on her feet. 'Coralie! She's at the nursery! The children's granny has turned up to take them away!'

'Ellie's not back yet!'

'I know! It must be someone pretending to be her. How soon can we get there?' Susan hoisted Fifi higher in her arms and made for the door.

'I'll take the Beast!' Rafael brushed past her and out of the front door, just as he was, no helmet, no leathers.

Lesley was slowly getting to her feet. 'What's happened?'

Susan gabbled, 'We've got to go! The nursery says Ellie's arrived to collect the children! Can you give me a lift?'

Lesley said, 'Yes, but . . .' She was on her feet. 'What's the address?' And to her sidekick: 'You drive!'

Susan couldn't remember the address, if she'd ever known it. 'Dunno. Follow Rafael!'

He started up his motorbike. Was turning out of the drive. Lesley hurried Susan to the police car. Rafael would get there quicker than them . . . wherever it was . . .

Susan hoicked Fifi on to her hip and tumbled into the back of the police car. No baby seat, of course. Susan fastened a seat belt around herself and Fifi, even as Coralie came back on the phone.

Coralie was crying. 'Susan, they've found us!'

Susan could hear shouting and banging. Angry voices. Someone kicking at the playhouse?

Susan sad, 'We're on our way! Listen, Coralie! The children's grandmother is in Canada. Whoever that woman is, she's not Ellie. Tell the nursery people that. Rafael's on his way, and so is Lesley!'

Lesley ordered her sidekick to put the siren on!

They raced around the corner and . . .

Lesley shot out, 'Where is this place?'

Susan gulped. She couldn't think. She must have heard . . . she'd heard where it was yesterday or the day before, hadn't she? 'Off the Avenue. Along the bus route, I think. I can't remember. Coralie, are you still there?'

Coralie was gabbling. 'Evan, it's all right. Don't cry! They're on their way. They'll be here in a minute . . .' More banging. Shouted threats.

Coralie was sobbing. So was Evan.

Would they be in time?

'There!' Susan pointed. 'Rafael's bike, ahead of us in the traffic!' Susan's heart was thudding. She knew, she just knew that the children were in danger, though why . . .? Why would anyone target a child? And surely it couldn't have anything to do with Evan's death . . .?

Ellie would be praying by now.

The nursery was in this street, wasn't it? But which number . . .?

It was a quiet street of big houses.

They slowed to a crawl. Rafael's bike had disappeared . . . or was that it, ahead?

The windscreen wipers were switched on. An early morning mist was becoming more insistent.

Susan clenched her hands into fists. She closed her eyes tightly and thought, what Ellie would do? *Dear God, if you are there . . .? You didn't want children hurt . . . Not that I know why anyone should . . .? But, please?*

Without warning the police car swung across the road and double-parked, shutting in Rafael's bike, which had been left across the pavement. A hedge and high railings protected a strip of garden in front of a large house with brightly coloured children's pictures in the front windows. Another car was doubled-parked in front of them, but facing the other way.

Uh, why was that car parked like that?

It wasn't a police car, was it?

Lesley was out of the car in a flash.

Susan struggled free of the seat belt. She was still holding Fifi who, so far, was more intrigued than annoyed at being given a ride in a car without being strapped into her baby seat. Illegally.

Well, Lesley wasn't going to arrest Susan for an infringement of the rules, was she?

Rafael had opened the gate and bounded up the path to a big, solid-looking front door. Ringing the bell. Banging with his fist.

Susan screamed. 'Round the back! In the playhouse!'

A strange woman came round the corner of the house, carrying a child in her arms.

From behind her they heard someone . . . Coralie? . . . screaming, 'Stop her!'

Rafael reached for the child. 'Give him here.'

The woman avoided him. Late middle-aged. Unremarkable. Beige clothing, puffy features. 'Out of my way. My grandchild needs hospital treatment urgently.'

Evan had one arm over his eyes, blocking out what was happening. He was gulping. Sobbing.

Coralie, looking rather the worse for wear, came screeching round the corner of the house. 'I told you—'

An older woman followed her. Angry face, rigid stance signalling that the situation was out of hand. Fortyish, competent looking. Carrying a white-faced, wailing Jenny in her arms. The manager of the nursery?

What was her name? Mrs Meadows? Mrs Field?

The manager was out of her depth, barely containing her anger at this unprecedented situation. 'Please, slow down. This is not right, indeed it isn't. Children cannot be removed from my care without due authorization. Please, put that child down!'

Rafael stepped in front of the woman who was carrying Evan. 'I think there's been some mistake. That child has officially been placed in our care and we authorized his attendance at the nursery. So who, may I ask, are you, and what do you think you are doing?'

'Ridiculous!' The woman flushed. 'Out of my way, or I'll have the police on you!'

Coralie was bobbing up and down, appealing to the nursery

manager. 'Mrs Field, these are the people I told you about, Rafael and Susan, who are looking after the children for the time being. Rafael, tell her that I'm—'

The woman who was carrying Evan tried to step around Rafael. 'Out of my way! I'm these children's grandmother and I have every right to remove them from unsuitable premises.'

Lesley was at Rafael's side, holding up her shield. 'Detective Inspector Millburn. And my colleague is outside in the car. Let's all calm down, shall we? What did you say your name was?'

'Mrs Quicke. Eleanor Quicke. I am these children's grandmother, and I am taking them home with me, this minute!'

Lesley said, 'There seems to be some misunderstanding. I know Mrs Quicke well, and I know these are her grandchildren, but I don't know you. So, as Mrs Field suggests, why don't you put the child down, and we can talk the situation through?'

A new voice broke in. 'What's all this, then?' A man, tall, well-built, thirtyish, dark of hair and chin. 'Are you refusing to let a grandmother take her children out of nursery? Social Services will have something to say about that!' Casual, cheap clothing. Puffy features. There was a family likeness. Mother and son?

Lesley turned on him. 'You have documents from Social Services? Show me.'

'They're in the car.' And to the woman: 'Give me the child. We're holding up the traffic.'

It was true that somewhere in the road a driver had started to toot his horn because traffic was building up behind him.

Lesley got herself between the man and the woman. 'Just a minute. There seems to be some confusion here. I am willing to believe that there are two Mrs Quickes, that this lady has been sent to the wrong address and that Social Services have become involved. The paperwork should tell us what's what. So, let's have a look at it, shall we?'

The strange woman's eyes narrowed. 'I'm not hanging around waiting for you to sort anything out. I told you, my grandchild needs hospital attention, now! So let me pass!' She tried to thrust past Lesley.

A mistake. Lesley blocked her.

The woman tried to dodge round Lesley . . .

The man reached forward to take Evan . . .

Rafael grappled with the false Mrs Quicke, causing her to loosen her clasp on the child . . .

Susan, hampered by holding Fifi on her other arm, grabbed Evan, one-handed.

Evan was all arms and legs, but she had him safe!

Fifi muttered her discontent at being tossed around.

The woman broke away from Rafael . . .

She swung at Lesley, who stepped back to avoid her, only to be side-swiped by the man, who landed a punch which lifted Lesley off her feet and left her crashed out on her back on the ground . . .

The man held the gate open . . . the woman fled through . . . and banged it shut behind them . . .

They were off! Pounding across the pavement and into their car, which immediately set off. The police car was facing in the wrong direction to follow them.

Rafael ran after them, yelling at the police sergeant who, getting the message, frantically tried to do a three-point turn in the road, hindered by oncoming traffic . . .

They all heard the would-be kidnappers' car accelerate away. Round the corner and off they went.

FIFTEEN

Monday morning, continued

Rafael rushed back through the gate, to help a shaken Lesley to her feet.

The DI shook herself and winced. 'Nothing broken.' But she wobbled on her feet and her eyes didn't look right. She clutched her neck. 'Ouch.' And then: 'Assaulting a police officer. I'll get him for that!' She reached for her phone and gabbled into it, 'Officer down! Officer down! A man and a woman in a black sedan.'

Susan thought, Lesley's losing it.

Rafael said, 'I have the licence number, and we are at . . .' He gave the address and licence number of the car. Trust Rafael to keep his cool.

Lesley repeated the information Rafael gave her and, tottering slightly, limped to the gate and leaned on it for support. 'Our car . . . where is it? Where did he go?' Her phone quacked at her. She listened for a moment, and said, 'Reinforcements on their way. I need to take statements.' She sounded dazed, not at all her usual self.

Mrs Field was not going to help. Frozen with anger, she rapped out, 'I think I am due an explanation!' She was still holding Jenny, who continued to wail. The child wasn't hurt, but was reacting to the tension.

'Let me. Poor Cuckoo.' Rafael took Jenny from the woman and jiggled her up and down. Jenny burrowed her nose into his neck and sniffled to a halt.

Lesley was suffering from shock. She could hardly hold herself upright. She tried to laugh, a high, false sound. 'I wonder how long my poor sergeant will be, racing up and down the streets, trying to find the would-be kidnappers.' Was she going to burst into tears?

Evan was stiff in Susan's arms. And mute. She'd have liked it better if he'd bawled his head off.

Susan whispered in his ear. 'It's all right, my love. All over. You're safe now.'

Evan drew down his arm, which he'd been using to block out his sight of what was happening, and curled himself into Susan's body. His little heart was beating far too fast.

Coralie wrung her hands, speaking to Mrs Field as much as to Susan and Rafael. 'I tried to stop her! I thought you'd have told me if their granny was back and was going to collect the children, but I'd never met Mrs Quicke so I didn't know who to believe! Only, she didn't know how to pick Evan out of the group and I didn't know what to do!'

'You are a very brave girl,' said Susan, trying to keep her balance while holding the two children. 'I don't like to think what might have happened if you hadn't phoned us. You are a brave, brave girl.'

Coralie was shaking. And crying. 'The thing was, I ought to

have kept my head and not run away to hide. I always thought I'd be so calm in a crisis and look at me!'

Coralie was going to have hysterics, now the worst was over. Susan knew she ought to comfort the girl, but she couldn't seem to move. She gulped. Her stomach informed her that she'd eaten too much breakfast and that stress was bad for her. Extremely bad for her.

She dumped the two children on the ground, dived for the hedge at the front of the house and threw up.

Mrs Field was not amused. 'Oh, dear, oh dear. Whatever next? Never in all my days! And what will the gardener say when he sees that mess?'

Susan tried to control the impulse to vomit again. And failed.

Lesley lunged for the porch and straightened herself up by holding on to it. Her knees wobbled, but she tried to retrieve the situation. 'We've all had a nasty shock. I could do with sitting down, myself. Let's go indoors and sort ourselves out.'

Mrs Field stepped back into the porch, barring her from entry. 'Oh no, you don't! I've never had such a thing happen in all my born days. I've been running this facility for nineteen years, and never had a minute's trouble. What, may I ask, are the parents of my children going to say when they hear about this? It could be the end of everything for the nursery! I don't care who you say you are. I'm asking you to leave, right now! And take those troublesome children with you. I never want to see them again. Oh, and I've just thought – who is going to pay for the repair of the playhouse which that woman has wrecked?'

Lesley was making an effort to return to her normal self. 'Mrs Field, you forget yourself. A serious crime was attempted and only averted by the prompt action of young Coralie here. As I see it, you were willing to let a child in your care be removed without proper authority. Am I supposed to turn a blind eye to your behaviour? One word from me, and your licence is cancelled.'

Mrs Field gaped. 'No-o-o-oh!'

Susan almost threw up again. She wanted to lie down and die somewhere quiet.

The children? She hadn't dropped them when she'd felt sick, had she? Oh, how could she!

Ah, Fifi had managed to get to her feet and, wailing softly, was tottering towards her father, who crouched down, ready to pick her up in his free arm.

And Evan? Was Evan all right? No, he was far from all right, but not making a sound. He looked up at Susan. No tears. Yes, he was in shock. His eyes were huge.

Susan held out her hand to him. He stumbled towards her and clutched her leg to anchor himself in a shifting world.

Rafael switched the charm on to save the situation. 'Inspector,' he said, giving Lesley her title for once, 'I'm sure Mrs Field acted most properly, and there is no question of her losing her licence. She saw off the criminals who'd assaulted a police officer. She kept her nerve and thwarted a kidnapping! What a hero she is! When the newspapers get to hear about it, they're going to be flocking to her door. And, while I do see that it might be good for business, it's going to be really tiresome for her to have to keep interrupting her daily tasks when reporters want to take pictures of her and the playhouse.'

His charm would have melted the heart of the hardest of businessmen, and it worked on Mrs Field, too. She pulled herself up to her full height and preened. Yes, she really did. 'Oh, well, if you put it like that.' And to Lesley: 'Inspector, you don't look at all well. Come into my office. Perhaps a cup of tea?' She held the front door wide open.

Rafael dumped Jenny on Coralie. 'Can you look after Jenny?'

Coralie took Jenny while Rafael, still holding Fifi, came back for Susan and Evan, who still clung to her like a limpet. Susan found she couldn't move and she couldn't lift the boy into her arms, either.

Rafael looked down at her with an expression of mingled concern and irritation.

She tried to smile. Didn't quite make it.

She saw his face change. His eyes narrowed. He was wondering why she'd been sick. His brain clicked through various permutations and came up with the right conclusion. She was pregnant.

His lips tightened. This development was not planned. He was, almost, annoyed.

Then his expression relaxed, and he put his arm more closely around her. He was not annoyed. Tentatively, he was . . . yes, he was discovering that he was pleased. In fact . . . his smile morphed into a grin . . . he was ecstatic.

He kissed her forehead. He was still carrying Fifi, but somehow he managed to detach Evan from Susan's leg and carried the little boy to the porch and left him there while he returned to fetch Susan.

Once everyone was safely inside the hall, he shut the front door on the outside world.

Now they were in a different world, a world in miniature where children played happily in half-size Wendy houses and sat at low tables in small chairs. There were no more threats and no more tension. In the big, sunny room ahead a motherly-looking helper was measuring out drinks for the little ones.

Susan made a beeline for the only adult chair she could see. Evan followed to press himself against Susan's side and she put her arm around him.

Rafael knelt beside Susan and kissed her again. 'Why didn't you tell me?'

Susan said in a tiny voice, 'Sorry. I know you didn't want another just yet, but . . .'

'If she's anything like Fifi . . . Well, wow!'

'It might be a boy.'

'Fantastic!'

Lesley had sunk on to a baby chair. Her legs sprawled. Her phone slipped from her hand to the floor. 'The police are on their way. Let them in, won't you? I should be at the hospital to see if that tiresome girl Lucia has washed up there. Perhaps someone else . . .? Can you let them in and explain?'

Susan knew there'd be statements to be made and phone calls and everyone wanting this and that. All she wanted to do was lie down and have a nap. And here they came . . . more police . . . questions, questions. Attempted kidnapping . . . descriptions of the would-be criminals . . . where's the mother? . . . where's the father?

Susan retreated into silence, nodding or shaking her head when required.

Monday, late morning

The muddle seemed to go on for hours. People on phones and people shouting. Comings and goings.

Susan was bored. Fifi was bored. Fifi felt that her dignity had been severely compromised by being tossed around in unfamiliar surroundings. She wanted to be soothed. Susan obliged.

Evan remained catatonic. Susan was worried about him. Any attempt to unstick him from her side resulted in his closing his eyes and imitating a pillar of salt. Susan held him close with her free arm and gradually, very gradually, he began to relax.

Jenny ran off to play, with Coralie trying to keep an eye on her.

Lesley rubbed her neck more and more. Rafael noticed and made a fuss. Lesley was whipped off for a hospital check.

An older DI took Lesley's place: icy in manner and efficient, if unlikeable.

Rafael asked that Susan's statement be given first so that she could be taken home with Evan. He also insisted that a police officer be assigned to guard them in case the would-be kidnappers tried again. And no, he had no idea why anyone would want to kidnap Evan. No one did. It was crazy. The only conclusion he could come to, was that the attackers had mistaken Evan for some other child. Only that didn't work, because the fake Ellie had claimed to be Evan's grandmother by name.

Different theories were propounded as to why two strange people would want to kidnap Little Evan. What strangers would have known Ellie's name and her relationship with the children? Perhaps they were chancers, seeing his father's death in the papers, and looking for ransom money? The family had, after all, lived in a big house and belonged to the golf club.

Susan took no part in any of this. She couldn't make sense of anything that was happening. All she wanted was to go home and rest. The newly arrived DI said she wanted to know if little Evan had anything to say about his narrow escape. Perhaps they could see him again when he'd got over his fright?

A car was summoned to take Susan, Fifi and Evan back home, with a stout policewoman to act as protection. Jenny had wanted to stay and it was agreed she'd return with Coralie at lunchtime.

Ah, home. Susan discovered they'd left the front door open in their haste to rescue the children, which was fortunate as she'd left without a key.

Their protection officer wouldn't let them beyond the entrance hall till she'd checked that the rest of the house was empty. Which it was.

Ah, the kitchen. Home sweet home. Susan told herself what to do and managed to obey orders. Dirty plates left over from breakfast were still on the table. She put them in the dishwasher. She made tea. She changed Fifi and took Evan to the toilet and got some elevenses for all four of them.

How quiet and peaceful everything was.

The children were quiet, too. Too quiet, really.

Their protection officer said Susan must leave it to her to answer the door – or the telephone. Susan nodded. All she wanted to do was lie down and sleep.

Someone did ring the doorbell. It was Marcy, the cleaner Diana had sacked, curious to know why a police officer should prevent her from speaking to Susan. Susan explained to the officer that she'd arranged for Marcy to organize cleaning up next door, and in return Marcy shouted over the officer's shoulder that she'd hoped the agency would have kept a key to Mrs Quicke's place and they had, and so she'd been able to start the cleaners earlier that morning and was that all right? Susan said it was fine.

Evan drooped. So did Fifi. Susan felt the same way. She spared a thought for Rafael, who would now be sorting everyone out with his characteristic efficiency. At least they didn't have to cope with Jenny, too. Somewhat surprisingly, Mrs Field had agreed that Jenny and Coralie might stay on for a while.

Perhaps, thought Susan, Mrs Field had been short-staffed that day, which helped to make sense of how the would-be kidnappers had nearly managed to lift the children?

Susan wondered whether Rafael would arrange for the broken playhouse to be removed and replaced by something bigger and better, or that he would repair it himself. Either way, Susan suspected that Mrs Field would be all smiles when Rafael had finished with her.

Susan took the children into the big room. She found Evan his Hippo and Fifi her Gonk. She got as far as the big settee and put her feet up, with Fifi spread-eagled on her tummy, and Evan holding Hippo solidly warm against her side . . . and they all three relaxed and gradually drifted off . . .

A clock ticked somewhere.

Susan half woke and checked the children were still there and asleep.

She told herself she must get up, or she wouldn't be able to sleep properly that night. On the other hand, sleep was probably the best thing that could happen to Evan.

Her feet were beautifully warm. How was that? Fifi was on her mother's tummy? No, she wasn't. She was sitting up and chewing on Hippo's ear. Susan moved her legs, and somebody objected . . . Evan, newly roused from sleep and stroking something that purred and was warm against Susan's feet.

Susan hauled herself more or less upright. Fifi was sitting beside her with a large ginger cat pressed to her side. Fifi wasn't taking any notice of the cat, but Evan was.

Evan said, 'Puss, puss! I remember him. He's called Midge, isn't he? He likes Fifi, and he likes me. He doesn't like Jenny, does he?'

Brilliant! Evan was relaxed and interacting with a cat. Susan had never had all that much to do with Midge. He was Ellie's cat. In the past, before Ellie and Thomas left and the house had been handed over to builders, Midge had accepted Susan as a visitor who was a useful provider of snacks. Fifi hadn't had much to do with the cat before, but Susan knew that neither cat nor child would be sitting in close contact with the other unless they'd reached an agreement to coexist.

Susan yawned. 'Ah, Midge has come back, has he? When the building work began he went over the wall and made his home at the hotel, where he earned his keep, catching mice. I suppose he saw us and thought your granny had returned. He must have got in through the front door this morning while we were out.'

Evan said, 'Mummy doesn't like cats, but I do. What does he eat? Can I feed him?'

Food. Goodness, how time flew. It was lunchtime already. Susan heaved herself to her feet, collected the children and made for the kitchen, closely followed by Midge who had always appreciated Susan's cooking.

Now, what could she find for them to eat? Would Rafael join them? Did she have to feed the protection officer?

An undercurrent ran through her thoughts. Why had the false Mrs Quicke wanted to get hold of Evan? And would she try again? How had she known that he would be at the nursery?

Who was this woman who had pretended to be Ellie, and who was the man who'd come to her aid? Had Susan imagined the resemblance between the two?

Surely their attempt to kidnap the children had nothing to do with Evan's death? How could it?

And oh dear, was Lucia all right?

Round and round, up and down, in and out. The answer to the questions was just within reach but not yet clear.

Monday noon

Well, at least she knew how to provide food for the masses. And, cheered by the brilliance of a sunny day, Susan opened all the windows and turned herself back into the Great Provider. She scanned the contents of fridge and freezer. Perhaps they could have a baking session that afternoon? That would keep Jenny and Evan occupied. She managed to open another two boxes of kitchenware and distribute the contents around the cupboards before Coralie brought a tired Jenny home from nursery. Jenny had had a great time. She liked having new toys to play with in a place where she didn't have to play second fiddle to her brother.

Coralie was indulgent, saying Jenny was going to be a real bossy boots, if they weren't careful. Twice she'd snatched toys from other children and had to be reproved for it.

Coralie had bounced back with the energy of youth. She was looking forward to retelling her morning's adventure to her friends and family, and wondered if they'd have her on the telly news and what should she wear if that happened?

She'd regained her normal good humour, partly because – as Susan had guessed – Mrs Field had been short-staffed that morning, and had been grateful for another pair of hands about the place. Coralie said that Mrs Field had recognized she was good with children and had hinted that she might well offer her a job when she'd left school and been trained.

Jenny looked forward to returning to the nursery on the morrow. But Evan? No, he shook his head when the idea was mooted and looked relieved when the PO, their protection officer, said that it was unlikely that either of the children would be allowed to go anywhere until the police had found out why they'd been targeted in the first place.

Rafael arrived back, preoccupied with business but sparing a moment or two to check that Susan was all right and bring her up to date with the news.

He said that Lesley was being detained in hospital suffering from concussion and would probably be put on sick leave when she was released. He had diverted to the hospital on his way back, and had identified the assaulted girl as Lucia, who was now being guarded by another PO. Lucia had been gravely injured but was still hanging on to life. Someone would come from the police to search Lucia's room that afternoon. They were going to try to locate her next of kin, just in case. Finally, the police were still looking for the would-be kidnapper's car but no luck, so far.

There was no news of Diana.

Rafael kissed Fifi, gave Susan a hug, eyed Evan's fragile composure with a worried air but didn't comment on it, rubbed Midge behind his ears and disappeared on some business of his own.

As Susan busied herself with the meal, Marcy came round to speak to Susan. Once again she was blocked at the door by the PO, who interrogated Marcy as if she were a criminal till Susan intervened and vouched for her and asked for her to be let in.

'Well!' Marcy was both flustered and excited by the police-woman's presence and had to be filled in on what had happened before she could state her errand. 'Well, what I came round to say was that one of the curtain rails had been broken by the decorators. Should I order another? And Ellie's old gardener turned up, only to disappear without lifting a finger to help. What a waste of space he is.' In tones of deep disbelief, Marcy said, 'He says he can't work because he's got gout! I'll give him gout!'

Susan, spinning plates of minced meat and creamed spinach on to the table, and deterring Midge from feeding from Evan's plate, said, 'Do you know of a decent gardener who can tell one plant from another and what he should be doing at different times of the year? And would you like some food?'

Marcy said, 'Looks lovely, but I brought something for myself. I'll think about another gardener. Maybe the husband of one of my friends might be able to lend a hand for a while, since that lawn looks as if it could do with a good haircut, and I'd better get back for goodness knows, some people don't know how to clean a toilet properly nowadays.'

And off she went.

The policewoman graciously consented to join them at the table, remarking that *her* mother was a Michelin-starred chef, which made Susan feel rather low.

So while Jenny had a nap upstairs after lunch, Susan and Coralie took the other children and Midge outside to see if they could start the electric lawnmower. Which they failed to do.

But lo and behold! Their policewoman, who seemed to be constantly on her phone, liaising with whoever was now in charge of the case, said she thought she could see where there was a poor connection, and whirr, whirr! They were off!

Coralie laughingly reverted to childhood, demanding first go at the mower. Midge chased flies. Fifi crawled off into the long grasses and wailed that she was lost until rescued. Evan refused to leave Susan's side, and showed signs of panic if she moved more than a metre away from him.

The policewoman said she'd searched Lucia's room and had removed certain items. She said she'd placed tape across the door so no one could go in until Forensics had given it the once over. That was all right by Susan, who rather hoped they'd seen the last of Lucia, and then chided herself for being uncharitable to someone who might be dying at that very moment.

Susan took a stool out on to the patio to sit in the sunshine and relax.

The fact that there was as yet no hedge or fence to divide the garden in two worked well when it came to cutting the lawn and it did give the children space to roam around and explore.

Susan could hear Marcy's voice next door in Ellie's part of the building as she alternately praised and upbraided the cleaners. Curtains were put up here, windows thrown open wide to air the rooms, a hoover whined. All the comforting sounds of normality.

Ah, if only Ellie were back, they could sit and have a cuppa together in the garden, and gossip about nothing in particular.

Susan showed Evan how to make a daisy chain for Fifi. Well, there weren't any daisies in the newly cut lawn, so he picked some blooms from the neglected flower beds which had once been Ellie's pride and joy. There was no harm in that was there? At least it meant he had become brave enough to venture a little way from her side.

Oh, the poor garden! Some plants had survived and rampaged through the undergrowth but ivy had crept in here and there and the roses! Oh shame! They needed pruning and training and . . . Susan's head ached at how much needed to be done. She was no gardener. She wouldn't know where to begin. Perhaps with pruning the roses? Only, she didn't know how to do it.

Perhaps Marcy's contact would work out. They must get the garden back to a semblance of its old self before Ellie returned.

And what of Ellie's once delightful conservatory? It was the haunt of spiders. In fact, it looked derelict, with its outer door hanging ajar and a broken window. Fifi had tried to get in there and had to be removed so that she didn't cut herself on the broken glass.

Coralie and Susan together tried to close the door of the conservatory and failed. It would need the services of a handyman to do that. Coralie checked that the door from the hall into the conservatory was locked as indeed it was.

Susan amused Coralie by telling how Diana had broken into Ellie's house through the back door and had spent the night in Ellie's bedroom before disappearing again.

Coralie emptied grass cuttings into the compost bin, announced she was flaked out, and lay down at full length on the grass . . . only to bob up five minutes later to take Fifi on a tour to explore the garden away from the invitingly open door of the conservatory.

Evan sat down beside Susan and watched. Evan probably needed professional help. Susan wondered who you went to when someone has tried to kidnap you, your mother has dumped you on strangers, and your father has died. Especially if you might have seen that happen, though we won't ask about that yet, will we? Or will we?

Susan's eyes drifted up and up, over the wall to the pale blue sky and the sliver of roof that she could see of the hotel next door. Was Diana holed up there, binoculars in hand, watching her children play in next-door's garden? Or was she out somewhere, trying to talk her way out of her financial problems?

Was it too soon to ask Evan questions? He had relaxed now, and at some point he would be asked to talk to the police. Perhaps it might be a good idea for Susan to get an idea of what he knew?

Susan didn't look at the boy but said casually, 'We do make silly mistakes sometimes, don't we? That funny woman this morning, the one who said she was your granny and wanted to take you home with her. She needs her head examining. Have you ever seen her before?'

He shook his head. No.

'Or the man who came with her?'

Another shake of the head.

'He wasn't in the hall when you went down the other night to see what all the fuss was about?'

A long pause. A frown. Finally, a shake of the head and a shrug. 'Dunno.'

'But you did see a man who told you to go back to bed.'

A nod.

'Was he an old, old man, or someone young?'

A shiver.

Susan put her arm around him. 'All right. That's enough.'

A long, long pause. Then, in a tiny voice, Evan said, 'I smelled his smell. I knew his voice. Mummy says no one is to smoke at home. But he does.'

Susan controlled her excitement with an effort. 'You've seen him smoke in your house?'

A bigger shrug. Evan had had enough. He got up and went to join Fifi and Coralie, who were examining an ancient stone birdbath which had fallen over on to its side.

So Evan had seen something? He'd recognized someone from the aura of cigarette smoke he carried around with him, and from his voice?

Perhaps Diana would be able to tell them who it was. How annoying that she wouldn't give them a contact number! Susan got up to tell the policewoman what Evan had just said. The woman was in the living room, walking to and fro, on her phone as usual. When she saw Susan looking at her she turned away, keeping her voice low. Perhaps it was correct procedure for the officer to keep communication with her superiors a private matter, but it was frustrating for someone who had information to impart.

But then she wondered if Evan's story could be relied on. Susan wondered when Lesley might be allowed back. Lesley would be good at getting the truth out of Evan, wouldn't she?

Jenny woke up and wailed on finding herself alone. Coralie went up to deal with her.

Susan shivered. The sun's warmth was fading. Next door Marcy was going around, slamming windows shut and making sure they were secure.

Would Marcy be able to say who might have been smoking in Diana's house? She'd been on duty there every weekday.

And that set up another train of thought.

SIXTEEN

Monday, late afternoon

Susan called Evan and Fifi into the house. Evan helped Fifi over the lawn, encouraging her to walk. She moved unsteadily because she was dragging Hippo along and the clumsy size of him unbalanced her.

Susan caught Fifi up and kissed her. And then hugged and kissed Evan, who responded with a fleeting caress of his own. Ah, the first sign that he cared for her! Susan thought her heart would burst for joy!

She brought in the stool she'd been sitting on, closed and locked the French windows.

She was not particularly surprised to find that Midge had sneaked into the house while her back was turned. He'd decided to move in with them, hadn't he? What would happen if Jenny went for him again? Mm. Susan wondered who would come off best and decided it would be Midge. Well, Jenny would have to learn to treat him with respect.

Now, what to do? Ah, yes. A cookery session. Fifi loved to lick the spoon when Susan made her chocolate cake with black treacle. It was one of the few times Fifi didn't mind getting dirty.

Coralie brought Little Miss Crosspatch Jenny to sit at the kitchen table with them. Jenny was still tired from her activities at the nursery, but Coralie coaxed her to drink some milk and play with her tablet.

The policewoman loomed up, unsmiling. It was odd how she seemed to occupy more space than she did in reality. She was like a large black cloud, dampening everything in sight. Maybe she wasn't at her best with children? She said, or rather proclaimed, 'DI Millburn's been discharged from hospital. She's supposed to take it easy but she says she'll pop in here later. It's ridiculous. She's been taken off the case but won't let it rest.'

There was more than a suggestion here that DI Millburn was making a bad situation worse by interfering in a case which was no longer hers.

Susan stood up for her aunt. 'I always like to see Lesley. She's family, you know, and has always been very good to me. Now, I'm going to start a chocolate cake for tea and a beef stew for us oldies for supper. Then I'll bake some biscuits so that the children can have fun with the dough. Will you be joining us for supper?'

The woman went all thin-lipped. 'I expect to be relieved before that.'

Susan shrugged. She'd tried, hadn't she? And now, to cook and bake and forget about bad men and even badder women.

Of course the landline phone would ring as soon as Susan had started to knead the dough for the biscuits. The protection officer took the call, relaying the message to Susan. 'It's that woman from next door. The cleaner. Wants to know if she can hire a polisher for the hall floor.'

'Tell her yes,' said Susan, thinking she'd got the mixture a trifle too moist for the children to handle yet.

'And,' said the protection officer, 'she says that Cal, the gardener from her old place, has been round asking if there's any work here. She says she doesn't think much of him, but he might be up to clearing the conservatory out for you, and she's suggested he pop round to see you.'

'Definitely,' said Susan, thinking he'd be the answer to a maiden's prayer, even if she were no maiden.

The doorbell rang and there was a clatter as Evan slithered off his chair and dived under the table. Jenny stared, open-mouthed.

Fifi, safe in her highchair, tried to see where Evan had gone.

Susan froze.

The protection officer finished relaying the message and clicked the phone off.

Susan said, 'No! No, it couldn't be! Or . . . Evan? Evan, darling!' Her hands were covered with sticky dough. She tried to clean them. She said to the officer, 'Don't let him in! Do you hear me? Don't let him . . . No, wait a minute. Arrest him!'

'What?' The protection officer looked at Susan, open-mouthed.

'He's the killer. No, perhaps not. But he's involved. He's come for Evan because the child recognized him. Whatever you do, don't let him in!'

'Don't be ridiculous!' The woman looked out of the window. And there, with his good-looking profile presented to them, standing at the front door, was a young man with dark hair, wearing a sloppy T-shirt and jeans. Cal, the gardener from Diana's house.

Susan had never seen him before, but she knew the type. Superficially attractive, vain, he would have left school without taking any exams. He spent money on trainers and haircuts. Unreliable.

A strong, sweet scent invaded the kitchen through the open window.

Under the table, Evan sneezed. Jenny, sitting perched on a cushion on her chair, waved happily at the sight of the newcomer. Both children knew him.

Susan took a deep breath. Told herself not to panic. Wished they had thought to put up a blind to shield anyone in the kitchen from the gaze of people who came to the door.

The protection officer was not amused by Susan's reaction. 'I thought you wanted a gardener. Judging by the state of this place . . .! Look, this lad's nothing like the man who tried to take Evan this morning.'

'I know, I know!' Susan frantically ran her hands under the tap. 'He's not . . . oh dear, I know what I know, or rather, Evan knows . . . What am I to do?'

'You'll have to speak to him,' said the protection officer, being ultra-reasonable with a woman who'd gone to pieces. 'You agreed he should call.'

'No,' said Susan. 'Don't let him in. Tell him to go. Tell him I've changed my mind, tell him anything but get him to go. Only, yes, first get his name and where he lives so that you can pick him up later.'

The woman sniffed. 'Don't you think you're being rather unreasonable?'

Cal was becoming impatient. He tried the bell again.

Evan whimpered.

Cal tapped on the kitchen window. Susan turned away from the glass, presenting him with her back view. She knew it was childish, but she didn't know what else to do.

Cal rapped louder. The window was open. He was getting annoyed. She sneezed. That scent!

He said, 'Hey, missus! Open up! Macy said you had some work for me.'

And she had. Yes, she had. And then Evan, frightened at the sight of him, had slid under the table.

The protection officer took her time getting to the front door. Susan heard her open it, and say, 'So sorry. It seems it's not convenient today. Give me your details and I'll see they contact you tomorrow.'

He was not amused. 'She asked me to call.'

'So sorry. Not today.'

'I'll be round tomorrow morning, then.'

'Suit yourself. Where can they contact you?'

'I'll be here, on the dot of eight. Right?'

The front door shut. The man crunched away over the gravel drive.

Susan sat on a chair and pulled Evan out from under the table and into her arms. 'There, there. Nasty man's gone away.' She rocked him to and fro. He was rigid with fear.

Finally, he relaxed and gave a long, long sigh. She continued to cuddle him on her lap. Susan looked at the protection officer. 'I'm going to ask Evan some questions. Want to tape his answers?'

'Really?' The woman rolled her eyes, but set her phone to record.

Susan said, 'Evan, it's all right. Cal's gone and I'll make sure he doesn't come again. Now, your mummy doesn't like people to smoke in the house?'

He shook his head.

'But sometimes people do, when she's out?'

He nodded.

'Lucia doesn't mind it?'

A nod. 'Lucia likes the smell.'

'I suppose Cal smokes when he comes in for his elevenses?'

A nod. 'Lucia likes him.'

'She likes the smell, too?'

Another nod. 'I don't. It makes me sneeze.'

'You smelled him just now, didn't you?'

'Lucia opens the doors and window when he goes because Mummy doesn't like the smell.'

'It's a strange smell. Sort of . . . sweet?'

He nodded. 'Can I do some cooking now?'

The protection officer drew in her breath. 'You mean, the gardener smokes cannabis? Yes, well. I thought I smelled it, too. Perhaps it's best if you don't have him work for you.'

Evan looked at her enquiringly. He didn't know the word 'cannabis'.

Susan said to Evan, gently, 'The night your father was fighting the bad men, you came down to the first landing looking for your mummy and saw a man in black. He told you to go back to bed.'

Evan hesitated. He didn't want to talk about that, did he? Susan felt bad about pressing him to do so, but if he could only feel safe enough to say what he'd experienced, the whole horrible matter could be put to bed. At last, Evan nodded.

'He spoke to you and you smelled that same sweet smell? You knew who it was?'

Evan closed his eyes and went stiff in her arms. Susan cuddled him, stroking his head, telling him what a good, brave boy he was.

The protection officer regarded her with amazement. 'You cannot be serious!'

'I am. Deadly serious. The gardener smoked cannabis. Lucia knew it. Evan knew it, though he doesn't know its name. Evan smelled it the night his father died. He heard the man's voice and he knew who it was. The criminals knew that Evan could identify them and that's why they tried to kidnap him this morning.'

The protection officer's colour rose. 'And you really want me to tell the DI that you've identified the gardener as a killer because a small boy dislikes him smoking around the house?'

'It's not as simple as that.'

'I should think not! Look, I'm trying to make excuses for you, but you are trying your hand at being an amateur sleuth without knowing the first thing about it. You do realize that what you have just done has contaminated any evidence the boy might have been able to give us? You've asked him leading questions which means his replies are meaningless. What's more, you didn't always ensure he spoke when he answered you. There's nothing I've recorded which I can use.

'And another thing. You've dreamed up this scenario whereby the gardener killed his employer for some unknown reason, but you haven't explained why that woman and her son were connected with the crime. Was it the gardener who tried to kidnap the boy? No. Of course not. That was a simple attempt at kidnapping a wealthy woman's child. Admitted, they bungled it, but in my lengthy experience of criminals, they often do bungle it. Ten to one, you'll never hear from them again.

'Please, leave police work to those who are trained for it. If you've decided you don't want to employ that lad because he smokes cannabis then that's your problem, but police work is about proof and this' – she waved her phone – 'is not proof.'

Susan felt her eyes fill with tears. She had thought she had stumbled on the truth, but perhaps she had let her imagination run away with her. Perhaps she *had* led Evan on.

The protection officer loomed over Susan. All three children looked on in amazement. What was the woman so cross about?

Jenny's mouth was open. Perhaps the child was getting a cold?

The protection officer patted Susan's shoulder in a modified form of assault. It was not meant to encourage or console, and it certainly didn't.

'Come on, now. No harm done. Naturally you're upset, with someone trying to lift the boy this morning. Let's get you back to what you know about. You are a stay-at-home woman, who keeps house and likes to cook, right? Now, you were going to show the children how to make biscuits? Well, why don't you get on with doing that, and we'll forget your little attempt at being a police officer, shall we?'

Susan nodded. What else could she do? It was true that she didn't know anything about the laws of evidence, and she had led Evan on to give her the answers she thought fitted the problem. She ought not to have done that. A trained policewoman would have known better. She'd done more harm than good.

She hid her distress and got out a blunt knife to divide the dough into smaller pieces. She gave one to Fifi to play with, found a rolling pin and an empty bottle so that Evan and Jenny could flatten their lumps of dough.

Coralie helped. Jenny even abandoned her tablet in order to play with some dough. Finally, Susan helped the children cut out shapes and lay them on baking trays. She decided to use her top oven for the biscuits, as the chocolate cake was now ready to be taken out, and the stew was already cooking in the bottom one.

Coralie suddenly said, 'Jenny! No! Stop it!' Jenny had shot a lump of dough at Evan and laughed when he ducked. Evan gave her a long, thoughtful look and moved around the table to be next to Fifi, who pawed his arm with her sticky fingers and crowed. He liked that. It cheered him up no end.

A phone call took the protection officer into the hall. Coralie sidled up to Susan and said, very quietly, 'I don't care what she thinks. I think you're right. My dad's always said to steer clear of boys who smoke grass.'

Susan said, 'Thanks, but she's right, you know. I shouldn't have interfered.' She took the tray of misshapen biscuits out of the top oven and set them aside to cool. 'I jumped to conclusions. It's true, the gardener smoking cannabis doesn't mean anything.

Evan probably did smell it that night, but that doesn't mean it was the gardener. At least, I don't think so.'

Coralie helped Susan to clean up the mess, and they fed the children soft-boiled eggs and soldiers for tea, with a small slice of chocolate cake, one of their own biscuits and some fruit for afters.

When her father arrived in his taxi to take his daughter home, Coralie didn't want to go. 'I don't like leaving you. Suppose that gardener comes back?'

'Another officer is supposed to relieve this one, and Rafael will be back soon. We'll let the children run around the big room and keep an eye out for intruders.'

Coralie sighed. 'I suppose that's all right. Ring me if anything happens and you need me, right? What a day! What a lot I have to tell the family!' She departed.

Susan was sorry to see her go.

Rafael drove up on the Beast and put it in the garage. Susan felt safer when he arrived, and even better when he gave her a kiss and a hug and wanted to know how she was feeling. She managed to smile and say she was fine, and to tell him what the kids had been up to that afternoon. That worked. The lines of strain on his face vanished and he went off to greet the children, throw them in the air and catch them again, and finally to listen to *their* detailed account of what they'd done that afternoon. Fifi sat in the crook of his arm and contentedly chewed on Hippo's ear. That tooth was a long time coming through, wasn't it?

The surly protection officer came off the phone to announce that there'd been some kind of glitch and her replacement would arrive in half an hour or so. And, as she'd been on duty now for twelve hours, she was going to leave as the master of the house was home. And leave she did.

Susan didn't know if she were glad or sorry to see the woman go, but soon she and Rafael were caught up with the business of getting the children in and out of the bath, into pyjamas, reading them bedtime stories, and finally tucking them up in bed with a prayer.

Evan asked for the prayer to be said twice. Evan wasn't going to sleep well that night, was he? Susan still hadn't solved the problem of putting three beds and a cot into the nursery. Fifi was being remarkably good-tempered about sleeping in her buggy top, but how long would that last? Ah well, she'd see to it tomorrow.

Monday, supper time

Downstairs, Susan closed all the windows, drew curtains and turned herself back from being a mother-of-three to being the wife-who-is-always-welcoming when her hunter-gatherer-husband returns from earning a crust.

She could see he was hungry, so she dished up supper and made small talk. She asked if he'd contacted their builder about putting on a porch, and mentioned she'd like to have a blind or shutters made for the kitchen so that they had some privacy. But even as she ladled the first helping of stew on to his plate, the doorbell rang.

No, it wasn't another protection officer. It was Lesley, wearing a neck brace. She looked pale and rather the worse for wear. She said, 'Are the children all right? Not suffering from the nasty fright they had this morning? May I come in for a bit? And is that stew I can smell?'

'Do you need to ask?' Susan got another plate out of the cupboard, ran it under the hot tap to warm it. There was nothing worse than putting hot food on cold plates. Susan didn't ask why Lesley didn't want to go home to her husband. They all knew he wasn't any kind of support to her in her demanding job. Ellie had been anxious about that marriage from the beginning but had hoped it would settle down.

If he were running true to form, the dear man would have been thinking – even if he didn't actually say – that it was inconsiderate of his wife to get herself injured and therefore unable to provide him with the care and attention due to the Head of the Household. He would probably be at the cricket club tonight, or out drinking with his mates. It was best not to enquire after him.

Lesley eased herself gingerly on to a chair. She looked as if she had a headache. She said, 'I've been signed off work for a week, but I couldn't rest. I've heard you've lost your protection officer, shortage of staff, but someone will pass by in a car several times a night to make sure you're all right. Oh, and the news from the hospital is good. I understand Rafael identified the girl who was assaulted behind the shops in the Avenue last night. They say she's probably going to pull through but she isn't well enough to talk to officers yet.'

Susan and Rafael made appropriate noises and got down to the food. As did Lesley, who ate two helpings of stew with steamed vegetables, followed by two pieces of Susan's famous chocolate cake. With cream.

Some colour came back to Lesley's cheeks and eventually she sat back and patted her stomach. 'That's better. Can't remember when I last had such a good meal. So what's new?' She ignored Susan and looked to Rafael, the Man of the House.

Susan put dirty plates into the dishwasher and wished she were not such a dimwit. The protection officer's remarks had struck home.

Of course Lesley would ask Rafael what he knew first. I did mess up this afternoon, didn't I? The officer had been right to point out what I'd done wrong but, well, it still hurt. And though I might have got some things wrong, surely she ought to have discussed it with me, respecting my point of view, instead of dismissing what I said as the chit-chat of a dum-dum? Oh well, I shouldn't have interfered. Obviously.

Lesley wouldn't expect me to have anything worthwhile to say. Why should I? I'm just the person who looks after the children while the professionals go about their daily tasks with their heads in the air, not listening to a child who might have something very important to say.

Aargh! Stop being so sorry for yourself, Susan. Sit down and listen to the adults for a change.

Rafael did indeed have something to contribute. 'Well, first of all, I phoned Ellie and brought her up to speed. She was saddened but not particularly surprised to hear what Diana's been up to because Ellie knows exactly what her daughter's like. I half expected her to say I ought to give Diana the benefit of the doubt, but she didn't. She said that if she had a penny for the times she's helped her daughter out of trouble, she'd be a very rich woman. I did say I might have an idea of how to help Diana, and Ellie said I shouldn't go out of my way to do so, because I might get drawn in to something unsavoury. She was concerned about the children until she heard how brilliantly Susan was coping, and she said how pleased she was that we had Coralie to help. Ellie says that Jenny needs watching, but that Evan is a little soldier.'

They all smiled at that. Ellie, as usual, had hit the nail on the head.

Rafael said, 'I said Susan had got Marcy to put the house in order and asked if she and Thomas were going to fly back early to deal with Diana and her problems and she said she was taking a back seat on this one, and that we were perfectly capable of sorting it out ourselves.'

Lesley looked doubtful. 'I wish she were here. She sees things so clearly. She understands people better than anyone else I know.'

Susan made a cup of tea all round and offered her aunt some aspirin.

Rafael continued, 'I wish Ellie were here, too. We're doing our best, but there's so much that doesn't make sense. I spent a considerable amount of time today on the phone at work, researching Cynthia Cottrell's family business empire. The balance sheets are healthy. They pay dividends to shareholders as and when they should. Gossip says that some of their contracts were obtained through the Old Boy network and others through the system which says, here's a nice holiday for you in the Maldives in return for a favour. But the only link I can find between Cottrells and Diana is through her agency selling houses at that one site. I've put out feelers with various business acquaintances asking for their opinion on the Old Man but didn't find anything of interest except a general feeling that it was better not to cross him.

'I went on to see if he could trace Diana's bolthole. Susan and I did wonder if she might be using one of the top rooms at the hotel next door because it overlooks the back of our house and the garden, but even when I described her to the receptionist there, she denied they'd ever laid eyes on her. I'm not sure that I believed her. The police might have more luck?'

'I suppose so,' said Lesley. 'I still can't believe she's gone to ground without leaving us a contact number. What would have happened if the children had been kidnapped this morning and we couldn't get hold of their mother!'

Susan said, in a quiet voice which they could ignore if they wished, 'They weren't after Jenny. Just Evan.'

'You think so?' Rafael wasn't that interested. He produced his smart phone. 'I researched houses and flats advertised by her agency which have recently been sold at a knock-down price. I came up with two addresses which might be of interest. Both are studio flats, one is in a prestigious development down by the canal and one in a block of flats just off the Avenue. Both were sold to a builder as the buyer moved to a new house in Keith's company, the Betterment project. Diana handled the sales.

'Builders do this sometimes: they buy a smaller property that's not moving in the market, in order to sell a much larger one. Usually the first property goes back on the market but in this case one of them has and the other hasn't. I wondered if perhaps Diana might be renting one of these studio flats for herself, by special arrangement with the builder. It's a long shot, but you might like to send someone to check them out?'

Lesley said she was supposed to be off work for the time being, but would pass the tip on in the morning.

And that concluded the business of the day for Lesley and Rafael.

But not for Susan, who nerved herself to speak. She cleared her throat, and the other two looked at her with slight frowns. Did she really want to say something?

She said, 'It may be nothing. Your officer thinks I'm off my rocker. It seems I've been extremely stupid and compromised the evidence, because I don't understand grown-up police business.'

Lesley patted Susan's hand. 'My dear. Why should you?'

'No. Well. The thing is, I don't think Evan died because Diana wanted to rescue incriminating papers from their safe. Why should she get someone else to do that, when she had every right to go into the safe at any time to suit herself?'

'I agree,' said Lesley. 'We've been over and over this and it doesn't make sense that Diana organized a break-in. It must be one of the Cottrells who arranged it.'

'The timings don't fit,' said Susan, sticking to her right to be heard. 'If Keith had been threatened with divorce by Cynthia then yes, he might at some point have realized the papers could give her ammunition and want them back. It might well have come to that but in fact, as of the night Evan died, there was no hint of it being on the cards. So I can see no reason why Keith should stage a break-in.'

'True,' said Rafael. 'It was either Cynthia or her father.'

Susan shook her head. 'Cynthia only realized that Diana might become a problem when she talked to Evan that evening. I don't know who instigated the phone call and it really doesn't matter because although they might have spoken about divorce, neither of them really wanted it. What Cynthia and Evan both wanted was for Diana and Keith to break off their relationship. Cynthia liked keeping Keith around rather like a pet dog, and Evan needed Diana to keep the household and business running. Neither of them knew at that point about the papers. If they had, that might indeed have become an issue. But they didn't. Cynthia didn't consult her father about getting rid of Diana till after Evan died.'

Lesley managed a weary smile. 'Dear Susan. If you get rid of all our suspects, who are we left with?'

SEVENTEEN

Monday evening

'Who are we left with?' Susan nerved herself to share her theory. 'We're left with someone who had a different motive. Someone we hadn't considered. Someone Diana had upset. Someone who knew she kept valuables in the safe but didn't know where the safe was.'

Rafael frowned. 'Oh, I see. You mean Marcy, her cleaner?'

Susan said, 'No, I don't mean Marcy. It's true that Diana sacked her so that she didn't have to pay Marcy her wages, but Marcy is a realist. She was furious with Diana. I would have been, too. But once she'd thought things through, she accepted the status quo and set about getting herself another job straight away, and that has paid off. As of today, instead of being just another cleaner who's paid by the hour, she's become a project manager. They're as rare as hens' teeth and she can negotiate her own contracts in future.'

'That's true,' said Rafael. 'If she does a halfway decent job on Ellie's house, we could use her on trust properties that need to be brought up to scratch between lets. Because we've got so many more properties to handle – thanks to Monique's gift – our current team is stretched to the limit and we were thinking of employing someone to help out.'

Susan said, 'We've been working on the assumption that the burglary was masterminded by professional people who would have worked out the odds of doing this and that. But it wasn't like that. It was Amateur Night at the pub and it ended in tears.

'Look, let's start out at the beginning, with Diana having a cash flow problem. Her husband was declining into Alzheimer's and a wheelchair. He was a drain on their family's finances. The downturn in the economy meant nothing much was happening at the agency. So what did she do? She cut staff wherever she could and pawned a diamond ring belonging to Evan's family to get some cash. She sacked Marcy, refusing to pay her wages. Finally she got rid of her live-in nanny, although there was another reason for her doing that as well.

'Now, Marcy didn't think Diana would have gone to the pawnbrokers herself and I agree, because if someone had spotted her the word would have streaked around all her friends and acquaintances that she was on the skids. Marcy considered who Diana might have asked to go to the pawnshop on her behalf and came up with the name of their gardener, who Marcy described as young and untrustworthy, willing to take chances, not a reliable sort of person.

'You remember how Diana got rid of Marcy? She accused her of stealing and pawning a valuable ring. Diana tricked Marcy into holding the pawn ticket in her hands for a moment, so as to get her fingerprints on it. We know now how Marcy reacted, and we can discount her as having masterminded the burglary.

'But the gardener was something else. He'd done a sneaky job by taking the ring to the pawnbrokers for Diana. Did she pay him an agreed fee for taking the ring to the pawnbrokers? If she ran true to form, she didn't. Now the young man described to me would not have taken this lying down. He's not like Marcy, able to calculate the odds, draw a line under an unpleasant experience and get on with life. No. He'd have gone spare. Diana chose the wrong man to upset. I've seen the lad – he's called Cal, by the way – and I agree with Marcy's assessment of him. He's a no-hoper with poor education. And he smokes cannabis, which means he's always going to be short of money.'

Lesley concentrated, with an effort. 'It's true that lads excluded from school tend to drift into gangs where drugs are readily available, even if they're not dealing themselves. Yes, some of them do get odd jobs, nothing too onerous, just enough to keep them supplied with their drug of choice.'

'Exactly,' said Susan. 'Let's look at it from this Cal's point of view. He's been cheated of his due by a lady who lives in a big house, runs an expensive car and operates what appears to be a thriving estate agency. He himself is most likely living in sub-standard accommodation, probably in a block of council flats, eking out some sort of living as a gardener, paid by the hour, and with a habit of smoking weed which has to be paid for.'

Lesley got out her notebook. 'Cal . . . what? We'll check him out.'

'I don't know what his surname is or where he lives, but he's turning up here tomorrow morning at eight and you can arrest him then.'

'What for?' Lesley made a stab at taking Susan seriously.

'Well, for conspiracy to burgle? That would do for a start.'

'What! But there were three of them.'

Susan was eager to share her thoughts. 'Don't you think Cal would know some more youngsters as stupid as himself? They meet at the pub and at football games. They hang around street corners together, chatting up girls. They spend time in games arcades. They're on the fringe of real crime, paying for some weed here, nicking the odd mobile phone there. I think it would have been easy for Cal to find a couple of like-minded lads to help him burgle the house of someone he had a grudge against.

'They were amateurs. It was a messy, badly thought-out plan probably hatched in a pub over a few drinks. A couple of Cal's friends would start off by sympathizing with him for having been so badly treated. One of them would say that it shouldn't be allowed, and another would follow that up by saying someone ought to teach her a lesson. From there they'd float the idea that it would be a lark to break into Diana's house and nick something to pay her back for her bad behaviour. They thought the house would be an easy target what with Evan being an invalid and all.

'Diana must have mentioned getting the ring out of the safe. He assumed, wrongly as it turned out, that it would be in the front room. He recruited a couple of like-minded idiots, one of whom would act as lookout while he and his mate found the safe and forced it open, or lifted whatever small valuables they could lay their hands on to sell.'

Lesley tried to nod and then held on to her head. That hurt. 'The boy whose DNA we found on the scene – the one who ended up dead on Saturday night – was as you describe, a hanger-on. A no-hoper. Left school without taking any exams. Never had a job, lived on the fringe of crime. He was known to have acted as a runner for drugs, yes. He's on record for having acted as look-out for a couple of break-ins from shops, but nothing heavy. At the moment we're trying to trace his associates. If we find that he was at school with our gardener, then certainly we can look into that connection.'

Susan felt a flicker of pleasure. Perhaps she hadn't got everything wrong, after all. 'I think the three of them set out on what had meant to be a walk in the park until it turned, shockingly, into murder. Evan woke up, tackled them, they fought back and he died. I imagine the would-be burglars were shattered by what had happened. I don't know which of them carried a knife but I'm sure they didn't intend to kill anyone. Once Evan was down and injured, they fled without having got into the safe or stopping to nick anything else. They'd have been horrified to discover the next day that Evan had died of his wounds.

'I think Cal and the second, unidentified conspirator, met up to compare notes the next day. They'd reassure one another that there was nothing to link them to the burglary except, possibly, their lookout boy. And we know he was dealt with on Saturday. Oh, and there was one other who might be a threat to them.'

Rafael followed this line of thought up. 'They'd known Lookout Boy for ever. They'd know he'd been in trouble before and that his prints were on file. They'd know he couldn't be relied on to keep his mouth shut if the police started to make enquiries. So they dealt with him?'

Lesley said, 'Evan's death could be put down as manslaughter. Killing Lookout Boy was murder.'

Susan shuddered. 'Poor lad. He didn't stand much of a chance, did he? I wonder if he even knew why he was killed.'

Lesley said, 'All right, Susan. Who's the other person who might have been able to betray them? You think it's Lucia? But I could have sworn she hadn't a clue about that, or about anything else, come to think of it.'

Susan said, 'I think she helped Cal without realizing it. Let's look at her life as a nanny. She was young and lonely, stupid and available. He was young and reasonably good looking. He would go into the kitchen for a cuppa when he was on his break. She would arrange to be there on some excuse. Using the washing machines, perhaps? There wasn't one upstairs. She'd have the children with her. Both Evan and Jenny knew him by sight. Lucia probably had romantic dreams about him.'

Lesley sniffed. 'What, Gormless Lucia meets the gardener and falls in lurv?'

'We know she covered for him. He smoked sweet-smelling cigarettes, and we know that Lucia would open the windows and doors when he'd gone, so that Diana – who hated anyone smoking in the house – wouldn't know. Yes, of course she would gossip to him about what Evan and Diana were up to. He knew their timetable, when the children were out and when Marcy was around. But Marcy wasn't there at weekends. I can see him chatting her up and arranging to meet him when she was off duty of an evening. She might have hoped for more, but I don't think she'd have got it.'

Susan said, 'Marcy told me he'd already got too young girls up the duff. Has anyone checked to see if Lucia's pregnant?'

'Nasty thought,' said Lesley, squeezing her eyes half shut. 'I'll have a word. So why did Cal try to kill her? If it *was* him, and not just a random mugging?'

'Remember that on the day Evan died and Diana threw her out, Lucia kept on about a friend who lived in Acton. She said she'd tried to contact him or her but failed to do so and she'd been left walking the streets till we rescued her. I think it was Cal that she was trying to contact, but he was in panic mode that day on discovering that Evan had died, and he refused to accept her calls. It was only later, after he'd calmed down, that he began to take her calls again. After that, as we know to our cost, every time Lucia came off her phone from someone, she got more and more stroppy, demanding this and that. Transport back home, four-star hotel accommodation, money, and so on. Conclusion: he was egging her on to make some money out of the situation.'

Lesley said, 'She could have had other friends. We're asking at the abbey if anyone recognized her. Someone might be able to point us in the right direction.'

Susan said, 'He doesn't strike me as the type to go to Mass, but if she was in any sort of relationship with him, she'd want to keep in touch, and he'd want to meet her to find out how far the police had got with Evan's murder.'

Rafael was frowning. 'Granted, she's no great brain. But surely when Lookout Boy was killed, wouldn't it occur to her that Cal might have had something to do with his death?'

'Why should it? She didn't recognize him when Lesley showed her his photograph. If she'd never seen him with any of his friends, she wouldn't have any idea there was a connection. I think Cal invited her to meet him on Sunday and she agreed, probably expecting a kiss and a cuddle. Some girls think that's the way they pay for the attentions of a man. I think Cal was seeing shadows where there were none.

'He hadn't meant Evan to die, but die he had. That Saturday night he'd dealt with Lookout Boy. Maybe he'd acted alone, maybe with the friend who'd made a third at the burglary. Perhaps his guilty conscience told him Lucia would soon begin to suspect him, or perhaps even she had begun to put two and two together. So he tried to wipe her out. He scarpered with her handbag to delay identification and so that he could sell her mobile phone and, if she'd taken it with her, her passport as well. Inefficient as ever, he left her alive and at some point she should be able to talk.'

Lesley sounded doubtful. 'It's a nice story, but you've no facts to link him with anything that's happened. Look, I'm officially off the case. I can always drop hints, I suppose, but . . .' She stretched and said, 'Ouch.'

Susan made one last try. 'Let's imagine, just for a minute, that there was a witness to Evan's murder. Someone heard shouting and went down to the first-floor landing to see what was going on. He saw a man in black who told him to go back to bed. He knew who the man was because, although he wore a black balaclava, he recognized the scent and the voice.'

Lesley said, 'Hold on. Who told you what happened that night? It wasn't Lucia, and there was no one else there. Unless . . . Ah, it was the child? No! Really? Little Evan told you this? But we can't act on the word of a four-year-old? No!'

'I know.' Susan felt miserable. 'I asked him about it, and I shouldn't have done it without proper witnesses, should I? I thought I was being so clever. He told me this and that at intervals when he was feeling relaxed. I got your police officer to record what he said eventually, but I didn't do it properly and . . . I feel such a fool.'

'Yes. Well. He probably made it all up.'

Susan felt as if her face was on fire. 'No, I don't think so. I really don't. He went down to the first floor looking for his mother, only she wasn't there. He was frightened. He heard a lot of shouting. He saw someone who told him to go back to bed. He knew the voice and he recognized the man who smoked cannabis. That's a realistic story, isn't it? Not one a little boy would make up.'

'Oh, I don't know,' said Lesley. 'Children nowadays watch all sorts on the telly, and some of the books they read, well, they'd scare me into having nightmares. No, I can't face the thought of basing a prosecution on the word of an imaginative four-year-old boy.' She moaned, hands to neck brace. 'I think I've had enough for one day. Am I fit to drive home or shall I call a cab?'

Susan had one more try. 'What about the attempted kidnapping? Every time I think about it, my blood pressure goes through the roof. It doesn't seem to me that the police are taking the matter seriously. Where's the replacement protection officer we were supposed to have? Oh, if only we could get in touch with Diana! I'm sure this all goes back to her and the way she treats people.'

Lesley pushed back her chair and stood up. 'I'll check. I know we're short-staffed and they may have to prioritize. If there's a riot outside a nightclub or a multiple car crash somewhere, there won't be any officers to spare. Look, I can't think anything will happen tonight with the children safely in bed here, looked after by two adults.'

Susan was not convinced.

Lesley blinked. She was in pain but trying to keep going. 'I may not be thinking straight. We'll talk about this again tomorrow. You've convinced me we need to look into Cal's background, but the rest of your scenario doesn't hang together. I'm not convinced this is all about a teenager needing to fund his drugs habit. If you'd made out a theory that that crazy woman this morning had been behind the burglary, then I'd be right on to it. But you can't, can you?'

Susan twisted her fingers in her hair. She couldn't, no.

Lesley was beyond tired. 'Look,' she said, 'every now and then we get a woman crazed with grief because she's lost her own child and tries to pinch someone else's. Sometimes it's an issue in a divorce case, with one party trying to get possession of the child. And there's always a market for pretty children to be sold abroad. I'm far more worried about her than about some gardener who might have considered himself misused by Diana. If she's fixated on one of Diana's children, then she might well try again, probably while they're outside on a walk, when it would be easy to snatch a child, shove him in a car and drive away. I'll see that someone gets back here on duty first thing tomorrow.'

Susan was close to tears. Nothing she said seemed to have got through. She said, 'The woman used Ellie's name.' She turned to the window, where her own image was reflected back at her in the glass. Outside, all was dark.

Lesley rubbed her eyes wearily. 'You're overreacting, and I'm worn out. We'll talk again tomorrow. A patrol car will pass by every now and then through the night. You should be safe enough with the doors locked and Rafael on the premises.'

Susan thought of the empty house next door, which was only too easy to break into, as Diana had proved. Once in, you could get out into the garden through the conservatory. Then you could break into their own big room through the French windows. She felt they were all too vulnerable.

But maybe Lesley was right and she was overreacting.

Rafael had stopped listening to her, too. 'If we see either of those two strangers again, we'll dial nine-nine-nine.' His tone was almost patronizing.

'They're not strangers,' said Susan, sounding like a child who'd been scolded for something she hadn't done. She put two and two together and made it five. 'The woman is Cal's dealer. And the man is her lieutenant, possibly some relation of hers.'

'Now you're making it up,' said Rafael, and this time his tone was sharp.

She blinked tears away. 'I suppose I am.' The truth was hanging there, at the back of her mind, but she hadn't got it quite right yet.

Lesley was white of face. 'Sorry, Susan. I don't say you're not on to something, but I'm too tired to take it all in.' She looked around. 'Did I come in my car? I don't think I'm fit to drive. Can you get a taxi for me?'

'I'll take you home,' said Rafael. 'It's getting late, and you look ready to drop. All right, Susan?'

She nodded, because they expected her to agree. Inside, she knew it was not all right. Ripples of fear crawled up and down her spine. They didn't believe her interpretation of events. Who could blame them? She hadn't any proof. None. But the more she thought about it, the more she knew she was right. Or mostly right, anyway.

Rafael took Lesley out, inserted her into his car, and drove away.

Susan cleared the table and loaded the dishwasher. She couldn't stop thinking.

If that woman is a drug dealer – which is a big 'if' but it does fit the picture – then she must be furious with Cal for embroiling her in his crusade against Diana. Cal in turn must be feeling desperate. He's responsible for Evan's death. He's murdered his lookout boy. He's tried to silence Lucia and failed. Any minute now she might wake up and name him as her assailant. What would instinct tell him to do?

Run away and hide.

For this he needs money. Where can he get it?

From Diana, of course.

Diana would make a good target. She's a woman, alone. But she's disappeared.

He knows from Lucia where Diana's children are living now. He knows I'm a pint-sized homebody with a formidable husband.

He suggests one final ploy to his drug dealer. 'Let's even things up by kidnapping Diana's children and making her pay through the nose to get them back. Susan should not present any difficulty. We might have to wait till Rafael is out of the way, though.'

Ah, why didn't I see it before?

When Cal met Lucia on Sunday evening, he asked her about the children and where he could contact Diana. For the first time, Lucia became suspicious of his motives, and SHE LET HIM SEE IT. He realized she knew why he was asking those questions and he panicked and attacked her.

Susan considered the links in her theory and thought that yes, she'd probably got it right this time. There was no proof, of course. It was all based on her assessment of the characters of the people concerned.

If she were right and Cal was still out for revenge and money, then the children were still a target. Oh dear . . . and Rafael had just left!

No, of course Cal wouldn't break in here tonight. Would he?

Wouldn't it be easier for him to turn his attention back to Diana's big house? Burgle it again in the hope of finding the safe this time? No, he wouldn't do that in case there was still a police presence there.

Susan realized she was alone in the house except for three helpless children . . . oh, and Midge, the cat, who had just decided he could do with some company. He had set about making sure she agreed by winding to and fro around her legs. She fed him and switched the dishwasher on.

She held on to the back of a chair, trying to still the shakes.

I'm all right. I'm perfectly all right.

The landline phone rang. It would be the baddies, checking that she was home and alone? No, ridiculous. It couldn't be them. And why should it be, anyway?

She didn't recognize the voice at first. 'It's Sam, Coralie's Dad. Are you all right there, missus?'

She was so frightened, she spoke the truth. 'No, not really.'

'Ah. The thing is, you must say if I'm overstepping the mark, but Coralie told us about what's been going on and, well, we said she was grounded and not coming back to you tomorrow. But she's very much her mother's daughter and she said she'd leave home and doss down with you and wouldn't let you cope all by yourself. So we had a bit of an up and downer and we've sent her off up to bed in a right old state.'

There was some confused shouting in the background. Coralie, wanting to know if her father was speaking to Susan?

Sam took the phone away from his ear to yell, 'Shut it!' and then came back to Susan. 'Sorry about that. Coralie's worried about you.'

'She's been just great,' said Susan. 'But I do understand if you don't want her to come back.' She moved away from the kitchen window because it gave on to the great big dark space out there. Anyone standing in the road could see her moving around inside. How soon would Rafael be back? Would Lesley invite him in for a cuppa?

'The thing is . . .' Sam didn't seem to know how to go on. 'I've just come back from my last shout of the day. I had to collect a man from the hotel in the next road to you and take him to the station. I passed your place to get there and I noticed there was an old Volvo parked in the road a little way along from you. Three people sitting in it. There's so much off-street parking in your area that you don't often see cars left in the street. Now, two people having a chat in the front is OK, and two people in the back is something different, but three people . . .?' Another pause. 'The thing is the car was still there when I come back on my way home. I can't get it out of my mind. Coralie said you'd got a police officer with you, so that's all right, isn't it?'

'She's been withdrawn,' said Susan.

The line went dead. Sam had clicked off.

Susan shut off the kitchen light. It was too revealing. Anyone passing in the road, anyone coming into the drive, would be able to see her.

She withdrew into the hall. She listened for sounds. Nothing. Thankfully the three children were quiet, sleeping peacefully, unaware of what might happen.

Well, what might happen?

Nothing might happen.

Sam didn't think it was nothing. He'd taken the trouble to ring me, to see if I were all right.

Of course I'm all right. Just a little . . . wary. Just a tad scared of being left in a well-lit house when it's dark outside and I'm all on my own. If those three people in the car are watching the house, checking how many people are here and how many might be left before they . . . well, what would they do?

They're not after Evan now. They're frightened and angry. They want revenge and compensation. They've seen Rafael and Lesley drive off, leaving me on my own. The odds are three to one.

Well, change the odds.

Of course. She rang Rafael's number.

She heard his smartphone ring . . . *in the kitchen!*

He'd left his smartphone on the table in the kitchen?

She was going to scream.

Er, that won't help.

Think, Susan! Think! What would Ellie do, apart from pray.

Well, I can pray, of course I can pray. But the sensible thing to do is to ring the cops and scream for help. Come on, now. You can do it!

Nine-nine-nine. Ring, ring. Ring, ring. Weren't they supposed to answer within so many seconds?

'Which service do you want?'

'Police! Quickly, please!'

Pause, pause, pause. 'What is your name . . .?'

Susan told herself not to howl down the phone. It wouldn't help. She managed to state her problem clearly, and without giving way to hysteria.

The phone said, 'You're worried because you're alone in the house and there was an attempted kidnapping earlier in the day?'

'Yes. Sort of. A friend has just reported a suspicious car hanging around in the road outside. It's been there some time. And there are three people in it.'

'Just a moment.' Long pause. The phone handler was consulting someone?

Susan fidgeted.

The phone spoke. 'A patrol car will be passing by your house every hour on the hour to check that all's well. If anything happens to disturb you, ring us again.'

The phone went dead.

Haven't I just told them I'm scared to death?

Susan heard a car start up in the road outside.

A car was driven forward and parked across the entrance to their driveway. It turned off its lights.

The streetlights were few and far between. They didn't help much to identify the make of the car, nor its colour.

Rafael wouldn't park across the driveway, would he?

And the shape of the car was all wrong.

It wasn't Rafael's car.

So whose was it?

EIGHTEEN

Monday, late evening

Susan scrambled around the darkened kitchen looking for a weapon.

I can bolt the front door, but oh, it's got that big glass panel in it . . . and there are French windows leading into the big room at the back! Why didn't the architect advise us to make the house burglar-proof? We should have had a stout oak door put in, and shutters and . . . I would like a moat and a drawbridge as well.

What am I going to do?

Pray!

She looked wildly around for something, anything, to defend herself with.

A dark shape loomed outside the kitchen window. It tapped on the front door. It was a man, she could see that much.

She wasn't going to let him in. No way!

She dithered, closing her eyes tight, fervently wishing the caller could vanish, which he didn't. It was Cal, the gardener. Of course.

He rang the bell. Firmly.

She shivered, clutching her arms. 'Rafael, where are you?'

Pray!

Dear Lord above, help! I don't know the right words, I'm no good at this thing . . .Would that old iron doorstop do as a weapon? It was here when we moved in . . . No, too heavy. I can't even lift it . . . *And I know it's all wrong to ask You for help when I haven't been in touch for a good while, but* . . . If only I'd played hockey, or cricket, or . . . umbrellas are no good . . . *and it's not for me, in particular, but those poor children! Oh, Fifi! Don't let them hurt Fifi! I'll kill them if they touch her! Oh, what am I saying?*

Round and round the kitchen she went. She didn't turn the light back on, it was too revealing. A knife, perhaps? *No, I might kill someone which would be awful and I don't know where to aim, anyway.*

Poor little Evan. Look after him, please! He's had such a bad time . . .

Ah! Got it. My heavy frying pan. If I swing it high . . .? No, I must try for low. Low down, see. Yes, I know there are three of them, and only one of me, but if the Lord is on my side . . . *You will be on my side, won't you?*

The bell rang again. There was only one man out there.

Where were the other two?

Ah, the man at the door was a diversion. The other two would have gone round to the far side of Ellie's house. They'd break in through Ellie's back door just as Diana had done. Then what would they do?

They'd go across the hall and down the corridor to see if there was a doorway into this part of the house. That will give me a few minutes. Where's my own phone? I must ring the police again . . . bother! I've dropped it!

She could have wept with frustration, trying on her hands and knees to see where it had gone and . . .

No time to waste. Can I make some kind of barrier across the bottom of the stairs and . . . We do have locks on the bedroom doors, don't we? If I lock myself in with the children and . . . What then? Wave a white flag or a sheet out of the window . . .? Where's my rolling pin? That would make an excellent weapon, but . . . Where did I put it?

The man has gone from the window. I can't find my phone!

They will have gone back down the corridor now and opened the door into the conservatory, or smashed it. I can't remember whether there's a lock on it or . . . No, a bolt. I think.

Abandon the frying pan. Drag the two baby buggies out, and the scooter, and the bike. Can I tie them to the newel post at the bottom of the stairs? I can use the straps! My fingers are all thumbs. Add that dratted easel which we've never been able to find a proper place for and Fifi's highchair and some saucepans.

Crack! It sounded like a rifle shot. They'd smashed their way into the conservatory and the door there was hanging open on to the garden, wasn't it?

She'd left a small passage through the clutter on the stairs so that she could somehow wriggle through and up to the landing. She closed that gap after her, with a chair from the kitchen which she hauled into place from where she stood above. Her Heath Robinson construction now blocked the stairs completely.

She stood on the landing, wondering what to do next.

I'm the King of the Castle, and you're the dirty rascals.

Midge the cat inspected the barricade and inserted himself into it. He probably thought it was some game invented by grown-ups for his amusement.

Shall I hide?

But where?

In a minute they'll be round the house and standing outside the French windows looking into the big room. They'll smash them or lever them open. Yes, that's them now. Oh, bother! The windows have only just been re-glazed.

Her brain went into overdrive. She'd left the frying pan downstairs and had never found the rolling pin. She was no good at this lark!

Good Lord, protect us!

Keep calm. Keep cool. Breathe deeply.

Think!

'Susan?' A small boy's voice. Shaking with fear.

Oh, my God! Evan's woken up and come to see what's going on!

'Go back to bed, Evan. Please!'

He pattered along the corridor towards her.

He was hindered by carrying Hippo. No, he was helping Fifi along, and she was towing Hippo behind her. *Oh my God! Not Fifi, too!*

Evan's eyes were wide with fright. He knew something was wrong and he'd come to her for reassurance. He said, 'Fifi's frightened.'

Susan snatched Fifi up and cuddled her. She was warm and cuddly. She was not frightened. She was interested in this new experience. She was chewing on one of Hippo's ears. When will that tooth come through?

'Go back to bed, Evan!' Susan's voice cracked. He wasn't going to obey her, was he?

'No.' His chin wobbled. He clutched her leg. He felt safer with her than in his bed alone upstairs. He'd got that wrong, hadn't he? He'd be a lot safer hiding under the bed . . . or . . . could she stow him in a cupboard?

Boudicca, completely unarmed, prepared to repel invaders.

I'm hysterical. I'm fighting on the beaches and wherever else it was supposed to be that Britons fought the invader.

I can't see that my defences will hold, and they'll take Evan and they won't leave me alive as a witness because that's their way . . . oh, let them spare Fifi! They might! Oh yes, they might! She can hardly talk! If only . . . where could I hide her? In the linen chest at the top of the stairs. No, she'd suffocate.

Oh, dear Lord above!

The three of them came banging through the big room. They'd swept away the outer defences of the house and were homing in on their prey.

The two men came first. One was younger than the other and looked fit. That would be Cal, the gardener. Yes, the sweet scent of his cigarettes floated up the stairs ahead of him. He and his friend were all in black and wearing balaclavas.

This second man was the bulky bully who'd tried to help the

pseudo Ellie to kidnap the children that morning, and who had laid Lesley out. And, he had a knife in his right hand!

Light flickered on the blade. This was a knife that liked to cut and thrust! Was this the knife which had helped to end Evan's life and that of the lookout boy?

Susan shuddered.

She turned her attention to the woman. And yes, this was the woman who'd tried to lift Evan from the nursery that morning. Perhaps it might be possible to reason with her? Judging by her bulk and noisy breathing, she was not very fit. She wore a bulky black tracksuit and a scarf tied round her head in the fashion made famous by the queen. The scarf was of silk with a black and purple pattern on it.

She carried a walking stick. This was not the sort of prettily decorated fold-up-and-put-in-your-handbag stick. This was the sort you took on a hike for whacking at brambles and cattle that dared to cross your path.

The three stood in a group in the hall, assessing the barrier Susan had created on the staircase.

'Well, blow me!' The woman was the first to speak. She cracked out a laugh, not because she thought the situation amusing but because she was astonished that Susan had dared to oppose her. Her voice was sharp.

She thrust the two men aside to stand, arms akimbo, at the foot of the stairs. 'Give him up, dearie, and we'll leave you in peace to put your baby to bed.'

The blade in Knife Man's hand flickered as his hand twitched. He was more than ready to use it, wasn't he?

Susan felt Evan clutch her leg even tighter. She jiggled Fifi, who seemed interested but not particularly bothered by this interruption in her night-time ritual. 'They're both my children,' said Susan. 'You're not having either of them.'

'Nonsense, Ducky,' said the woman. 'The boy's ours. His mother owes us, and we're going to keep him safe and sound till she pays her debt.'

'With what?' asked Susan. 'Monopoly money? Diana hasn't a penny to her name. Her house is being repossessed, likewise her car. Her husband's assets go to his children by his earlier marriages and she's been trying to raise a loan from people who don't want to know. Her lover has deserted her, and his family are pressurising her to hand them over the agency and leave town. She hasn't a hope of raising money for herself, never mind the boy.'

'His grandmother—'

'Has had enough of bailing Diana out. Anyway, Ellie isn't even in this country at the moment.'

'She's bound to come up with—'

'You've been misinformed. The only money Mrs Quicke has is her old age pension. Everything else, including her house, belongs to a trust fund and they're a hard-headed lot on the board, who certainly won't want to pay ransom money for Diana.'

'Why, then . . . you and your husband seem fond of the lad. You'd lend Diana enough to—'

'We're stretched to the limit having done up this place, which also belongs to the trust, by the way. Sorry. There are no bottomless pockets around here. And the police are keeping an eye on this place throughout the night, calling in every now and then. They should be here, oh, any minute now. Why don't you cut your losses and get out? You've three deaths on your conscience already. I know you personally didn't set out to kill anyone, but your two companions have let you down big time, lashing out when they should have known better. I don't think you were in on the original raid on Evan's house—'

'I wouldn't have been so stupid! Those three idiots—!'

'Exactly. But all the police could have charged them with was manslaughter. I don't think they intended to kill, did they?'

The younger man . . . Cal? . . . made as if to speak.

She clobbered the back of his head. 'Shut it! Haven't you done enough damage?'

He flinched, but didn't strike back.

The woman shook herself. 'They made their bed, and they'll have to lie on it! But I'm out of pocket and no one, but no one, does me down and gets away with it. We saw the police drive past a quarter of an hour ago, and they'll not be back for a while. Your husband's off with some woman or other, isn't he? He won't be back before morning, if I'm any judge of the matter. So it's just you and me, ducky, and I'm not going home empty-handed. If there's no ransom available, then there's always a market for a nice-looking young boy in the Middle East, right?'

What a terrible fate! No! Dear Lord, save Evan! Give me some chain mail . . . a sword . . . some arrows, preferably poisoned. Help!

Her throat tightened. 'No way!'

The woman smiled. 'Fond of him, are you? All right, we'll take the girl instead. Pretty little thing, I'm told. She'll fetch a good price.'

It's true that I don't care for Jenny as I do for Evan. I could give Jenny up without a qualm . . . or could I?

No, I couldn't live with myself afterwards if I had to choose between them. Besides, this woman takes no prisoners. She wouldn't make the mistakes the other two have. She would ensure someone was thoroughly dead before she left the scene.

That knife! It keeps moving in the man's hand, looking for somebody to hurt.

She managed to say, 'No,' before her throat closed up on her.

The woman gestured to Cal and his sidekick. 'What are you waiting for? Pull that stuff down and take the boy.'

They grinned, enjoying their superiority under fire and Susan's helplessness. This was, they were sure, going to be a doddle!

Cal gestured to Knife Man to take one side of the barricade while he took the other.

Fifi shifted in Susan's arms to look down and across the hall to the front door. Was that a shadow pressed against the glass panel?

Someone rang the doorbell. Long and hard.

It couldn't be Rafael. He would use his key.

Midge the cat streaked out from under the barricade brushing past Cal as he made for the safety of the kitchen.

Cal, caught off balance, teetered.

He put his foot down on the frying-pan which Susan had abandoned and skidded across the floor . . .

. . . into Knife Man, knocking him off-balance . . .

The two of them fell in a confusion of arms and legs.

'What the . . .!'

The knife clattered to the floor and slid into the shadows.

The doorbell continued to ring.

Susan screamed, 'HELP!'

Fifi, sensitive to Susan's distress, joined in.

Evan took a deep breath, closed his eyes, and screeched.

The woman shouted at the men. 'You stupid . . .!'

Knife Man managed to get up, grunting, looking round for his weapon, reaching for it, only to tangle with the scooter and fall flat on his face.

Someone standing at the front door yelled, 'Are you all right?'

Susan screamed, 'HELP!' again. And, 'Go round the back!'

Cal, on his knees, attempted to pull himself upright by leaning on the buggy, only to find it was linked to the highchair, which toppled on to him.

He swore, losing his temper, kicking at the buggy . . . which folded up on his leg, trapping it as if in a vice. He tried to free himself, flailing around, dragging the buggy with him . . .

Till he collided with his mate, who was shaking his head, trying to get back on his own feet . . .

A commotion in the big room at the back, and a large, hunched-over figure burst into the hall . . .

The woman swung round, striking out with her stick at the newcomer . . . who picked her up and flung her against the wall. She slid down the wall. Slowly. Her eyes crossed, and the stick fell to the floor.

Cal screamed, 'Let's get out of here!' Despite the buggy enclosing his leg, he dragged himself to the front door, hauled himself upright to reach the latch. He pulled the door open to confront a wild figure in a black jacket over pink and white pyjamas. It was wearing bunny-rabbit slippers.

'What!' He tried to swipe the figure out of his way. It used its fist to connect with his undercarriage, toppling him back over the pushchair.

Snap! His leg?

Coralie? Her father and mother might have sent her up to bed, but she'd refused to be left out of the fun. She flexed her arm. 'Ouch!'

Knife Man wavered to his feet, clutching at one wrist. He focused on the front door and took one limping step towards freedom, only to fall over the much-abused pushchair. Clonk!

Cal screamed.

Knife Man lay still, chest heaving. Sobbing. Unable to move.

The woman whimpered. As did Cal.

Susan stopped screaming, and so did the children.

A lot of heavy breathing went on, mixed with moans from the wounded soldiers.

Sam, the taxi driver, who'd donned his enormous leather jacket for the foray, kicked the heavy walking stick out of the woman's reach and stood over her, watching her recovery.

The woman closed her eyes and made no attempt to rise. Had he knocked her out, or was she faking it?

Sam straightened up. 'Well, missus. Coralie thought you might be in a spot of trouble. She insisted on coming round with me and told me how to get in the back way. Good thing I did, eh? Though, I must say, they're not up to much, this lot, are they?'

Fifi peered down the stairs, interested to see what was happening.

Evan looked up at Susan. And, very tentatively, grinned.

A large shape loomed in the front doorway. 'Is there a problem?'

The police had arrived. At last.

Susan said, 'How many pairs of handcuffs do you have on you, Officer?'

Won't Rafael be annoyed to have missed all this!

A detective inspector arrived to take charge. This was most necessary as everyone present was trying to talk – or rather, shout – over everyone else.

Except Jenny upstairs – who slept through everything – and Fifi, who fell asleep in her mother's arms as soon as Susan was helped down the stairs in order to collapse on to the settee in the big room. Oh, and Evan, who crawled on to her lap and went out like a light, too.

While Sam and Coralie were trying to explain what had happened, Rafael returned, astonished to find his house invaded by the constabulary, two paramedics, Sam, Coralie, and three strangers who were all rather the worse for wear and at least one of whom required hospital attention.

The final count of injuries was: one slight concussion, one sprained wrist and one broken femur. All on the side of the intruders.

The damage to property included a dent in Susan's large frying pan, a pushchair which looked as if an elephant had sat on it, and no less than three damaged glass doors, which would all need to be attended to before the children could be let loose in the house again.

The newly arrived detective inspector pounced on Rafael to explain who he was, and why he'd been absent when the invasion of the body snatchers had taken place.

Rafael said he'd no idea he'd left his phone behind. He said he'd been delayed when delivering Lesley back to her place as her husband hadn't quite understood that his wife needed care and attention. But what was that compared to the mess he found on his return home?

'Why,' Rafael demanded, 'has my family been put at risk? Why didn't you take our problems seriously? My wife was left to confront a bunch of incompetent murderers without any support from the police! Look at her! Exhausted, in shock, having defended the children with her life!'

Susan lowered her eyes, and heaved a great sigh of content. Her part in the proceedings was over now that her hunter-gatherer husband had returned home to defend his family from all comers.

While the DI was still trying to sort out what had happened, a large ginger cat stalked through the assembled company, making the point that as he had been responsible for the defeat of the baddies, he needed to be fed *now*!

Chaos ruled OK!

It turned out that Susan had got one thing wrong. The woman with the walking stick – whose name turned out to be Mrs Chapel – was not a drug dealer. She'd been Diana's office manager for many years. Six weeks ago Diana had sacked her to save money. Her son was a mechanic who worked at the garage where Evan had his and Diana's cars serviced. When Evan stopped driving, Bob Chapel – the Knife Man – had offered to find a buyer for the car which was no longer needed and, true to form, Diana had failed to give him the commission he'd been promised.

A chance meeting in the pub found Bob Chapel and Cal bemoaning their lot and vowing vengeance on Diana, which had led to them teaming up with Lookout Boy for the aborted raid on her house.

When that burglary had gone wrong, Bob Chapel's panicky reaction had triggered his mother cross-examining him as to what he'd been up to. He'd confessed his part in the event and she'd been grimly pleased to hear that they'd tried to get back at Diana for short-changing them.

Lookout Boy had indeed panicked on hearing that the police were looking for him as having been involved in Evan's death, and had threatened to spill the beans, which was when Cal and Bob had dealt with him.

It was Mrs Chapel who thought up the idea of kidnapping one of Diana's children for a ransom. Cal had heard all about the nursery and the family situation from Useless Lucia. The plan had been for 'Mrs Quicke' to pick up Little Evan. Bob had taken his mother to the nursery in his car and double parked in the road outside, ready to back his mother up if necessary. When Lesley had intervened, it was he who had knocked her for six. Their getaway car had been stowed at the back of the garage in which Bob worked, thus avoiding the attentions of the police, only to be brought out again in the attempt to snatch one of the children.

Given all that information, it was not difficult to find proof of their misdeeds. Bob's knife had traces of blood from Evan and Lookout Boy, and Lesley identified him as her assailant. It turned out he'd been in trouble twice before so was sure to be banged up for a long time.

Ditto Cal, whose DNA matched the second sample found at the scene of Evan's murder. The gardener's link with Useless Lucia was established by a quick look at his calls to and from her on his phone, whereupon he threw the blame for everything on Bob who, he said, had been the one to suggest they pay a visit to Diana's house in order to pick up something – anything – to compensate them for their trouble, and subsequently to silence Lucia.

It turned out that Cal's leg had been broken in three places. Two operations failed to restore mobility. He also got a nice long sentence in jail.

Mrs Chapel was in some ways more fortunate, in that although it could be proved she had taken part in the attempted kidnapping at the nursery, and had accompanied Bob and Cal in their foray to Susan's house, no one but Susan could swear to her intention to sell one of the children abroad. Bob and Cal were so much in awe of her that they refused to confirm her threat, and so her brief got her a shorter sentence than she might otherwise have merited.

However, there are some crimes which disgust even long-term prisoners, and somehow or other the truth got out. Mrs Chapel did not have an easy time in prison and did not live long after her release.

Afterwards

Useless Lucia was released from hospital, earned some money by giving an interview to the tabloids titled 'My Lover, the Killer' and flew back home on the proceeds, swearing to return for the trial and probably not meaning to.

Lesley recovered after a fashion, spending most of her recuperation at Susan and Rafael's house in the daytime, helping Susan with the three children, or just lying around, gazing into space. When it was clear that she dreaded returning home to her uncaring husband at night, Rafael offered his aunt-in-law use of the flat he had lived in before he was married, and into which he'd fitted himself, Susan and Fifi while the big house was being renovated.

Lesley gratefully accepted and gradually replaced her 'lost' look with the air of one who had lived through a storm and come out the other side. She often dropped in for supper and a chat. Why not, when Susan was doing the cooking?

Rafael soon realized it was no use trying to work from an office downstairs particularly as Jenny had an uncanny ability to sneak in and fiddle with his computer, so he put a gate across the stairs to the attic floor and made himself a nest at the top of the house. The reception for his computer was better there, too.

The police checked out the two flats in which Rafael thought Diana might have taken refuge. They discovered that yes, she had been using one of them but had since departed. And yes, she had stayed for a few days at the hotel in a room on the top floor overlooking the back of Susan's house . . . but hadn't been seen since. Oh, and the bill was still outstanding.

Marcy masterminded the final polish on Ellie and Thomas's house, even finding a gardener who knew what he was doing and who set about restoring the grounds and the conservatory to what they were meant to be. Fortunately or otherwise, Ellie and Thomas's return was delayed yet again – this time to be present at the christening of one of his granddaughters – which allowed time for the new planting in her garden to settle down.

Marcy then moved on to working full-time for the trust, which suited all concerned. Her first job there was to make Evan and Diana's old house ready to re-let.

Evan's funeral was arranged by his elder daughter Freya. Diana did attend, as did both Rafael and Susan. Evan's will was simple. He'd left the agency and the contents of the house to Diana, expressing the wish that his daughter Freya might be allowed to take some pieces of furniture from what had been her childhood home if she so wished.

After the funeral, Diana said that she was in consultation to sell the agency and the contents of the house – less the one or two pieces which Freya might wish to remove. She said that as she had not yet settled where she would live, it was not convenient . . .

Not convenient!

. . . for her to reclaim her children at the moment, and that she assumed they might stay with Rafael and Susan for the time being.

She suggested that the children's half-sister, Freya, should become their guardian while Rafael and Susan were appointed long-term foster parents. The nerve of the woman!

So various agencies had to be consulted and involved.

Neither child seemed to be missing their mother, but taking on the two children officially was an enormous commitment for Susan and Rafael to have to make. Evan had already wound himself into Susan's heart. She loved him to bits and he seemed to understand that and to reciprocate. Jenny was another matter: a toy-snatching, whiny, telly-and-tablet-watching couch potato.

Susan quailed at the thought of taking her on.

Then she remembered that Ellie used to say it didn't matter where the love for a child came from, so long as they were given it from somebody. Could Susan manage to love such a spiky child? She decided that she must try. No matter what it cost, and no matter how many battles there would be ahead. With Rafael and Coralie to help her, fostering the children was the right thing to do.

Rafael bought the children a rocking horse, a trampoline and a set of cricket bats, and taught the older two how to play in the back garden. Susan taught Evan to read and write, while Fifi and Midge worked out how to deal with the enlargement of their family. They ignored bad behaviour and rewarded good, just as Susan did.

Then one afternoon, the doorbell rang and there she was, the Wicked Witch of the North.

Black and white, with a flash of scarlet at her throat. Susan estimated that Diana's handbag and shoes alone had cost as much as the council tax on a three-bedroom house. She was backed by a brand-new car which had a self-satisfied gleam to its paintwork.

Susan, with Fifi on her hip, thought for one awful moment that Diana had come to reclaim the children. And if so . . .? Oh dear. How ever could she bear to let them go?

She instructed herself not to gape, conscious of wearing baggy T-shirt and maternity jeans, both of which were patched with flour from the shortcrust pastry she was making with the children.

Diana said, 'I understand my mother has delayed her return by yet another fortnight. I suspect she's allowed herself to be taken advantage of by Thomas's family, and has forgotten all about us. Anyway, I'm on my way to the airport for a long-overdue holiday, so I thought I'd drop in some presents for the children. Otherwise' – a tinkling laugh – 'they might forget their mother.'

What a relief!

Diana handed over two perfectly wrapped boxes bearing a Harrods label, which Susan fielded with some difficulty. Susan said, 'You'll come in for a while?'

Diana hesitated. Was that a twinge of regret? She glanced sideways at the car with its tinted windows. Was someone sitting in the car, waiting for her? Keith Cottrell, or some other helpful 'friend'?

'No, no. No time. It would be too painful for me . . .' Did Diana really wipe a tear from her eye? Well, if she did, she soon recovered. 'When I'm settled, I'll speak to them on Skype. I see you're due another baby yourself? A pity you can't find better maternity outfits. I always tried to look my best for my husband.'

Susan set her teeth. So, Diana thought Susan dressed badly? Well, yes. By comparison, perhaps she did. Susan thought of how Diana's selfish actions had led to the deaths of her husband and the lookout boy, had landed Lucia in hospital and Lesley in a neck brace. Acid words burned Susan's tongue. And then she relaxed. Diana had done her best to keep her husband, his house and the business running when money had been short, and she'd sat beside him and held his hand when he was dying. There must be some good there, wasn't there?

So she said nothing but watched as Diana inserted herself into the passenger seat of the expensive car and was driven away.

'Pooh!' said Fifi, as a gust of car fumes drifted back to them.

'That's right, poppet,' said Susan, closing the door on the outside world. 'That car looks good, but its engine requires attention. You can't always judge by appearances. Now, where were we . . .?'